Move Over, Mountain

Also by John Ehle

Fiction

Kingstree Island
Lion on the Hearth
The Land Breakers
The Road
Time of Drums
The Journey of August King
The Changing of the Guard
The Winter People
Last One Home
The Widow's Trial

Nonfiction

The Survivor: The Story of Eddy Hukov
Shepherd of the Streets: The Story of the Reverend
   James A. Gusweller and His Crusade on the New
   York West Side
The Free Men
The Cheeses and Wines of England and France, with
   Notes on Irish Whiskey
Trail of Tears: The Rise and Fall of the Cherokee Nation
Dr. Frank: Life with Frank Porter Graham

MOVE OVER, MOUNTAIN

JOHN EHLE

PRESS 53
Winston-Salem

PRESS 53, LLC
PO Box 30314
Winston-Salem, NC 27130

PRESS 53 *Classics*

Move Over, Mountain
50TH ANNIVERSARY EDITION

First Edition

Second printing, 2015

Cover design by Mike Davis

Cover photograph © 2007 by Kenny Johnson,
used by permission of the artist

Background photograph © 2007 by Benita VanWinkle,
used by permission of the artist

John Ehle photo courtesy of Rob Neufeld

Printed on acid-free paper
ISBN 978-0-9793049-8-9

1

Jordan lay in bed and remembered the night before when his luck had run out and he had lost all his money. The odds had been high toward the end of the game, and he hadn't been able to stop. So he had lost all he had.

He rubbed his dark arm across his forehead to blink out the light, and turned part way over in bed so that his back rested on his wife's shoulder. After a while he swung his legs off the bed and began to dress. Today he would get a job, he thought. He would get a regular job. He would get one no matter what. He tied the laces of his shoes and swung his shirt from the bedpost. When he put it on, he noticed that one of the sleeve buttons was broken.

"Damn," he muttered.

"What you say, Jordan?" his wife asked without turning over.

"I busted a button on my sleeve."

"Leave it. Wear your other shirt."

"I busted my other shirt up the back."

She rolled over in bed and looked at him.

"I'm too big," he said. "My muscles are too big."

He pulled on his pants, fastened the belt, as his wife turned back over. He wondered why she didn't get up to fix his breakfast. She didn't know he had lost the money. She didn't even know he had lost his job at the coalyard.

"Annie, you goin' to get up?"

She pushed herself up on one elbow and looked at him sleepily. He stumbled past the painted washstand and out of the bedroom into the small hall. On his left he threw open a narrow door and called out, "All right, up and at 'em in there, boys. Hit the floor!"

He heard not a sound. He went on into the bathroom and began to shave. Today he would get a job. No matter how hard a job it was, he would take it. Even laying concrete blocks, he'd take a job laying blocks. He laid them before, thousands of them. They made your arms ache at night for a week or two after you went on a job, but he would do it again. He was stronger than the other Negroes. If they could lay blocks, he could too. Or maybe the Thompson Company would let him work in the lumberyard again. Moving lumber was easier than laying blocks.

He washed his face with cold water, dried, threw the towel into his bathtub. Then he beat his fist on the wall behind him, which was also the wall of the children's room.

"I said hit the floor in there! Let me hear you."

From the other room he heard the two boys tumble out of bed. He grinned. He almost laughed. Good boys were hard to come by. Boys who could handle themselves. Strong boys.

He put the shaving equipment back in place, rubbed his chin and cheeks with his hand. It was a good shave. Well, that was as it should be. He ought to look his best. He had to get a job today.

Thompson Company was a wood building on the corner of Wilkins and Circus Street. It was named Circus Street because the circus ground was about a block down from Wilkins, or it had been before the lumberyard began using it. Now there weren't any circuses anyway, for a town the size of Leafwood. When carnivals came through, they pitched their tents beside the lumber on the north side of the lot.

Jordan hitched his pants higher. His sleeve was rolled up inside his jacket and he kept mashing down the rolled cloth.

Inside the Thomson Company building was the odor of a wood stove that was taking the chill off the room. A Negro named James Hogan, a next-door neighbor of Jordan's, stood up when he came in and came over to him, his hand poked out.

"Jordan—Jordan, how are you?" Hogan was glad to see him, no doubt about that.

Jordan and the old Negro talked for a minute. They said something about the way things used to be when they worked on jobs together. They had built the textile plant together.

"How many years ago was that?" Jordan asked, for the old man never forgot about anything.

"That was six years ago, come spring."

"I wish another job like that textile plant would come to this town. I lost my job at the coalyard, Hogan. Got to find another one."

The old man wrinkled his face. "Oh, now, Jordan, don't say. Don't say."

"You know of any jobs around?"

Hogan sat down beside the stove and thought seriously for a long while. "You might talk to the boss," he said at last. "He might help you. But you know the trouble with you is— " He hesitated and Jordan had to tell him to go on. "The trouble is you're too big, Jordan."

Jordan knew this was the truth.

"When the average man gets mad, he might hit somebody, might get in a fight. When he gets drunk, he might do the same. But when you get mad, Jordan . . . it's like—it's like thunder. You almost killed Sam Marshall."

Jordan nodded.

"He almost died," Hogan said.

"I know," Jordan said. "I'm too damn big."

"Too big, and too angry when you're mad."

And so they sat and talked about that until the boss got in. He was very polite to Jordan. Everybody was. They didn't ignore Jordan as they did some of the other Negroes. But there just wasn't anything for him to do now. Maybe in a month or so. Or maybe in the spring when construction work picked up.

"Sure, I can get a job in the spring," Jordan said his voice rising angrily. The boss and the old man looked at each other, and the old man shifted nervously from foot to foot. "But I have a family to feed right now."

He stood there looking at the two of them for a minute more. Neither of them said anything. So he turned and went out.

They were nice to Jordan over at the trucking company, too. They told him they might need a driver before long. He gave them his address and told them to be sure and find him. They said they would. When he went out he remembered that the man hadn't written down his address. But that didn't necessarily mean anything. They expected they could always find a Negro by asking another Negro. They could just ask somebody to go find that big Negro with the high forehead, the one that looks like a fighter.

Jordan crossed the railroad track and went up into the business section of Leafwood. He stopped at the drugstore where, years before, he had worked in the stock room. The boy behind the counter didn't know anything about the stock room. Jordan went on down the street, asking about jobs, even a part time. He had to find some money to tide him over for a day, at least.

He was almost to the end of the block when he saw her, the Taylor widow, window-shopping and coming along, a woman almost too light-skinned to be a Negro. Men were staring after her, as always, but she glanced at no one until she saw Jordan, then she stopped stock-still; so he hastily made his way through the traffic and across the street.

Got to stay clear of that woman, he thought, hurrying along. Once he glanced back and thought he caught her looking after him. He asked at two restaurants for a job, explaining how he liked to wait tables or work around the kitchen. It was a big lie and he told it and it got him nowhere. Finally, at the corner filling station, he got on for a few hours washing cars.

He worked hard, taking pride in the way the metal would come out shiny under his hand. "Workin' for Annie," he said in time with the clean sweeps of the wash cloth. "Workin' for the boys."

But at the same time, he was trying to figure out what he was going to do. No matter how much he thought, nothing turned up. He had quit most of the employers in town and the rest knew about it. He was too restless and dissatisfied.

"Got a thorn in my spirit," he mumbled. "Got the northern thorn. Lord, I got to get up to that country."

Up in the North—that was the country. That was where his brothers were, and he was just treading time until he got up there himself. Only poor to ordinary luck had held him back in North Carolina this long. Luck and Annie. His real life wouldn't start until he got away.

Even thinking about leaving cheered him some. Soon he was singing—
If my girl refuse me
Shove me in de sea,
Where de fishes an' de whales
Make a fuss over me.
He chuckled aloud. Time was when he was a singin' fool, but it took a guitar to make music flow. His guitar was pawned in Durham, and for all he knew was sold off by now. But never mind, he had the songs.

So he worried and worked and sang songs until about noon, when the attendant gave him two dollars and sent him on his way. "No more cars," he said. Jordan buried the money in his pocket and headed out. He went by two construction yards and neither put him on. Just as well. He had worked for both of them before, building houses. He had mixed mortar and dug foundation holes, even masoned some, and his work had been done well; but he had never taken pride in it. Nothing he did in that town was for himself. His own work would start after he got North.

Finally he trudged down to the ice plant and made his plea, but the owner turned him down flat. "Icehouse is no place for a colored man," he told them, grinning as if it were a joke. "Wrong climate."

Jordan figured it for the truth. Nothing human about a cold place. Lord, he wouldn't have gone there at all except he was growing desperate. He was almost desperate enough to go back to the hospital and take up where he had left off there. For almost a year he had moved up and down its sick halls, peering at the patients. The suffering had troubled him so much he could hardly stand it. Even now he had a heavy dread of the place.

But Doctor Morgan had told Jordan once he should have been a doctor, then he could have helped relieve the pain. That was about as high a compliment as any man in that hospital had ever received, and Jordan knew he could count on a good word from Doctor Morgan any time.

He started walking toward the place right then, but as the pile of brick and silent windows came into view his steps grew heavier. Finally he sat down on a tree stump on the hospital lawn and worried his way out of the notion. He would rather go on like he was, without a penny in sight, than work in those halls again, hear the weeping, see the bodies carted to and fro. No good to come of it, not for him.

So he started out, growing more and more tired as he felt the day closing in.

Along about five-thirty, he reached Jake's beer hall and waited around while Jake put the finishing touches on a sketch of Jackie Robinson. Jake had his beer-hall walls decorated with faces of Negro athletes, one looking just like another, so far as Jordan could judge, and nobody looking like he did in real pictures. Even Jake's own portrait, showing him as a young man in boxing tights, didn't look much like him. It was a devil of a sight better-looking than Jake—that was the truth of the matter. But what Jake did in the beer hall was his business. Nobody criticized and nobody corrected Jake.

"Hey," Jordan said. "Hey, Jake, how 'bout lettin' me work here for a while?"

"Come off that talk, big boy. You know I just need help on Friday and Saturday nights. Look at the place right now—not a soul in it. Ain't goin' to pay nobody to stand around."

"Well, I got to find somethin', Jake. Seems like my luck's hit bottom."

"Did you go talk to that young widow woman that turned you in to the coalyard?"

"Naw. Not goin' to, either."

"Sorry damn mess," Jake said, erasing part of Robinson's chin and taking a new start on it. Then he looked up sharply, his tiny eyes alive. "Say, big boy, don't that damn Patrick work at the coalyard?"

Jordan shifted uneasily. "Ain't goin' to crawl to no coalyard people for my job back."

"Not sayin' that. But he's dispatcher, and he went and let that woman get you fired. Did he say anything in your behalf?"

"Well, you know Patrick—how he is—just laughs and carries on for the white men down there—"

"Godamighty," Jake boomed, throwing aside his pencil. He swung to the wall phone behind him and started dialing a number. "Goin' to get him down there."

"Jake, you look here now—"

"Pour yourself a beer, Jordan. Goin' to have you back workin' by tomorrow mornin'."

Jordan started to object again, but he couldn't bring himself to do it.

So he poured a beer and found a booth. A few minutes later he looked up as Morris Coltrane came in, glancing about to see if anybody was there he knew. Coltrane was the only prosperous Negro businessman in Leafwood.

Jake told him to stick around until that "that damn Irish nigger Patrick gets here. Goin' to have the fireworks fly!"

So Coltrane brought a beer over to Jordan's table and sat down to wait for the show. He said not a word to Jordan, nor had he anything to say to Jake. He was secretive all the way around, Coltrane was. He sipped his beer, then offered Jordan a cigarette. Jordan hadn't smoked a cigarette since the night before, so his hand went out automatically to take it.

Then he wished he hadn't, because he saw a faint smile on Coltrane's face, a superior smile that always came when he did a favor for a man, as if he had bettered him.

"What's funny, Coltrane?" Jordan said evenly.

The smile left his face at once. He leaned back importantly in the booth, fixing Jordan with his eyes. He was a black Negro, so he was held in low esteem by the whites and by most other Negroes, to boot; but he had climbed to the top, and now had a light-skinned wife and plenty of money, which came to him from his cleaning establishment.

"What's this about Patrick?" he asked.

Jordan explained about losing his job and how Patrick had not taken a stand. "That woman complained, and I had no chance to argue 'bout it."

"Well, you can get a job somewhere, can't you?"

Jordan nodded right off. Lord, he wasn't going to let Coltrane think he was done for; and he wasn't going to work for Coltrane, either. Possibly that's what Coltrane would like—to get him in his sweatshop and work him down, try to lord it over him. Wasn't going to do it, though. Jordan wasn't working for any colored man, except maybe Jake. The whites were lordly enough for him.

"What you goin' to do?" Coltrane said.

"Well, I'm thinkin' about openin' my own business."

Coltrane's eyes blinked as if they were thinking on their own.

"Tired o' workin' for the other man. Thinkin' about openin' up a taxicab company, by God." Jordan figured it out as he said it, remembering the night before when he had vainly tried to get a white taxicab driver to take him to Durham. "Goin' to get me some cabs on the road and take off makin' money."

"Well, see here, Jordan, sounds good."

Jordan peered around at the face on the wall. "Think maybe four cabs ought to do for a start." Lord, be well to settle for one, but if a man was bragging, might as well go the whole distance.

"I'd—uh—be interested in investin', Jordan. Do you . . . need any money?"

"Yeah, I do." Jordan said easily, smiling to himself.

Now Coltrane was leaning across the table, peering at him so intently Jordan didn't know but that the man was lost to his senses. Jordan would have led him further, but Patrick came bursting through the doorway, demanding to know what Jake wanted with him.

Coltrane, shaken by the interruption, caught Jordan's arm. "Say, Jordan, when I get ready to leave, you come along, hear? Let's talk some more about this taxicab company."

Jordan nodded just as Jake started bellowing at Patrick. Jake was fighting mad, and Patrick, a slight man who was afraid of his own shadow, was bouncing around in front of the bar, trying to get in a word of explanation.

"Let the best worker in this damn town get fired, Patrick," Jack boomed, striking the bar with a mighty blow. "Goddamn hole, this town, and Jordan the only good man left in it. Why didn't you resign, stomp out in protest?"

"I . . . I—how could I do—" Patrick shook his head in bewilderment. "Resign?" he blurted out.

"Well, you're a trained white-collar worker. We all know those white men at the coalyard would've bent down on their knees to keep a smart man like you weighin' the God-damn coal trucks. Where else could they find a man to read the scales?"

Coltrane stifled a laugh, but Jordan shifted uneasily on the wooden bench.

Jake came out from behind the bar, grabbed the terrified little man by the collar of his coat, pulled him over Jordan's booth and pounded him on the back with the flat of his hand.

"Now, God knows, here he is," he boomed. "Jordan, meet your redeemer, the man that's goin' to get your job back at the coalyard."

Jordan clenched his fists nervously.

Patrick stammered, "I . . . I didn't come down here . . . to stand no trial—"

"Trial, hell," Jake bellowed. "I'm praisin' the power you got at—"

Jordan interrupted. "Let him be, Jake." He didn't look up from the table, but his body was braced, ready for anything.

The aged boxer looked at Jordan for a moment, then his face slowly unfolded in a smile. "Just thinkin' on your behalf."

"I know, I know. But let him be."

"That's right," Patrick said, quivering and looking to Jordan to save him. "I can't go gettin' involved whenever somebody gets in trouble—"

Jake swung on him, now furious.

"Let him be!" Jordan shouted, standing now, his eyes narrowed in anger.

Jack backed off, then glanced away, nodded. "Yeah," he said. "All right. It's your job, big boy."

Patrick began to laugh, a high, nervous cackle that seemed to roll out of him against his will. At the coalyard the laugh was something to entertain the white men, but in the Negro beer hall it sounded painful and unreal. As if to stop it, he began to speak. "It was just what you said to that colored woman, Jordan—that Taylor widow." He stepped back, angrily unable to say more.

Jake looked at Jordan, put his heavy, flat hand on his shoulder. "What did you say to her, big boy?"

"No need to go into that."

"Come on. What did you say?

"Well—I called her a whore."

"Godamighty," Jake said, impressed.

Patrick interrupted. "She's been callin' down at the coalyard ever since. Phoned twice today—"

Coltrane took special note of this and spoke up for the first time. "You got an answer right there, Jordan," he said. "Maybe you made her mad enough to make her like you."

"Huh? You mean she likes me so she gets me fired?"

"Stranger things than that can go on in a woman's mind when she lives by herself, no man about. You've read about it, haven't you?"

"No," Jordan said, half-thinking. He never read books, or anything else. It was hard enough to figure out the words without having his mind sent into a spasm of wonder by what was said.

"Might be wise to stop by her house tonight." The gleam in Coltrane's eyes was bothersome. "Not a prettier woman in this town—'cept my Helen."

"Lord knows," Jordan said, "not me go by there." Then he looked at Patrick. "Saw her uptown today and she near stared me through."

"Well, you shouldn't 'a' talked to her the way you did."

Jordan's eyes darkened and his hands moved ever so slightly on the table top. "It was the way she talked to me, superior-like. Standin' there on her back step, actin' like anybody deliverin' coal is a servant." He struck the table with his open hand. "I'm no damn servant!"

The three watched him closely, caught by the power of the man. It was clear enough that there was a difference in him—a surging inner hunger, a savage remembering quality. They saw he could lead a dangerous course before he was through.

Coltrane cleared his throat uneasily, got up from the booth. "Well, I'll run along."

"Huh?" Jordan said. "We was goin' to talk, don't you remember?"

"Oh, yes," Coltrane said vaguely. "Yes. Later—sometime."

He went out quickly and without looking back. Jordan saw him hurriedly swing into his car and head on down the road.

Jake put his hand on Jordan's shoulder and leaned lightly on him. "Look, Jordan, why did you have to go callin' that woman a whore?"

"It's the truth, ain't it?"

"Well, I dunno."

"That's what I hear. She was a dancer up North, and she come down here and married old man Taylor for his money. All dancers are whores, ain't they?"

Patrick began to laugh, his cackle going on and on.

"I don't think so, Jordan," Jake said.

"I think they is," Jordan said. "At least, all I ever seen was whore of one kind or another."

As Jordan reached home, a fall wind was blowing the leaves down the street and across the lawns. Next door he saw Sarah Hogan watching him from her living-room window. Some said she could be had, but he liked girls older than sixteen.

He ran up the clay bank into his yard, which Annie kept swept clean between the patches of grass. The house before him was covered in pieces of tin, some of them patched and rusted in places. The two front windows were mist-colored now, and glared out like shining eyes. To Jordan, the door would pass as a nose and the long, sagging porch as a mouth, giving the house a gaunt toothless face. He liked the idea of an unfriendly house, unfriendly on the outside, so that nobody would drop by except those who ought to.

He stepped onto the porch and stomped the dirt from his shoes. The floor shook under him a bit; not much of a place, but it cost him only twenty-five a month, so he couldn't complain. Rented it from a coach at the high school, a white man who always sent a student to Tin Top to collect rent. That way he never heard a complaint, never had to be reminded that his house needed work.

Jordan pushed a rocker away from the door and went inside, closing out the Tin Top world, clinging, as it did, to the red hills, huddled beneath twisting lines of telephone poles, shrouded down in the smoke of cookstoves. He stepped into his living room, warm and clean, furnished with a sofa, a big chair that he liked to use, a rocker and odds and ends. The pillows were colorful, and Annie had fashioned draperies out of spare pieces of cloth. A single yellow bulb, dangling from a cord, sent a mellow glow over the scarred floor and pine walls. The place was as informal as the family, and as friendly as Annie could make it.

"You have to speak to the boys," she called to him from beyond the kitchen door. "Jordan, is that you?"

"It's me."

"They been actin' up."

They could act up all they pleased, so far as he was concerned at that moment. Deeper worries bothered him, not the least of which was how to tell Annie about losing his job and their savings.

Now she was standing in the kitchen doorway, her somber, dark eyes on him, a pretty woman of twenty-eight, dressed in a blue housedress and worn, white apron. About her was a feeling of warmth and care. Her face shone with perspiration from kitchen work. "Why you late?"

"I been out lookin' for a job."

He didn't realize for a moment what he said. Slowly the meaning came to Annie, too. She stared at him, too stunned to trust herself to speech.

He sat down uneasily in the worn armchair. "I was heavin' coal yesterday afternoon, when the woman in the house told me I hadn't brung her a full four-ton."

"Woman? Who you mean?"

"That youngish Taylor widow." He leaned his head back on the chair. "So—I told her she was bad wrong. But she got mad and complained, oh, my Lord! Called up the yard. Mr. Crawford laid me off."

Annie sank down weakly on a straight-backed chair near the kitchen door. "What about the man with you on the truck?"

"Jenkins? Oh, I dunno."

"Lay him off, too?"

"No, don't reckon they did." It was a problem he hadn't considered before. "But Jenkins didn't say much of anything."

He closed his eyes momentarily, then abruptly pulled on the lamp beside his chair. The light fell on a glass tank in which some goldfish swam lazily, a gift from a white woman who had hired Annie for a month to help with a new baby. Jordan was always startled by the calmness of the fish.

"You—you goin' to try to get back on?" Annie asked.

"Let me be, Annie," he said softly, wanting to forget about it for a while. She went on off, and he sat there thinking about his problem, wondering what he was going to do. He started to call the boys out of their room so he could talk to them, but it was better to leave well enough alone, he decided. Always, as he approached the house, he would hear them call out happily that he was in sight. But they had learned from experience not to be around him when he first came home from work, for he was always tired and sometimes he was angry, and they would take to their room and stay there until supper. That was as it should be, and he decided not to interfere by calling them out now.

When Annie ordered him and the boys to supper, he got up lazily, stretched, and went into the bathroom and washed up. Nobody said anything to him while he took his place at the head of the kitchen table and stared around at the hominy grits and sausage, potatoes and applesauce.

As he ate, the warmth of the food cheered him some. "This is all right," he said. "This is good. You boys don't know how lucky it is here, eatin' good food."

Both boys chewed thoughtfully, proudly, as they watched him.

"When I was on the farm years ago, we ate this way, except we had more real pork. I'm gettin' tired o' sausage, Annie."

Annie glanced at him. "What you expect?"

"But it's okay. I like sausage. This ain't hot enough though. Lord, I remember my pa would pepper sausage till it damn near tore your tongue out. My ma once gave me some of it when I was a tiny boy, and I howled. I thought she had done me in."

"How can you remember when you was a boy? I can't remember the first sausage I ate."

"You're forgetful then. I recollect accurate what happened to me. I was the oldest, and by God, I was the best. That's the story anyway. Yes, and I remember my pa makin' me stand afore him as he told me about when he was a boy, and how lucky I was to have a warm room to live in. I tell you boys, it wasn't as warm as this. We're lucky here."

"Jordan, please—" Annie said bluntly. Then suddenly she seemed to be very weary.

He turned back to eating. He needed some kindness, that was a fact, but instead he was getting cold treatment. If he had just had ten dollars the night before, the reaction might have been different. Ten more dollars and a change in luck would have done it.

"They've put a sign up in the store now, Jordan, and write your name on it when you don't pay your bills."

"Huh? How's that?"

"Write your name on the board. Goin' to have 'Jordan Cummings' written on it afore long," she said.

Jordan chewed a piece of sausage that was in his mouth and glared at her. "They ain't goin' to put my name up in public view."

"We owe the store fourteen dollars for last week."

He swallowed and ran his tongue around the inside of his cheeks. "I had a bad run o' luck, that's all. I ain't the first."

"It'll be the first time for you on the board."

"I ain't goin' on the board. They got no right to write my name. Who runs that store now?"

"Mr. Lacock still."

"He ain't nobody. White man runnin' a store for niggers ain't nobody." He drank the last of his coffee. "How long he give us to pay up?"

Annie bit her lip for a moment, then sighed. "I reckon a month, since we haven't fell short in two years."

"Oh, well then," Jordan stuck his hands in his pockets and leaned back on the legs of his chair. "A month. Why, that's all right. We might all be in the North within a month."

Annie turned sharply away from him, and the boys looked up, startled.

"The North?" the older boy said.

"Never mind gettin' interested now, boys. Let me worry about the North." He didn't want them to get upset as he had been at their age about the great land up there. His own father had drilled the North into him, made him want to see it and live in it. Even as he plowed and harrowed, fed the stock and baited traps, he had rested on the good ideas he had of the North.

"We're goin' to have to buy some coal," Annie was saying.

"I put some money back from time to time, but I don't want to use up the savings to pay the grocer, you hear, Jordan?"

He looked up slowly. He hadn't told her he had gambled away the savings the night before.

"You boys go study," he said quickly, wondering how he would tell her about the money. "Keep your eyes shinin', boys. Ain't licked yet." He laughed. Those two boys were all right.

The boys went out, looking back of their shoulders.

"Study hard," Jordan said. "Learn."

They went into their small room as Annie began fiddling around with the pots and pans stored in one of the chests. Finally she straightened and turned slowly toward him. He knew that was where she had hid the money, because that was where he had found it. He fidgeted with the edge of his plate. "Don't fret, Annie."

"What?" She was still trying to make it out.

"Annie, I tell you how it is. I lost my job late yesterday afternoon, and

I figured it was goin' to take a while to get a new one, and things bein'
like they stand in this town. So I had to try to get on top quick, maybe
enough to leave this place."

"You—you lost the—"

"Had it up to a hundred dollars for a while, but afore I knew it, my
luck just went. Just hit bottom."

She didn't seem to know what to say, or what to do with herself,
standing near the center of the room looking around at him. "Ah, Lord,
Jordan—" There was a dullness to her face, almost the same expression
his mother had had in her late years. Now for the first time it was in
Annie's face, too.

"Seems like when a man loses what money he has, most of the smiles
fade away." He said it trying to joke her into smiling, but she moaned, as
if the words shook her, and turned to the sink.

Then she turned back, stared at him for a long moment. "Sometimes,
Jordan, I think you're plain no-'count."

"Huh?" He started, stunned and angry. "No-'count? Look here, I stayed
in this town because o' you. I been here because o' you and them boys—"

She swung away, hurried out of the kitchen and into the boys' room,
slamming the door after her. He rushed to the door and tried to force it
open, but she was leaning against it. With a shove, he threw it open and she
was thrown across the narrow room. He caught sight of the frightened faces
of the boys, and young Harris began to cry. "No, Daddy—no, Pa!—"

"Be quiet."

The boys began to cry aloud.

"Annie, come out of here. I want to talk to you. I want to tell you
what I know."

She didn't move.

"Annie—"

She watched him sullenly for a moment, then moved past him into
the hall. He started to close the door as one of the boys leaped from the
bed and grabbed at it. "Mama," he said.

Jordan pushed him inside and closed the door. He turned to find Annie
had gone into the living room. He followed her there. "Annie, listen to
me now. I been in this place all my life, and no hope is around. It don't
come to me. God, I try, Annie, and I work—"

"Listen, Jordan—"

"I work. I want to see us well, and I don't like kids cryin', but I don't fit here, and I can't stoop to beggin' for a job here. Now in the North—"

"You never saw the North! Coltrane was in the North, and he come back here! Others have been in the North, but they come back!"

"Drivin' big cars, yeah. Lord, they come back."

"Come back hungry, some of 'em, too. Coltrane come back hungry."

He slumped down in the chair, the strength going out of him, and rested his arm and head on the worn places of the upholstery. "I'll be a man when I die," he said, "not like some of the rest of 'em."

"Coltrane and Patrick are not as good as you, you think? Then why is it they're doin' better?"

He shook his head angrily, his hands pressed hard on his forehead as if his mind troubled him.

"They give and take a little, but not you, Jordan."

"Shut up," he said.

"I'll not shut up, either!"

"Shut up!"

She stood shakily before him. "All our lives you been wishin' over what you don't have, makin' me make do, and now I'm not goin' to listen to you—"

He twisted his head in frustration. Beside him the goldfish were swimming lazily in the tank. With one blow of his fist, he crashed in the side of the tank and the water gushed out onto the floor, the fish riding in it. Annie screamed and fell to her knees; tried to pick up the fish in her hands. Then she hurried into the kitchen and came back with a pot full of water. Jordan sat in the chair, his head back, his hand dripping small drops of blood onto the floor. "God-damn fish," he whimpered. "Caged in and slow."

Annie backed off from him, the pot in her hand, the goldfish swimming around in it crazily. "I'll . . .I'll sleep in here tonight, Jordan, on the sofa. Go to bed."

"I want to explain about the fish."

"It's too late for talk, Jordan."

He looked around helplessly. "I'll be the one to sleep in here."

"No." She stepped back until the wall was against her. "Go on, Jordan."

He rose slowly, heavily, and moved past her into the hall. The boys were sobbing. He pushed open the door and stood looking at them, their faces dimly outlined by the light that shone in from the living room. "Be quiet, boys," he said.

They looked up at him sullenly, still sobbing. He pulled the door closed and stumbled into the bedroom, fell across the bed. He heard Annie close the door behind him, then open the door to the boys' room and go inside. Through the wall he could hear her talking to them. "Tomorrow I'll take you down to the creek in the woods. We'll look for bullfrogs in the tall grass. Don't fret about tonight. Tonight is over. Go to sleep."

After a while he heard the sobbing stop, then the door to the boys' room opened and Annie stepped into the hall.

He heard the faint click of the lamp in the living room, then not another sound.

He buried his face in the pillows. "No-'count," he whispered. "Ah, God." Patrick was better, was he? Patrick—he could break Patrick with his hands.

Or Coltrane. Both of them driving in cars wherever they wanted to go. No bills that had to be paid that were beyond them. No troubles. Only he had misery—and he was the better man.

"You were the best of them, Jordan. I raised all four. You were the best." He could hear his father tell him that.

But the brothers were in the North, safe in the North, rocked in the North, in the wealth of the North. But he was in Leafwood, while his wife slept in another room and his children sobbed in their beds and he had no place to count on.

He threw the pillows onto the floor as he turned over, his face toward the ceiling. Lying there he could see nothing, not even the black shades drawn close against the windows. Beneath the soundless tin roof, alone, and without anyone making a sound, he had to think his way through. He had to solve it without his hands; it wouldn't choke, he couldn't strike it. No, Lord. He had to get hold of it with his mind.

Slowly his breathing became slower. He thought of the many places he had worked and lost his job. He thought of the fights, the jarring impact of flesh and bones. He thought of the taste of whisky and the laughter of Jake, the rolling laughter when he was drunk. He thought of his boys in the next room and how far away they were. He thought of his boyhood, and wanted to be back at the farm, wondered if he could go back there and take over and work the same land.

He lay on the bed, wrestling with his mind. He would sleep some, but would wake up, still thinking. Finally he saw the light creep in around the edges of the shades. He got up, flipped up the shades. Outside on the road, Hogan was trudging wearily toward the lumberyard, just has he had every workday for forty years. Jordan watched him until he was out of sight, then kept looking at the place he had last seen him, as if Hogan would help him understand his own place in the world.

He went back into the hall, stumbled into the living room. Annie was on the sofa asleep.

He nudged her awake. "Annie, I'll show you," he said softly. "If I have to break this town in my hands, I'll show you."

"Jordan—"

"But, I'm not sure what it's goin' to mean, Annie, or where it's goin' to lead."

"Jordan, what you mean by that?"

"I mean I'll beat whatever stands in my way. You think Coltrane and Patrick are—"

"Take care now. Don't go too far to the other side, do you hear me?"

"I'll show you," he said, backing off, enjoying deep inside the fear that crept into her eyes. "You just see me, Annie. I'll win out somehow."

He stumbled out onto the front porch, a stiffness in his body. A bolt of lightning flashed in the sky. The thunder rumbled after, and the great oak in Hogan's yard bowed its higher branches to the wind.

Yeah, goin' to storm, Jordan thought.

Well, that was all right. Didn't matter how late in the day he got started. It could even be afternoon before he went by the Taylor widow's house.

2

That morning, as the rain fell, Jordan slept on the big bed in his and Annie's room. It was about noon when he awoke, and he lay there listening for a while to the drops shattering apart on the tin close above his head. He pulled the blankets up around his chin and let the sound bathe his mind. The sound had weight and coolness and it flowed over his troubles, eased them out until he was smiling some.

Annie came in, hovered about. She brushed off the top blanket, then stepped back, peered at him anxiously. "You . . . all right, Jordan?"

He didn't feel like answering her. It was too comfortable there in bed to do much talking.

"I'm sorry for the way I got last night, Jordan." She took a pillow from her side of the bed, punched fluffness into it and put it under his head. "My temper got the better of my senses."

"Well, it's a new day," he said.

"Saved that money hard, though," Annie went on, "a little at a time."

"Yeah, I know you must have."

"Had a purpose for it."

"Huh? What?" he said, showing more interest.

She smiled briefly. "Just—emergencies. You know."

"That's right," he said. "Got to stay ready. Got to plan."

He stretched his long arms over his head, then lay back deep in the pillows, the good spirits resting in him. "I tell you, I could go on up the road right now and get my job back at the coalyard," he said. "By suppertime, we could be on the easy road again. I could go up there right now, Annie."

But she didn't urge him and he didn't go. He let Annie and the sound of rain comfort him. He wouldn't tell Annie where he was going when he did leave, either. Perhaps she thought he would ask all the white men at the coalyard for the job back, but he knew the Taylor woman could phone the coalyard and get his job back in a minute, if she could be persuaded to it.

No need to tell Annie that, though. No need to let her guess how hard it would be to go crawling to a woman, either. That was a man's worry. Annie had protected him from worries, Lord knows, taken them as her own. Never let him know there was much of a problem raising the boys, except once in a while she would ask him to do some talking to them. If she ever got sick, he didn't know it. Even if she felt the least bit weary, never let on much, not until last night. Then she let on, all right.

But every woman ought to have a night to let on.

So he reasoned until the rain stopped. The clock said midafternoon and he knew he had to leave. He washed up well and brushed off his jacket, kissed Annie, and headed on up the street, walking slow at first, but sure, for it was what he had to do. Whatever it was, it was what he had to do.

But when he came to the business section of town, he stopped by Coltrane's place, not that he was going to work there or anything, because he wasn't; but he could pass the time of day.

Coltrane came out of the press room, caught him by the front of his jacket and took him to one side. "Say, Jordan, you got a brother?"

"Got three."

"One in town?"

"No. Wish one was. They're up North."

"Hefty fellow in here a few minutes ago, lookin' around suspicious-like, askin' if there were other colored businesses in town and what I thought of the future prospects. Talked like a northern man. Had those eyes."

"Huh? Well, not one o' mine."

"He looked like you and he spoke your name, asked where you lived."

"My name?"

"But wouldn't tell me who he was, 'cept his name was Bryant."

Jordan grinned. He couldn't help it. It was the finest news he had ever heard. Maybe he wouldn't have to talk to that Taylor widow after all, maybe all his worries were over. For Bryant, his youngest brother Bryant, who had gone into the North at seventeen, was back in Leafwood.

Jordan went home with a song. Never could you tell about the way the world would treat you. He had spent the whole night in mournful worry, thought he would have to change himself all around; but Lord, good luck arrived in the nick of time with Bryant come home. Oh, he could remember Bryant—pudgy little fellow, clinging to his ma, his hands grasping for everything. Always was one to grasp for everything. Going to take Brother Bryant around and show him the sights of the town. Let him get a hold on Leafwood. Going to introduce him to folks at the beer hall, make him welcome, and make repair for all he hadn't done for him when they were boys together on the farm.

By God, going to ask Bryant to take him back North with him, too—that was the answer. Going to pack up with Annie and the boys, dump the clothes in the pillow cases, and go North.

It was a fine day, Jordan saw, with not a care in the world. Nothing in the world but clearing skies and Bryant come home.

Yeah, there was the big car parked out front of his house. Got to run. Hurry your feet, Jordan, get across Hogan's hedge there. God-damn— Bryant home . . . .

He pushed open the front door. Then pulled up short. On the other side of the room, sitting on the sofa, was a giant man, older than his years.

It was Bryant, maybe, but all grown.

Bryant stuck a plump hand toward him. "Hello, boy," he said.

Jordan shook his head, stared across the room at Annie, who seemed to be as perplexed as he.

Bryant blurted out, "God, doesn't anybody know me? Don't you know me, boy?" He chuckled, and a slow, boyish smile came on his face. Jordan saw his brother in the smile. It was the old way, and for an instant emotions almost overcame him.

"Bryant!" Jordan said, and clapped him on the shoulders.

But when he touched him, the smile became a crafty look that crept out of his eyes. Jordan peered at him as if trying to see through his face and into the years that were between them.

"Bryant, I—" Jordan smiled, a lazy, warm smile. "You've come back."

Bryant's face clouded. "Not back, Jordan." Then he muttered, "A day or two." He moved heavily to the stove, laid his hands on the iron sides. "It was cold up North, is all. So I said, what the hell, I got folks back home. I got Jordan there, waitin'. And Annie—" He turned to them. "You got kids?" he asked.

"Two boys," Jordan said, still unable to get over the shock of seeing him and the changes that had come about.

"Yes," Bryant said. He looked at Annie longingly for a moment, then turned his brooding eyes on Jordan. For a moment a flare of anger seemed to rise in him, but he put it down. "I'm hungry," he said. "You got some eggs?"

He ate more than enough, Jordan thought. As fast as Annie cooked the food, he chucked it in by forkfuls.

"How's the world, Jordan?" he said. "Pa always said you was the best of us. How's life?"

Jordan smiled easily. "I been movin' along."

"Movin' along, huh?" Bryant tore off a piece of bread and stuffed it into his mouth. "Makin' progress, huh? Where you work?"

Jordan glanced at Annie. "Coalyard."

Bryant swallowed, then ran his tongue around the inside of his cheeks. "What do you do there?"

Jordan hesitated. "Drive a coal truck."

A slow smile came over Bryant's face, then he looked quickly down at his plate and started eating again. "You got a good house here, Jordan. How much is it worth?"

Jordan ran his tongue over his lips. "It ain't mine. I dunno."

"You rent?"

Jordan nodded, feeling still more uncomfortable.

Bryant shrugged. "It's all right to rent. Nothin' wrong with that."

When Annie put the other two eggs on the platter, he grabbed her arm. "Annie, how long has it been since I seen you, huh?"

"I don't know, Bryant. More'n ten years." She pulled away.

"Ten years," he said, releasing her. "Think o' that, Jordan—ten years, and now we're back together again! When did Mama die?"

Jordan tried to recall the year. It was difficult to think with his brother there, because he kept trying to see Bryant as a kid. What kept coming to his mind was an afternoon twenty years before, when an almost human cry had come from behind a thicket, and Jordan had gone to see what it was. He had come upon Bryant, a boy of eight, staring at a kitten which he had just nailed to a wooden cross. Jordan had gone out of his mind then and had beat Bryant until he was weak.

"Say, Jordan—you with us, boy?" Bryant reached across the table and punched his arm. "When did Mama die?"

Jordan blinked. "She died—she died six months of the time you went into the North."

"Huh?" He smiled. "Because I went?"

"She died o' pneumonia."

"Ah, yeah, I remember. Somebody wrote and said she went a-singin'."

Jordan knew that was the truth. He remembered.

"Yeah." Bryant pushed the remainder of the food onto his fork and downed it with a single swallow, then emptied the coffee cup and set it to one side for Annie to refill.

"Yeah, God help us. She was a good one." For a moment Jordan saw there was a deep sympathy inside him for her. Bryant drank more coffee, steaming and black, as all of the boys had done on the farm when there had been coffee to drink.

"God rest her in the ground," Jordan said, feeling ashamed for not remembering her, for not having gone to the grave to take flowers.

"But many a rain since ten years ago," Bryant said. Then he leaned back on the back legs of the chair, so that the chair creaked under him.

Annie brought mugs for Jordan and herself, put the coffee-pot on the table and sat down. "We was goin' to name one of our children after her," she said, "but they was boys. If they had been girls—"

"You want to see the boys, Bryant?" Jordan said suddenly. He could be proud of the boys. He would like to bring them inside and show them off. Nobody could take away the boys.

But Bryant ignored him. "I did good up in the North," he said easily. "I beat 'em." He chuckled. "Little Bryant beat 'em. Not hard. Just let them know what you want—that's the thing, and then don't let 'em stop you. Get it, by God. And I did, Jordan. I had three dollars left when I got up there, just three dollars of the money Mama gave me—"

"Pa gave it to you," Jordan said suddenly. "It was Pa and me that gave you the money."

Bryant stopped, remembering. Then abruptly he finished off the coffee in his mug, watched as Annie poured some more, looking at her thoughtfully. He had a hunger, Jordan saw, a great hunger. He appeared to want to devour whatever was around him.

"I got up there with three dollars left of that money," he said, "and I got a job working as a janitor in a factory building. I swept floors. I didn't get anywhere that way, so I quit; without even the three dollars to my name, because I wanted something. When you want something, and know what it is, you can get it." Bryant pounded the words, as if that was the one truth he had learned in the North.

"What did you want?" Jordan asked easily.

Bryant's eyes went around the room for a moment. "God, Jordan, you ought to paint these walls," he said.

Jordan sat back in the chair, stunned.

"Yeah, hell, Jordan, you ought to fix up this place." Then Bryant smiled. "Good food, Annie. I'm full." He leaned back on the back legs of the chair again. "Where are the boys?"

Jordan went to get them. He brought them in the front way and took them to their room, got their best clothes off the hangers. He pulled the shirts on over their arms, doing the work, although he knew they could dress themselves. Then he ran a handkerchief over their shoes, stood back and looked at them. "You're good boys," he said. They glanced at him, surprised, then at each other. "Come on, now," Jordan said. "It's your uncle. He's come back and wants to see you."

He opened the door and preceded them. But at the kitchen door, as Bryant turned his chair to face them, Jordan let the boys go in past him. They halted, stock-still, when they saw the huge body peering at them from across the dim room.

"This is Fletcher," Jordan said, "and this is Harris."

Bryant stared at them hungrily for a long while. He took out a cigar and bit off the end of it, spit out pieces of tobacco. Annie came toward the boys and adjusted their shirts. There was no need to do that, but it helped to put them at ease. Then she stepped back. Once more they waited for Bryant to speak.

He puffed on the cigar, inhaling the smoke. Jordan knew that Bryant was having some trouble because of the boys.

Finally he said, "Come here, boys."

They didn't move.

"Go to your uncle," Annie said.

The boys hesitated, then went forward to stand within a few feet of Bryant. A big smile came over his face. He tossed the cigar into his empty plate, and put a heavy hand on each of the boys' shoulders. "Fletcher and Harris," he said. He looked at the older one. "You're named after your grandfather, ain't you, boy?"

Fletcher nodded, biting his lip.

Bryant turned his eyes on the younger boy. Suddenly he pulled Annie's chair around, and with his foot pushed Jordan's out from the table. "Sit down and talk awhile to your uncle Bryant."

The boys sat down at the table. Bryant poured a small amount of coffee into each of the mugs before them, then filled his own. Jordan stood ill at ease near the doorway, seeing that there was no place for him to sit down. There were only two chairs in the room, both children's chairs.

"I've been to the North, boys," Bryant said after a moment. "I been on a long trip. I seen the world, boys."

Harris' eyes widened and Jordan saw him lean across the table. A pang of pain touched Jordan as he remembered that he had not talked to the boys about the world outside Leafwood. Even when they had gone carefully over the pictures in the magazines, or in their schoolbooks, he had thought it best not to talk to them about the world—he knew the hunger inside himself would take hold on them. But the hunger was in their eyes now. It had made its own way.

"I've seen the subways—the trains—you seen trains?"

The boys nodded.

"I've seen buildings that was over fifty floors, boys, rearin' into the sky, damn near to the clouds. Think o' that."

The boys were thinking of it. Jordan saw that they had their eyes fixed on Bryant. Then Fletcher looked at Jordan with a furtive look, as if to say that Bryant was all right, that Bryant had seen the world and was a miracle, and that it was good that Bryant had come home. Jordan couldn't hold himself from going to the table. "I reckon it's time for the boys to be back outdoors," he said.

Harris and Fletcher looked up at him disappointed.

"Why, Jordan, I ain't started yet," Bryant said. He smiled a slow, disarming smile; then ignoring the glaring Jordan, went on. "When I first went to the North, I got off a truck at New York City, right smack in the middle of the biggest city anywhere. I stood there and looked at them buildings until I was dizzy. To think I was seventeen and had never seen them buildings, never even knowed they was there. My stomach got sick."

Bryant drowned a swallow of coffee.

"I got sick, and I was standin' right in the middle of the sidewalk with people goin' to and fro, so I wanted to get off by myself. There weren't no way to do it, boys, until I saw a stairway goin' down into the sidewalk, so I went down and under a gate, found a private place for a while.

"When I was feelin' better and was thinkin' about goin' back upstairs, I heard a rumblin' in the earth, and people started movin' around some. Then before I could decide what to do, there come a train, boys, right out of the belly of the ground."

Jordan didn't know whether Bryant was making this up, or whether it was so. He didn't know what he ought to do, either, but he didn't want anybody lying to his boys.

"What did the . . . train do, Uncle Bryant?" Harris said.

Bryant peered at him through the cigar smoke. He looks like the devil, Jordan thought.

"It stopped boys, right in front of me. And its doors opened, just sprung back. Any minute I expected to hear an order to get on, but not a sound was made by anybody as they stepped through the door. And when the train had had enough, the doors closed, not a hand a touchin' 'em, and the train went back into the ground."

Jordan started to interrupt and get the boys out of the room.

"Did you ever get on the train, Uncle Bryant?"

Bryant nodded, much to Jordan's surprise." I played it cool for a while, but the train seemed to be motionin' for me, so when the next one come, I climbed aboard." Bryant's face was animate with a strange light now, and his fat cheeks began quivering as he described his mad ride under the ground. "I was ridin' the rails into the dark, boys, with little lights on in the cars so you could see some of what went on. God, I was too scared to breathe. Then it hit me where I was a-goin'."

The boys leaned forward. Jordan ran his tongue nervously over his lips.

"We was goin' to hell, boys. I looked around at the others, and sure enough they seemed to know it, too. They was lookin' straight ahead, not an eye waverin', cold and death-like. We was goin' to hell, and nothin' to be done."

Jordan cast a helpless look at Annie, but she wasn't looking at him. She was standing stiffly erect, her eyes fixed on Bryant's face.

"All that afternoon I rode that train. People kept gettin' on and off and I didn' t know but what I should get off, too, so I picked me out a nigger that looked meaner than any other, and I followed him. When he got off, I got off. He got on another train after a while, and I did the same. Then he rode a long ways and got off. There was a whole flock of us now, mulatto and black-skinned, and I said to myself, 'Bryant, you done right. You got with your own people. They got segregation in hell.' "

Bryant roared with laughter, but Jordan only looked at him with a burning fear in his eyes, and he saw that his boys were clinging to the edges of the table top.

"Then we all went up the stairway. It was night up there, and the street was full of cars and other niggers, and I saw that hell was crowded. The cells where people lived was on top of one another and side by side, linin' the sides of every street, with people stickin' their heads out o' the windows and yellin' down—'Hello, Charley . . .hello, Stella, where you goin' now?'

"And I saw that the trees had all been burnt away, and every blade o' grass. There was nothin' left to burn."

The boys had forgotten all about their coffee. They were breathless with wonder and cringing with fear. Bryant sat back in his chair and wiped his perspiring face with the sleeve of his coat. Jordan told himself that it was just Bryant, not a devil. It was Bryant, and he had beat him up once that he could remember clear enough, and other times that he had forgotten the reason for. It was just Bryant sitting there talking to his boys.

"And the women, boys, was unlike anything I ever saw. They was not kinky-headed all around, but some of 'em was flat-haired, and they had paint on their faces. Well, sir, I followed. I walked up and down until I got tired, and all I saw was startlin', with the cells everywhere, and the people, people, people, boys. And finally I got to wonderin' about the time, so I found a man standin' over in the shadows at one corner, and I went up to him and said, 'Do you know the time, or do you have time down here?'

"He smiled. 'Down here?' Then he smiled again. 'Where are you from?'

"'The other world.'

"He commenced to laugh. 'Where is the other world?'

"'North Carolina,' I said.

"He roared, boys. He damn near died o' laughin'. Then he said, 'Where do you think you are now, son?"

"Hell-fire,' I told him.

"He bent double laughin'. Then he took me by the arm and led me down the street to a big room where about ten men was stretched out on cots—just layin' there, like they had all eternity.

"And he told them I was Bryant Cummings from the other world, and that I wanted to know more about hell. Well, sir, they laughed and carried on and passed me a bottle of whisky so many times I lost complete count of myself. It was a big night, and the last I remember as a fellow leanin' across a cot towards me and stickn' his face close to mine and sayin', 'Bryant Cummings, what do you think o' hell?'

"And I answered him right off. I remember sayin', 'Hell ain't so bad,' and the whole place fell to laughin'. 'Hell ain't so bad,' I said."

Bryant leaned back on the rickety chair and roared out his own laughter. Jordan watched him, his mind troubled by the story. He saw that Harris had perspiration on his face, as if it were a nightmare to him and he wanted to wake up.

"Uncle Bryant," he said. "Uncle Bryant—"

Bryant finally stopped laughing. Then he got his cigar going again.

"Uncle Bryant, was you in hell?"

Bryant puffed on the cigar. "That's right, boys."

Jordan stared at him. He saw that little Harris was shivering.

"I ain't been tellin' you boys anything but the solid gospel. Ask your pa. He knows everything."

The boys peered up at their father anxiously.

"Don't seem likely," Jordan said bluntly. "No. It's all a big lie, boys. Can't go to hell unless you're dead, and Bryant wasn't."

The smile went off Bryant's face slowly. The boys sat back relieved and now at ease. Bryant kept his eyes on Jordan. Then the smile came back, slow and growing. Suddenly he laughed, then clutched the boys hands until Jordan knew he was hurting them. He looked at the boys, a crafty gleam in his eyes. "I was in Harlem, boys, H-A-R-L-E-M. Don't forget it. Go to Harlem, boys. Godamighty, what a man can't do in Harlem."

Then he laughed again, leaned forward as much as his belly would permit, stretching toward Fletcher. "What do you think, boy? 'Hell ain't so bad,' I said. 'Hell ain't so bad.' "

An hour later Jordan led Fletcher and Harris to their room and told them to take off the Sunday clothes.

"Is Uncle Bryant your brother?" Fletcher asked.

"My youngest."

"Has he been everywhere?"

Jordan shook his head wearily. "Hard to say, boys."

He left them then, but stood in the hall listening for a minute as they began talking in low voices. He heard them mention the building and the trains in the ground. From the living room came the voices of Bryant and Annie as they got Bryant's suitcase and belongings stacked near the sofa, where Bryant was to sleep that night.

"That sofa ain't comfortable, Bryant," Annie said, "but it's the best we got."

"Never mind. Tomorrow I'll get me a room in a hotel."

Jordan went in. "Ain't no hotels for our kind here," he said.

"Huh?"

"No place to stay, except a small roomin' house."

"Godamighty!" Bryant sank down on the sofa, his arms hanging across his belly. "What a town. What this town needs, Jordan, is a little Harlem drive. By God, I got a notion—"

He stopped, then said impulsively, "Well, I'll sleep here tonight. Say, Jordan, you need any money?"

Annie glanced away. Jordan hesitated. "No. Got all we need, Bryant," he said.

A sly smile came into Bryant's face. He looked around the worn room for a moment, his eyes stopping on Annie's house dress which had been patched in small places and sewed together several times. "That's good," he said, the smile still on his face. "Always good to have all you need." He chuckled deep down inside himself. "Always did know you would make out well, boy."

Jordan went into the kitchen and waited while Annie got a light supper ready for him and the boys. Bryant came in soon enough and began to tell stories, one following another without break or separation.

Jordan ate quickly, then sneaked off. He got his jacket on and quietly opened the living-room door. In the kitchen Bryant was going on and on with the boys, and Jordan hated to leave just then. But he had important business.

More important than ever, now that Bryant had come home.

3

A clap of thunder rumbled as Jordan started out. He kept near the center of the sidewalk, staggering a bit from the weariness of his spirit, ignoring those who passed on either side. He passed the Texaco station where he had worked the previous morning. He went on by the drugstore huddled at the corner, its windows pasted with numbers. He passed the movie house where the whites were hurrying into the early show, and the coffee shop where the internes from the hospital held out on weekday evenings, meeting there with the student nurses. There were many stories the waiters told about the internes and the nurses, their blunt language and free laughter.

He passed the post office, then cut up past the inn, a three story colonial building with wide, white planks on its sides and a dozen false chimneys. On the porch sat the tourists and salesmen, caught in Leafwood for the night, watching the passers-by with the detachment of those who had little interest in what they see. Jordan had worked at the inn many years before, but the assistant manager has cursed him one morning for backing into a tray of dishes, and Jordan had brushed him up a bit.

It began to rain. Jordan hurried across the street to the side where the poplars shaded the walk. Even so, his shirt got soaking wet. He walked faster, noticing how the street lights reflected on the wet pavement and gravel paths, shadowing the eroded gullies. He walked by colonial homes, brick and wood, by cottages, bungalows, by porches with families gathered to watch the rain, by the window-closed homes of people away.

A block farther he crossed a street and entered the section of town where Coltrane and the other wealthy Negroes lived. The house of the Taylor widow was on a large corner lot.

It was a roomy place, and now, from one lighted window, it seemed to spread out into the night. He kept his eyes on that window as he approached. Quietly he mounted the steps to the porch. Only then did he hesitate. Warily he looked back at the street, expecting to see people watching him. But the street was empty. A car passed, its headlights flashing across the front of the house as it rounded the corner, but that was all.

For several seconds he was unable to decide what to do. Then, moving impulsively, he approached the window and peered in.

The woman was standing near the fireplace, looking at a small, framed photograph. His eyes swept around the rest of the room. No one was there with her—only the large, faded chairs, dark tables and richly colored rugs.

She turned, leaning back on the mantel. Her lips were moving, forming words, as she talked to herself. Jordan decided she was a mixture of white and Negro blood, with, perhaps, other kinds as well. Her features were fragile, almost oriental. Her skin was light; her hair was straightened and held back by pins.

My Lord, she is pretty, he thought.

She left the mantel and walked across the room, moving aimlessly. Now he could hear a few words: "Ben" and "years."

She moved back to the fireplace, laid her temple against the mantel, a weary, defeated gesture; her hand now touched the picture.

He backed off from the window, dismayed by what he had seen and, even more, because he has seen it. He started to run from the porch, but as he reached the steps, he stopped, hesitated, then slowly moved to the front door and knocked.

He knocked again, louder. He straightened stiffly when the light streaked into the hall as the parlor door opened. The woman peered curiously toward the front door. She reached at arm's length and flipped on the porch light, then blinked, startled, started to turn away, then stood confused.

"What—what do you want?" she called through the door.

"To talk," he heard himself say. His voice was about to break with tension. "To talk tonight."

"No." She shook her head, frantically.

Jordan waited as if held by the white circle of the porch light. "I have to get clear," he said.

She hesitated, then abruptly reached forward, unlocked the front door and threw it open.

"Ben, please—" she said, then swiftly turned away. "Wait here." She hurried up the hall stairs and was gone.

Jordan was stunned by the unexpected words and the painful voice. He backed out of the circle of light until he touched the porch rail. She had called him Ben. Perhaps from the start she had had him confused with someone else. That could explain the telephone calls.

Behind him on the street a car made swishing sounds as it slithered along the pavement. In the distance he heard a man call to another. Then the night settled down again.

A while later he heard her come slowly down the stairs. She unlatched the screen door, turned off the porch light. When she came out, the odor of perfume was faintly about her and make-up was on her face. "It isn't Ben, is it?" she said.

Jordan stood stiffly. "No. My name is Jordan."

"Yes, of course," she said. "It isn't Ben. It couldn't be, you know." She stood silently for a moment, as if considering it, then crossed to the swing. "I had been thinking about him this evening, and naturally when I heard the knock—"

Jordan nodded, leaned back once more on the rail. It was difficult to see her clearly, but occasionally a car would come by and he would see her face, now strangely animated. "I came to talk about when you and me had that argument."

She said nothing to that.

"I heard you phoned the coalyard two, three times." He thought he saw her shake her head, as if denying it. "I got a wife and two boys, and I can't get another job. It's got my mind too busy for me to stand."

There was silence for a moment, except for the porch swing moving gently, as if swaying in a breeze.

"It sounded so old-fashioned to hear the rain on the roof tonight," she said softly. "My mind went back. Then you came by, and it all seems to be part of the same pattern."

"I want to talk about the job."

"Let's not. It's not part of the pattern, is it? Let's not talk about bad feelings or mistakes. I'll call the coalyard tomorrow and explain. You'll get your job back."

He ran his hand nervously over his face and turned to look out at the street, as if removing himself from her presence. He didn't know how to thank a young woman, and he wasn't sure he should thank this one. She was only undoing what she shouldn't have done to start with.

"Is that all you want, Jordan—a job at the coalyard?"

He noticed the warmth of her voice, the softness of it, and remembered her face as he had seen it through the window, the fragile beauty. No need getting involved, though. To sleep with one of the girls at Minnie's was all right. That was over when you wanted it to be.

"Goin' to rain, I think," he said. "Goin' to rain a great deal before I can get home."

"Don't go now."

"Got caught in the rain a while ago. Was walkin' around, lookin' at the town. My wife probably wonders where I am. Been wonderin', I suppose."

The swing stopped moving. She rose. "I usually have coffee this time of night. Would you like some?"

Jordan hesitated, surprised by the question.

"We can go back to the kitchen."

She touched his arm. He stood nervously, not knowing for sure why she had asked him, but having no easy way to refuse, he followed her into the house. She led the way down the long dark hall and through the dining room, then clicked on the light, revealing a square room with a feeling of age and comfort to it in spite of the white, shiny appliances and creamy-colored cabinets built across the walls. Jordan sat down uneasily at the kitchen table and watched.

She moved efficiently between the electric stove and the cabinets, getting out coffee, running water into the percolator, then plugging it into an electric outlet. "Isn't it strange that we're here, Jordan?" she said, smiling. "Two people in the whole world, sitting in a kitchen, the world going on outside, not bothering us, we not bothering it."

He crossed his legs uneasily. It was true there was a feeling of safety there, as if he had removed himself from the problems that had worried him; but at the same time he was not sure of the woman.

"I like it this way," she said. "I'm afraid I always embarrassed the world when I was part of it. As a little girl, I used to go swimming in a creek near the town I lived in. Not many of us ever went there, and I thought of it as mine. And whenever anybody else would come near the place, I would yell at them, 'See, I'm in swimming naked!' I would be kneeling down in the water, so they couldn't see."

"Was you naked?"

"Yes. I was the one naked, but they were the ones embarrassed, and they would go running away through the woods and leave me alone. I've always gone through life embarrassing people until they left me alone, people I didn't want to be around."

Jordan shook his head, unable to adjust his thinking to what she had told him. "You don't talk like you did the other day."

"No. I'm sorry about what I said." She smiled. "Do you know why I got angry with you? Because you reminded me of Ben. Isn't that strange? Same big frame, same temper, almost same features. But you really aren't much like him, I'm happy to find out."

Jordan moved uneasily on the chair, which was too small for him. "I don't know Ben," he said.

She smiled at him, examining him thoughtfully. "Tell me about yourself."

"I need a job, that's the start of it."

"I'll call the coalyard. Stop worrying." Then after a moment she said, "Is that all there is about you?"

"I want to get away from Leafwood."

Her eyes closed for an instant, as if she were trying to hide her expression.

"This town has me hemmed in," he continued. "Thought I'd like to try to get North."

She nodded slowly. "You are like him, too, aren't you?" she said.

"Huh?"

"Yes. You are."

"Tell me about the North," Jordan said.

She smiled. "The North is—there, and if your luck is good—"

"My luck is good ordinarily."

"I was a dancer, and I got along. Then Mr. Taylor came up and saw the show I was dancing in, came back to the dressing room. The other girls laughed, because he was old. But I liked him. He was honest. Maybe old people can afford to be honest. That night he told me what he wanted, and I said I would marry him."

Jordan tried to take it all in, but she left out some of what he wanted to know. He wanted to ask her what it was that Mr. Taylor had said. He had an idea, but he couldn't imagine the old man saying it. Taylor had always gone around town with a walking stick in his hand, shooing away the kids and dogs with it. The idea of Taylor wanting a woman was too much for Jordan to take, unless he just wanted somebody to keep him warm.

"Where you from, Mrs. Taylor?" he asked her.

"Call me Mona. I'm from Minneapolis."

Jordan blinked, unsure of what she had said. "Where?"

"It's in Minnesota."

Jordan nodded.

"You know where that is?"

"Sure," Jordan said evasively.

"Jordan—"

He looked up at her.

"You don't, do you?"

For a moment he was angry, at himself first, then at her; but he got over it. She was so open and frank, he didn't mind admitting he had lied. "No, I don't."

"Don't lie, Jordan. Why pretend? Don't pretend with me, not here."

Jordan nodded solemnly, his eyes fixed on her. For a moment he wondered if she was a Negro. She wasn't like the Negroes in Tin Top; not even like Coltrane's wife, a girl who had also come from the North. She was like a white person, always thinking beyond herself.

"What else about New York?" he said.

She smiled, spoke gently. "Let's talk about here and now. Why do you want to talk about another world?"

"You live in another world," he said, the thought striking him as he spoke it.

She met his gaze only for a moment, then rose quickly and walked back to the stove, unplugged the percolator. She brought out the clean cups and saucers, took a box of cookies from the cabinet, and put it on the table. She poured coffee into his cup, then her own and sat down across from him.

They drank in silence, Jordan watching her, fascinated by her, but feeling that he did not belong.

"I have two fine boys," he said suddenly.

She looked at him quietly for a moment, as if trying to decide why he had said that.

"The boys is what I like."

"Do you tell them that?"

Before he could answer, she said, "You should, we should all say what we think. So many people go around with a curtain before them."

Jordan wiped his mouth with his sleeve, pushed his cup aside. He didn't understand about the curtain, but he didn't understand so much she said, that it didn't bother him. If she meant that he should say what he thought about her, he would be hard put to do it. He wanted her—he could say that. But he didn't want her, either, and he didn't know why, except that he had a feeling he couldn't deal with what he couldn't understand.

"I'd better go," he said.

She didn't look up. "Do you want to, really?"

He felt like a kid sitting there before her. He didn't want to go, but he didn't want to sleep with her. It would be like sleeping with Annie, but not Annie, either, for he understood Annie from the start. It would be like Annie only in that she wanted him, and only in that he wanted her in a deep way, different, that is, from the girls at Minnie's house.

He rose from the table, started across the kitchen to the hall. But as soon as he stepped through the door, he heard a sob, a breaking sound. "Ben—"

The pain in her voice stopped him. He stood there as if frozen to the floor, being touched by pain.

He heard her rise from the table and walk across the floor of the kitchen toward him. He turned slowly, saw her standing in the kitchen doorway, leaning on the door frame, tears in her eyes.

"Woman, just let me be," was all he could manage to say.

When he was outside her house, he wondered why he hadn't gone ahead with it. "God-damn coal truck," he mumbled, not knowing why.

But he did know she wouldn't phone the coalyard now. He had shut the door tight there, and it would be for him to go talk to Mr. Crawford at the yard, take the hard road. Nobody could be harder than Mr. Crawford.

And why had he done it?

Didn't he know full well that he couldn't get her out of his mind by running off like he had?

4

He lumbered down from Mona's house toward the dark recesses of Tin Top, a troubled but undefeated manner in the movement of his arms and legs, the high tilt of his head. The sky was clear now, the moon and stars were out. The rain had passed over, leaving the earth new-smelling, but it was chilly, too, and he pulled his jacket tighter around him.

Two blocks from Tin Top he changed his course and headed across the freight yard. If he was going to have to talk to old man Crawford, he might as well get it over with.

But the lights were out at the coal shack; Crawford wasn't there. Jordan gave the steel fence a blow with his foot and turned toward home. He would have to put up with another night of doubt and unrest.

But then he heard a freight train, heard its whistle. The sound went through him and sent him running. He reached the tracks just as the train came into view, rumbling toward him, moving fast, the diesel passing with a rush of air and the noise of rolling wheels. Behind came the freight cars, dull and dark, but as they clanked on, almost close enough for him to touch, he remembered the one time he had seen a passenger train, three years before in Durham. It had come by with windows brightly flashing, framing faces—a pretty girl, an old man bearded, a scar on the lip of a woman, a man smiling. Now his mind saw the windows and felt pride for each of the faces going out of that country, riding into the night, looking for something or somebody. He would see the faces again, somewhere, maybe in the North. Yes, in the North.

He stood there in the scorched weeds as the train, catching moonlight on its side, slithered along. Then the last car passed, leaving a dark, great empty space against the sky.

Goin' North, Jordan thought. He turned to look after it. When the train was only a faint light dimming, he knelt down, put his ear to the steel rail. And he heard it; the vibrations took sound. He heard the humming far away, wheels rolling. A singing going North.

When he reached home, Bryant was perched on one end of the sofa, talking away to Annie and the boys. Fletcher and Harris got right off, because it was almost half an hour past their bedtime, and their uncle extended his hand to them, as if they were grown-up. They shook it, giggling slightly, and hurried to their room; but through their closed door they could be heard to laugh and talk about what Uncle Bryant had done.

Jordan sat down restlessly on the side of the sofa opposite Bryant and knitted his hands together.

After a moment Bryant said, "Where you been, boy?"

"Oh—" Jordan ran his hand over his face. "Went to walk, but my mind got turned. Stopped down by the railroad yard for a while."

"Uh huh," Bryant said easily, as if he understood all about that. He didn't take his eyes off Jordan.

"Listenin' part o' the time."

"Was you?" Bryant said.

"Listenin' to New York, way off."

Bryant chuckled at that, but when he saw Jordan kept a serious face, he stopped and turned around on the sofa, almost self-consciously. "New York?" he said. "Well, you ought to go up there sometime, Jordan."

"Plan to."

Annie looked fretful at that, picked up a worn part of a magazine and started flipping the pages fast enough to tear the paper. But Bryant didn't notice anything about her; he was watching Jordan. "Why don't you just take off?"

"Well—" Jordan wished Annie would just go out of the room so he could talk to Bryant about it. "I got this family, Bryant, and it ties a man down." Annie suddenly glanced over at him. "I mean, it's a good thing," he said, "but it's bindin' on travelin' around."

"Take the family. That's what I'd do."

"Uh huh." Jordan said easily. "How much—how much it cost to get everyone up there?"

"Oh—" Bryant looked away. A small grin came to his face. "Little travelin' money—not much. Then something for a start. Maybe need five hundred dollars in all." He glanced at Jordan. "You have that much, don't you?"

Jordan wet his lips, embarrassed because Annie was there. It was hard to talk while she was listening to every word. "Well, not quite." Then he looked at Bryant straight out. "No, I don't."

Bryant folded his hands on his big lap, as if dismissing the subject. "No matter. Plenty of opportunities here."

Jordan shifted uneasily, feeling he was on the verge of getting somewhere with Bryant, but not sure. "Think Washington is closer?" he asked.

Bryant nodded. "Know it is."

"Well then," Jordan said quickly, "what about Washington?"

Bryant shrugged. "When I went up North, stopped by there, started to walk on from the freight yard to town and look it over, but I said, 'No, Bryant, go on up to New York first and see that.' So I stayed on the freight and we rolled into the train yard up in New York. Tell you what, boy, I knowed right then, first off, that my hunch had been right. You know what decided me?"

Jordan shook his head.

"The track. Washington and New York was just alike, except one had more track. And I said, 'Bryant, you got the big one; hold on." He sat back on the sofa and chuckled to himself, deeply satisfied.

Jordan poked around in his pocket and pulled out a handkerchief. "Well, New York is better, I know," he said, wiping the perspiration from his face.

"Much better. But no better in a way than Durham or Raleigh. I tell you these little places have boundless shores for growth. Stopped by Raleigh this mornin', bustlin' city. Stopped by Durham before comin' over here. Things are movin' in Durham. But you know that, don't you, Jordan?"

Jordan nodded, feeling more than ever ill at ease.

"Sure. Right here under your nose. Bound to know." Bryant smiled, almost gently. "Probably got so many opportunities you don't know which one to take, ain't that so?"

Jordan stared back at Bryant, seeing where the conversation was leading and becoming a bit frightened because of it. He didn't know what to say to him. He was about to stammer out some sort of reply, when suddenly Annie tossed the magazine half across the room and onto the sofa. She stood, pressed her dress down smooth in front and, without looking at either of them, said, "Time for bed."

It was very much like the final word.

A few minutes later, when Jordan closed the bedroom door, she was standing near the closet he had nailed together across one corner. She was just standing there at the curtain, not hanging up her clothes or taking anything out. He unbuttoned his shirt and threw it across the bedpost, let his pants drop to the floor, then hung them on a wall nail. With his underwear on, he climbed into the bed. Annie pulled her dress off over her head, hung it up carefully; then, with her slip on, climbed in beside him.

They lay there, one on a side, breathing toward sleep; but after a while Annie sighed heavily and turned slightly on the bed. "Storekeeper's not happy," she said.

"Huh? What does that mean?"

"Means we might not get more credit. If you can't get your job back, might have to ask somebody for help."

"Help? Who we ask?"

She breathed heavily again. "Might ask Bryant."

"Good God." He turned over on his back. "No, by God," he said. "Look, Annie, I'll have it straight tomorrow. I'll go up to the coalyard first thing."

Her hand came over and felt his arm; she tightened on it just a bit, as if to say she knew he would. But then she said— "Still, if you don't, Jordan—"

"Lord, I will. Honey, look, why—why if I don't, I'll ask elsewhere. Haven't had time to make a proper search since I lost out, anyway."

"Even if the coalyard turns you down—"

"Even so. Lord, just name a place. Plenty o' chances for work in this town. Go on, name a place."

"Well," Annie began, "you could go back to the mill."

"Well, they're layin' off, Annie. You know how textiles is."

"There's the hospital."

Jordan hesitated. "Yeah, that's right."

"They pay well, Jordan."

"They do," he said. "Name another."

"There's—there's the lumberyard. Hogan next door might could help you."

"Of course he could."

"And the construction places. You always said you could get back on there."

"Any day," he said, the weight of worry creeping into his voice. "Why, got a world o' chances."

Annie took his hand now, squeezed it. Gently he put his arms around her, drew her close. "You see, don't you worry," he whispered. He ran his fingers over her shoulder and through her hair. "Don't you worry 'bout tomorrow, Annie." He felt her breathe deeply, lying in his arms. "Don't nobody worry 'bout tomorrow, 'cept me."

5

Mr. Crawford peered through the dark interior of the coal shack toward where Jordan was standing. He sucked air through his teeth for a minute and then sat down on the corner of Patrick's table, a wiry, tall man of sixty years or more, with hair sparkling white except where the streaks of coal dust had colored it. His shoulders were bent from being around heavy work, even though he had not done much of it.

"You cussed any more nigger women?" he said.

Jordan looked at him evenly. "No, I haven't, Mr. Crawford."

"She phoned me, you know. Phoned a couple of times, breathin' fire and damnation."

Jordan nodded, wondering how he could ask about his job.

"Is she justified?" Crawford asked.

"I don't know what she told you, Mr. Crawford."

"Yeah, well you know more than you say, though, don't you? Know enough not to insult a customer, anyhow. Bad sign to do that, no matter who it is, and that woman does more than two hundred dollars of coal business every year."

Mr. Crawford spoke in such low tones Jordan could hardly hear him. But when he or Patrick spoke, it was loud and clear.

"Somebody told me she had led a wild life in New York City," Crawford said, "and all of it wasn't dancin', neither. Leastwise, there's a plainer word than dancin' for it."

The old man laughed in a throaty chuckle that graduated down to a hoarse giggle. Then he wiped his face with a handkerchief dirtied by coal dust.

"But—" he said, as if remembering an important point, "along with that same line there was a woman that used to work at my father's farm, about thirty-five she was, and a maid, never married, and there was no point in any boy tryin' to chase her, not that any boy ever would. But one night we heard a big commotion as she come back into the house from the woodpile."

Jordan was listening sullenly. The old man knew he was there to talk about his job, not about women.

"She come in weepin', her clothes tore, and carryin' a couple o' sticks o' cordwood. And she said she had been raped at the woodpile. Well, it was dark and I guess the fellow couldn't see what he was gettin'. Anyway she was a bawlin' and carryin' on. My father was hoppin' mad, went to get his shotgun, and he and me and my two brothers scoured the countryside lookin' for this fellow that had done it."

Crawford reflected on that for a long time, then slowly he said, "But you know, Jordan, after that happened, no wood was ever carried into the house in the daytime. The girl would make three or four trips ever night. And she was carryin' wood in the heat o' summertime."

Patrick let out a cackle and began to laugh uncontrollably. Jordan grinned, then laughed, thinking about the girl. The old man listened carefully as if judging whether or not they fully appreciated his story.

When the laughter died down, he nodded several times, then glanced up at Jordan. "Thought I could make you laugh, but I wasn't sure. When I came in here, you looked like the last rose o' summer."

Jordan grinned down at the old man. He liked him in spite of the way he cursed the workers as they sweated getting coal on the trucks. But he had never cursed Jordan, nor had Smith, the foreman.

Crawford rose, expelling a great deal of air. "Got to get out in the yard, so take over, Patrick."

"Yes, sir," Patrick said.

Jordan waited until Crawford was almost to the door. "Mr. Crawford, I need my job back," he said.

Crawford stopped with his hand on the knob. He turned around and slowly came back to him. "I figured you did. I was waitin' for you to say it."

"I need it bad."

"You never did feel you needed it bad when you had it, did you?"

Jordan hesitated.

"You see—" He stuck his forefinger in Jordan's chest. "I know nigger workers. And you was a rover."

Jordan wet his lips, stared at Crawford uneasily.

"But now you want a job, and that's a change for the good."

"Yes, sir." Jordan kept a loose watch on the old man's expression.

Crawford sat back down in the chair. "And you're a good worker, too, but why should I hire you? You would be in trouble inside a month."

"No, I wouldn't."

"Don't tell me you wouldn't. I'd have trouble, trouble, trouble right down to the line. And as much as I would like to help you out, I can't see takin' you back."

"I didn't mean you wouldn't have trouble, Mr. Crawford," Jordan said, trying to keep control of his voice. "I don't claim to be changed entirely, but I got a wife and two boys, and I intend to change. And I owe money already."

"How much do you owe?"

"I owe maybe twenty dollars."

Crawford slapped his open palm down on his pants leg. "Lord, think o' that! I'd have every merchant in Leafwood callin' me up, askin' why my help don't pay their bills—"

"I'll pay 'em, Mr. Crawford."

"Yeah, and raise children and everything else, won't you? And get all the whiskey you want, break up your furniture for firewood when you get cold. I know the nigger. Put five hundred Englishmen down in Tin Top for a year and then see how it would shine. But niggers set on the porches, or have a time, or enjoy their misery and produce young 'uns. You're a rover, Jordan, the worst of 'em!"

Jordan was about to blurt out a warning to the old man when Patrick suddenly interrupted, speaking swiftly and distinctly, and laughing happily. "Say, Mr. Crawford," he said, "watch what you include or you'll be firin' ever man on the lot."

Crawford started, surprised by the interruption, then amused by the laughter. Jordan glanced over at Patrick, knowing that he owed him a debt for breaking in when he did.

"Don't know what I'd do without that laugh, Patrick," Crawford said.

Patrick cackled a few more times, delighted with the remark, and strangely embarrassed.

Crawford looked up at Jordan again. "What were we sayin', Jordan?"

"I hope you was about to say I could have my job back."

"Oh, yes," Crawford said, a light gleaming in his eyes. "The job."

The room was quiet for a moment. "I can get a man to work for less than I was payin' you, Jordan. I was payin' you fifty, wasn't I? Well, I can get a man for forty, sir."

Crawford stared up at him. "Many manage on less."

Jordan knew not to challenge him now. "That's true, sir. That's true."

"Coal ain't sellin' proper. Time was when ten dollars a week didn't matter much, but it does now."

"Yes, sir. And I guess you have a family, too, don't you, Mr. Crawford?"

"You know I do! Seven grandchildren."

"Bet they're cute." Jordan saw it as a game and he intended to play it.

"They're the cutest kids in town, bar none. Oh, my, they are characters! One of them looks the spit'n' image of me."

"I bet he does," Jordan said quickly.

"Just exactly. He's smart, too. He can recite a poem that I didn't learn till a year older'n him. I had a fair memory a boy. Now I can't remember much o' anything."

"I don't remember well, either." Jordan said it in agreement with the old man, but when he saw the white head bob suddenly, he knew he had done the wrong thing.

"What do you mean—either?"

Jordan shifted uneasily from foot to foot, desperately trying to think of a way out of the predicament. He noticed that Patrick was looking at him, frightened now.

"I'll say this for myself," Crawford said emphatically. "Folks can talk as they please, but I remember many things that most people my age have long since forgot. I'm not ashamed to say that I still know many of the stories about the boyhood country I grew up in, and the ballads and all. I have a good memory, I think."

"I'm sure you do," Jordan said quickly.

"Many a man in this town with half my years can't outremember me.

I don't claim to be the sharpest man alive, but I can remember my childhood might nigh as well as I could when I was fifty, or even forty. I ain't lost much powers."

"No, sir," Jordan said.

They were quiet for a moment, Jordan feeling that the high hopes he had that morning were going to come to a short end. "I bet you do remember the old days," he said nervously, "All the old ways o' doin' things."

Crawford said nothing to that.

"Bet you broke many a horse as a boy, and saw many a calf born."

Jordan looked nervously toward Patrick, who shook his head quickly to indicate that it was pointless to continue.

"Bet you remember the old church services," Jordan said. He was going to keep trying until there was no hope at all, then he didn't know what he would do. "They don't sing the old songs like they used to, do they, Mr. Crawford?"

There was a pause, then the old white head tilted to look up at him, and a small smile came over Crawford's face. "Indeed they don't, Jordan," he said, almost fondly. "Why don't they sing like they used to?"

"I don't know," Jordan said. "They gettin' fancy, I guess."

"I like 'Amazin' Grace,'" Crawford said. "That was my father's favorite. He would stand in church and sing that song till the rafters rung. Was the loudest-mouthed singer in the congregation. Visitin' preachers would single my father out for comment when they got up to preach, speak out in his favor, as if they needed to defend him. And my father would beam with pride and look around at the others as if he had shaken the rag off the bush, and my mother would look straight ahead as if she didn't know a single member of her own family. He was just loud, Jordan. He couldn't sing a note."

Jordan laughed, deeply relieved to see that Crawford was talking to him again.

"He couldn't carry a tune." Crawford sat back, caught by the thoughts of the old church. "'Amazin' Grace,'" he said. "Patrick, do you know that old song?"

"Yes, sir," Patrick said.

"Sing it, then. Let's all sing it."

Jordan was stunned by the thought, but he had to have the job, and he wanted to win this game he was playing with Mr. Crawford.

Patrick stood, cleared his throat. Then on signal from Mr. Crawford, the three of them started in, there was just one thought in Jordan's mind, and that was to sing loud. He hit every word he knew with full force, and soon the small building was rocking on its foundation.

> *Amazin' grace, how sweet the sound*
> *That saved a wretch like me,*
> *I once was lost, but now am found,*
> *Was blind, but now I see.*

After the first chorus, Jordan, looking past Patrick and through the window, could see that the Negro workers had dropped their shovels over at the loading place and were all turned toward the building.

> *Twas grace that taught my heart to fear*
> *And grace my fears relieved*
> *How precious did that grace appear*
> *The hour I first believed.*
> *Through many dangers, toils and snares*
> *I have already come.*
> *Tis grace has brought me safe thus far*
> *And grace will lead me home.*

The foreman, Smith, came running in, breathless and astonished by the sight of the three men standing in the coal shack bellowing at the top of their voices.

"Now," Crawford yelled. "Now, loud, men, by God, loud!"

Their three voices came in a rumbling roar.

> *When I've been there ten thousand years,*
> *Bright shining as the sun,*
> *I'll have no less days to sing God's praise*
> *Than when I first begun.*

Crawford fell back exhausted in the chair, convulsed with laughter. Smith slapped his hand down on the table top. "Mr. Crawford, I could hear you clean over at the dump yard."

Crawford cackled out, "Was it loud?"

"The loudest I ever heard."

Crawford stood up shakily, much affected by the noise he had helped create. He cocked a thumb toward Jordan. "This Jordan is made of iron," he said. "When he hit the first note, it damn near lifted me off the floor."

"I heard all three," Smith said. "Damndest thing I ever heard. Almost made Jenkins drive a truck clean off the ramp."

Crawford stopped, turned his bright eyes back on Jordan. "Enjoyed the visit Jordan," he said.

He started out but, with his hand on the knob, he stopped, turned again and spoke to Smith, his voice so low Jordan could hardly hear him.

"I hired Jordan back at forty-five a week," he said. "Put him on a truck."

Then he was gone.

That night after supper, while Bryant had the boys out to ride, Jordan told Annie he had gotten his job back at the coalyard.

Tears came to her eyes, but she blinked them back. Then she came over and sat down across from him at the table.

"I didn't get the full fifty. Just got forty-five."

She nodded, still unable to find words.

"I had to sing for it," he said smiling, but not feeling the smile, not quite sure in his own mind whether he had done right, wondering on which side strength was.

Annie reached out and touched his hand.

"It was good to be back," he said to her. "Good to be back on the coal truck."

6

The next morning Jordan got up early to go to work, and was half-dressed when Annie turned over in bed and reminded him that it was Sunday. It was strange to Jordan that it was Sunday, because he hadn't gotten drunk Saturday night.

He lay back down in the bed. He would have to remember next Saturday. Trying to make his way in the town was one thing, but he needed a few beers on Saturday night—or a bottle of red wine.

He got up and stretched, went into the bathroom and washed carefully. So it was Sunday. For the whole day he would have to be with Bryant—Brother Bryant, come back from the North.

Bryant, who had not mentioned moving to the rooming house since his first night, got up at eight-thirty, rolling himself from the sofa onto the floor as the two boys, Fletcher and Harris, peered at him around the hallway door. He stretched, dressed slowly and stumbled into the bathroom where he stayed for over half an hour. Then he ate a breakfast that more than equaled any Jordan had ever eaten in his life.

"He's goin' to explode," Harris whispered.

"No. He wouldn't do that in our house," Fletcher whispered back.

Bryant looked up, having heard both remarks, grinning carefully so as not to permit food to fall from his mouth, and went on with the task at hand.

After Annie took the boys to Sunday school, Jordan went next door and asked Mr. Hogan to sell him the biggest hen he had in his lot.

"My brother is home," Jordan explained, "and what we had planned to have for dinner ain't goin' to do."

He and Mr. Hogan cornered a hen, and Jordan came back with it cackling away under his arm.

"What you got there, boy—dinner?" Bryant called to him.

"That's right," Jordan said. He asked Bryant to hold the chicken while he looked for a hatchet, and had no more than turned his back when Bryant said not to bother.

Jordan turned back and the hen was flapping around on the ground. Bryant had killed her with his hands.

When Bryant and Jordan arrived at the church, Annie turned the two boys over to them and went home to start preparing dinner.

They took their seats just as the service started, and Jordan could see, by the craned necks of the congregation, that Annie had gotten the word around about Jordan's rich brother being back from the North. Bryant was whispered about, gawked at. Even the preacher looked him over carefully before announcing the number of the opening hymn, and when he got to the morning prayer, he prayed especially "for the visitors among us who have come home."

Jordan knew he was talking about both him and Bryant. It wasn't because Jordan didn't go to church more often than not, either. In fact, he attended more than many members of the church who were in good standing with the current preacher. But the difference was Jordan would sit in church and squirm and make it clear to any and everybody that he was not satisfied with the way the service was being conducted.

The preacher was too simple-throated was the trouble. Not much tone to him, and he hardly made enough noise to stir up the dust under the piano. He had been to college way off in Louisiana, and now he was up there lecturing to himself, speaking in sentences that not even the Lord could follow, and going 'round and 'round whatever point he was making, like a pack of dogs swarming a hound in heat.

The preacher who had been there before was better. He was barrel-chested, so that his words would bounce around the walls before they settled down. He could scare a man right out of mischief. Reminded Jordan of the old-time preachers, the ones he had so enjoyed hearing as a boy, who would chant out their praise of the Lord, and their warnings about hell.

> O, hell is deep and hell is wide,
> Hell ain't got no bottom or side.

Those preachers had seemed to know the way of the whole world, and the worlds beyond, and to be on speaking terms with the participants.

Old Satan tole me to my face,
"I'll git you when-a you leave this place,"
O brother, that scere me to my heart,
I was feared to walk-a when it wuz dark.

And they knew Jesus, and a man would have sworn they had been there when he was nailed to the cross. "They nail my Jesus down," they would cry, their voices coming out full and agonizingly. "They put him on the thorny crown—look at that, look at that! Ohhhhh see my Jesus hangin' high!"

Jordan could see it, too, and he had never seen much worse. And those preachers knew all about Brother Paul and Brother Daniel, Brother Moses with the serpent-staff, doubtin' Thomas, sinkin' Peter, Elijah rising in the chariot, Jacob and his ladder, Noah tossing in the ark, David playing the harp, Jonah poking at the whale's belly; and they knew all the disciples that had any stories to go with their names, and the little children who came to Jesus, and about the Revelation, with the angels and archangels and the cherubims and the way heaven was without water—leastwise without a sea. They were offering a starry crown, full-voiced singing, angels flitting around, gospel shoes and silver slippers, bells ringing, milk and honey, with Jesus close at hand and Father Adam and Mother Eve walking around, clothed now, but smiling and forgetful of the time they stooped to listen to the devil.

That was the place. But this preacher was up there talking now and Jordan could hardly hear him, much less make out what he was saying. Seemed like he was reading from Jesus' sermon on the mountainside.

Good Lord, Jordan thought, Jesus spoke it out so five thousand could hear it and this man can't reach the seventh pew.

"The meek shall inherit the earth," this preacher was saying.

Not goin' to inherit the earth like that, Jordan thought.

So Jordan listened, his mind going on and on, his body squirming on the seat. Did seem like the preacher wasn't trying. He took the heart right out of the thing and just left the ideas. Jesus wasn't like that, Jordan knew. He must have had a voice with Godalmighty all the way through it. He must have shouted out, "The meek shall inherit the earth!" so that old Bryant, if he had been there, would have crumpled down inside and thought about how meek he had to get to gain the goal. Jesus was a shoutin' preacher, Jordan knew.

But this one was holy and not worth a damn.

Lord, why does Annie like him, Jordan thought, remembering that she did.

After a long while, he saw the service was about over. He sat there, limp from his own thoughts, as the preacher walked slowly up the aisle to take his place at the front door. From there Jordan heard him pronounce the final words, his voice giving them all the reverence he could manage, ending with "in Jesus' name and for His sake, A-men."

The congregation stirred, the chatter started. Jordan sighed wearily and wiped his face dry with his coat sleeve.

The two boys, who had sat through the sermon in silence, now asked to go outside where they could jump around. Jordan told them to go on, but the people started coming up to meet Bryant, so the boys stayed nearby.

Everybody in the church wanted to meet Bryant. They all knew Annie and liked her, and some of them knew Jordan and liked him, and the lot of them stood in awe of him. Everyone came down the aisle to meet his brother and shake his hand.

"God bless you," Bryant would say to them. "God bless each of you."

Jordan didn't know whether he was mocking the service or had been won over by the preacher. "God bless you, son," Bryant would say. "God bless you, sister."

But as the last of the members went on past, he turned to Jordan and put his hand on his shoulder. "God bless you, too, Brother Jordan," he said. Then a smile erupted on his face, a laugh came out of him and he smacked his stomach with the palms of his hands.

Dinner was a success. Noodles and dressing were among Bryant's many favorites. During the meal he entertained the boys by punching at his stomach with his finger to see if it was tight. If it gave before his finger, he would order another helping of the dressing, and the boys would scream with delight. Finally, when there was hardly enough food left to make a pass at supper, Bryant acted as if his finger wouldn't go into his belly, and asked the boys to try. Fletcher poked at it and didn't get anywhere.

"Go on boy, strike hard."

Fletcher looked up questioningly at his uncle, then his father.

"Hit it, boy," Bryant said. "Give it all you got."

Fletcher hesitated, but since his uncle nodded to him encouragingly, he hauled off and struck him in the belly with his fist, and then stood back stunned, for his fist had landed against a solid wall of flesh. His hand was numb.

Even Jordan was impressed. Bryant had muscle around the big bones.

That afternoon the five of them got into Bryant's car and drove out to the old home place. They drove north from Leafwood through the North Carolina countryside, the hills rolling gently from creek to creek. There were a few big dairy farms, and many small huts in which the tenant families lived.

After about a twenty-minute drive, Bryant parked his Buick on the road and they walked up the path to the old house.

Another tenant family lived there now and worked the fifty-four acres of worn land. Six children, ranging in age from three to twelve, were in the yard as Jordan entered it. Jordan didn't see the parents about, and he didn't speak to the children. He didn't feel that he had to have permission to be there. It was his home because of over twenty years he had lived in it, years they knew nothing about.

"You got no right here," one of the older girls said.

Jordan nodded and walked past her, the others following—the boys small moving objects around Bryant, like satellites to a planet.

Jordan led out into the field where the corn had been planted, the rows curving with the side of the hill. A rabbit sat not far from him, and both boys jumped with excitement as it dashed away.

At the foot of the hill a branch ran down from a spring which flowed twelve months of the year. Jordan had carried buckets of water up from the spring as a boy and a grown man. He looked down at the place his mother had put smooth stones so that the pails would not stir up the mud on the bottom.

"It's like it used to be," Annie said.

One of the boys knelt down and cupped his hands, drank from them. "In Sunday school they taught us this," he said. Jordan grinned, remembering there was a Bible story about it.

He stepped across the branch and onto the other farm. This had been Annie's father's farm, his land to work. Jordan started up the weed-choked path that Annie had used as a girl. He saw that pine trees were growing in the field now, some of them five feet high, so he knew that the land had not been worked on for five years, perhaps more.

From behind, Jordan expected to hear Bryant calling for them to go slower, but instead he was chatting with the boys, explaining how it was when he was a boy, and keeping up very well.

Soon Jordan and Annie came to a clearing from which they could see the house where Annie had lived. They walked more quickly now, hurrying over the rocky, red soil until they stood in the shadow of it, and could see, on the opposite hill, the farm Jordan had worked, the one they had just left.

Both tenant families had worked for the same landlord, so they were in the family, so to speak. But Jordan had never been to Annie's house before. There had been a secrecy about a house in the old days. It was the place of the family, where their secrets were lived out, and rarely did a visitor go inside. But Annie and Jordan often had met at the spring, where each would come to get water, and there they had talked about the day, or about the way the crops were. When they knew each other very well, she would talk about the brutality of her father, or the crudeness of her brothers, or the painful gentleness of her mother.

Jordan had wanted to take her away from her parents' house and to his own. He had asked his parents about it, and his mother had cackled in an embarrassed voice, her wrinkled hands clenching and unclenching nervously. She waited for Jordan's father to speak as he sat, one boot propped up high before the fire, and smiled at the boy. "No, it's better when you do not live in the same house with a woman," he said at last.

Jordan noticed that the smile quickly left his mother's face and she busied herself about the hearth.

"But I want to bring Annie here. She won't eat much and she can sleep with me."

"Sleep with you!" His father laughed at that until the stovepipe in the kitchen rattled.

As Jordan grew older, more and more often he waited for Annie. So it came about that they grew up, each in the other's life. And there was often an urge inside Jordan to hold her and not let her go, to protect her. But his father would roar at him to leave her alone. "Don't get tied down. You're to get out of this country, off farm land. You're to get away to a new start!"

So Jordan never touched Annie, never let her know he wanted her; and when they would walk from the spring, he would stop when they came in sight of her house, and she would go on alone.

Now, for the first time, they stood together at the house where Annie had lived. The kitchen door hung loose on a hinge and the porch floor was rotted out. The locust post on which the dinner bell had been strapped still stood, but the bell had been pulled down.

Bryant and the boys came up to them now, the boys laughing and panting, but Bryant not the least bit winded, though he had been talking every step of the way up the hill.

"God, what a house," he said. The boys giggled. "This is your mother's old place, boys," he said. "What do you think?"

The boys laughed with Bryant.

Jordan and Annie, seriousness overcoming them, paid no attention. They walked on to the front door and entered, Annie hesitating only a moment, as if she were not sure she could stand the sight of the rooms.

"This was the parlor, Jordan," she said.

He looked into a room on the right of the entrance door. The cement around the fireplace had been varnished. Here special visitors, too good for yard talk, would be welcomed; but without visitors, it was a room closed off.

Annie went on down the hall, Jordan following. They were entering the personal part of the house, and Jordan wondered about the smells and odors, the sounds and words that must have come from the throats of Annie's family over the many years.

They moved slowly, hardly aware of the boisterousness of Bryant and the boys outside as they played around the barn, swinging on the doors.

"This is where my parents slept," Annie said.

So many notions struck Jordan he could hardly hold them. He went inside the room. "Was you born here?"

"Yes," Annie said.

"Ah, God." He moved around in the empty room, smelling the mustiness of it. A slick, bawling baby held high by her feet—Annie— born in a wooden room with a single window at one side, in a bed long since broken up for firewood.

Jordan was not sure what to make of the room. He felt feelings about it, but could not think through them. He felt the room as a breeding place and a birthplace. He felt the breath of a hundred people starting here, each one of them holding onto life for a spell. Each one ending up somewhere. Each one falling in love, too, and some of them winning out and taking their lovers to rooms just like this one—perhaps it was this one—and there beginning the groaning pleasure that would bring along more babies to go their way and find each other.

Jordan left the house. He got outside in the air. He didn't want to see the other places. His mind wouldn't hold it.

Bryant and the boys were still playing around the barn. Seeing Jordan come out to leave, Bryant took one door in his hands and pulled it down. "Dangerous," he explained as Jordan approached.

Jordan, ignoring him, went on down the hill, his arms flung out from him, the wind cold in his face. Bryant and the boys were laughing, perhaps at him, but he didn't stop.

After a while he left the path and moved into a cove where he and Annie had sometimes met. It was smaller than he remembered it.

He lit a mashed cigarette. More than ten years before, he had taken Annie to this place to tell her he was going away. He and his father had made the plans. The next morning they would drive the wagon to the freight yard at Leafwood, Jordan with one hundred and fifty dollars in a pouch bound to his waist. From there Jordan would go to Washington, where one of his younger brothers, whom he and his father had previously sent on, had a good job. If nothing was doing there, he would go to New York, where Bryant was getting his start. Bryant had written only once, but it was to say that he could see strong days ahead.

So Jordan brought Annie to the small cove to say goodbye. He sat her down, the water pail beside her, to tell her of his plans. She was wearing a pink dress which her mother had made, and was fresh and alive, eager for any knowledge he might have for her.

"Annie," he said. She looked at him, her brown eyes quick, watching every movement of his lips. "Annie, I have saved money, Pa and me."

Annie nodded, still happily unaware of what he had to say, but sure it would not pain her. She had been with Jordan since early childhood, and all that was clean and strong was connected in some way to their lives together.

"And you know how Pa is about getting away. All three of my younger brothers is gone now, thanks to Pa and me, though one don't write to tell us where he is, and two don't write but seldom. But they are well, up in the North." He stopped, momentarily unable to bring himself to say it. Then he spoke the words. "And it's time for me to leave, too."

Instantly tears came into her eyes. She seemed to panic, like a small animal in danger. "Jordan—"

"No, Annie—listen—listen, Annie—" He could not think of proper words. He was leaving, and that was the end of it. He could not explain it away. "Annie, I'll send for you."

She began to weep.

"I'll send for you," he repeated.

She shook her head in anguish, tears rolling down her cheeks.

"I will!" But as he said it, he knew she could not rely on that. All any of them knew of travel were wagon rides and long walks; and he was going a far distance—he had no idea how far—and who could say how they could see each other again?

"Annie—" He knelt beside her, his knees going deep in the moss. He put his hand on her arm.

Abruptly she stood, saying nothing, but looking at him as if accusing him of a crime too common to be spoken. She wheeled about and started from the place. But Jordan held to her, held her back as she began to weep aloud, struggling to get away. He pulled her closer, wanting to explain, until she was close to him, pressed against him, trying to pull away. Until she was in his arms for the first time.

"Ah, Lord," he said. "Ah, Annie." His voice was deep and hollow, as if coming from a distance. "Lord 'a' mercy, Annie."

And as she wept, they sank down together to the bed of moss, moved by one mind. He could feel her pressed against him, and so, in the afternoon before he was to go away, Jordan knew he could not leave her....

Jordan suddenly was aware that Annie and Bryant were calling him. He started to answer, then heard Annie say, "I know where he is." Her footsteps drew closer, until she came up the narrow path and stood beside him. Their eyes met for a moment, each remembering.

"I'll be along directly, Annie," he said.

She looked down, as if embarrassed by the place. "Yes, Jordan." She went away.

He sank down on a rotting log. Then he shuddered, recalling his father's angry words when he heard Jordan would not leave the farm. "Ah, Godamighty, God, no, Jordan, no!" It was a wail that went out over the fields. "You're the best one. I watched all four. Don't be caught in a woman's hand. You'll die here like the mill dam, go down unknown to the ground! Oh, God, Jordan, get away, Jordan! You were the best of them."

He heard Bryant call to him now. "Jordan, where are you, boy?"

Jordan started to answer, but the words caught in his throat. Suddenly he started off through the underbrush, pushing through it, on down the side of the hill and around the place where Annie and Bryant and the boys were waiting, until he came to the mill dam. He came upon it by surprise, as one always did, for it was nearly lost in the plants and bushes, moss and creeping vines of the creek bottom.

The dam, thick and high, was stone piled on stone for a length of a hundred feet. Jordan sank down on a log and stared at it, unable to comprehend anything so staggering in size. There was no mortar in it. The stones were fitted closely, each one broken out of its age-old place in the earth by wooden poles and Negro hands, and pulled to the dam site. Then red clay was piled behind it as a fill to hold the water.

It was built in slavery days, but no one knew when. Some of the stones were so large that Jordan believed ten men his size could not have turned them over on the ground, yet there they were, high in the dam.

No one knew how many men had worked there, had strained their muscles, how many feet had been bruised, toes mashed, voices choked in cries of danger, joy, excitement, perhaps pain, as a rock was lodged in its place.

Jordan shook his head like a shaggy dog bothered by the sunlight. His mind would not hold to it. By whom? Who built it?

They had done a big thing. No doubt men had walked from miles around to see it. It must have been discussed for months, even written down when it was finished. Wine was drunk, people danced on the low rocks beneath it, and there was whiskey—maybe hams—there were songs from way back.

But who built it?

Now one came upon the dam by chance. One pushed through the brush and there it was. Even the dogwood trees, crooked and snakelike, grew on its top, their roots deep down in its insides; and the creek had long since filled the lake with clay and silt. Now the creek rumbled over the top as if the dam had not been built at all, as if not a single day had been spent gathering stones from the opened ground.

And the mill house was but three standing walls without a roof, with fallen roof rafters, one side open to the creek which fell there through the air alone. Long since, the mill wheel had broken, fallen from the pole to be buried, or washed away splinter by splinter, in the creek spray.

Who were the men who had built it? Where were the slaves who had danced around it? What year was it they ate the first piece of bread made of the first ground grain from its wheel?

There was not even a mark in the stone to name the white man who had wanted it done. He had planned for a work that would stand for all time. This was the work, now filled with red North Carolina clay, unable to hold a puddle of rain water.

The earth heals its scars.

From a short distance away Jordan heard Annie and Bryant call to him, then the boys were calling— "Pa, Pa." Jordan only shook his head uneasily. It was beyond him; he could not master the place. He was thirty-three, and already he could tell that he was less strong than he had been. His muscles grew tired earlier in the day. Like a pear turning yellow on the tree, he had reached his prime, and in time would drop away. And when he fell, it would be at the close of nothing that would remain, certainly nothing so large as a dam made of a hundred thousand closely fitted stones. The earth would cover him; all he had done or thought would be in the earth with him.

"Here one is remembered only as long as his works." Jordan could hear the words as if they were being spoken, but he could not place the voice. Perhaps his father's, the thinking voice that could never explain to him. "Here there is nothing more for us when our bodies are through. Get away, Jordan!"

At the mill dam, feeling the weight of the growing past, Jordan for the first time understood the words, knew beyond doubt what his father had felt, and it moved him almost to tears.

"For God's sake, Jordan, why didn't you answer us?"

Jordan looked up sharply to see Bryant standing over him, with Annie and the boys nearby.

"What you doin' here, sittin' like Pa, lookin' at the dam? There ain't nothin' here that's so holy, is there? You look like a ten-year-old milch cow."

The boys giggled.

"Shut up, Bryant," Jordan said.

Annie started and Fletcher's mouth fell open. Bryant stiffened suddenly, then relaxed. "We ain't boys no longer," he said bluntly. "This is the old place, but we ain't like we was."

But he said no more, nor did Jordan as they walked back to the car. But the children looked at their father uneasily, as if they were not sure he could tell Uncle Bryant to be quiet. Now they hovered about him, looked at him expectantly.

"Uncle Bryant said that he plowed the fields with a mule. Did you ever do that, Pa?"

"Yes, yes."

"And gather apples in the fall?"

"I remember," Jordan said, moving on faster now, not wanting anything to come between his warm memories and himself.

"Uncle Bryant said he would lick the other boys when they were mean."

Jordan stopped, then moved on down the road. "He never licked me," he said, but he said no more. Let Bryant talk. It would do no harm, he thought.

That night when the chicken had been picked over and the family was full again, Jordan told the boys to go to their room. They kissed their mother on her cheek, then nodded to Jordan and to their uncle, and left the kitchen. Bryant's eyes followed them moodily, and for a long while he looked at the empty doorway through which they had passed.

Annie said, "Why haven't you married, Bryant?"

Bryant laughed. "I never thought of it."

"You could have boys of your own."

A pain flashed in his eyes. His lips closed firmly, then he nodded. "I have thought of children," he said.

He and Jordan talked about New York, Bryant telling about the ships and the work at the waterfront, and how he had had one job and then another. But he never told how he had made his money, and Jordan didn't ask.

"How did she die, Jordan?" Bryant said again, coming back to a subject that bothered him.

"Mama? She went down with a hymn."

"Bible verses, too, huh?"

"Yes. And Pa standin' in the room—"

"Not cryin', was he?"

"No."

"He wouldn't be! Let her die, he'd say."

Jordan's eyes narrowed. "He didn't cry then, but he did later, Bryant, for I saw it."

"Him? Cry?"

"Yes. I saw it. He was sittin' in the kitchen when I come up from the barn. I just happened to glance through a window, and he was sittin' in her rocker by the hearth, rockin' back and forth, tears runnin' down his face."

Bryant shook his head as if he didn't believe it.

"Sittin' in her rocker," Jordan said. "I saw it."

"How did *he* die?" Bryant asked suddenly.

"Day by day. He never complained, but you could tell afore you went away that it was day-by-day dyin'."

"Yeah," Bryant said. Then after a while, "When did he go?"

Jordan thought of that. "Shortly after I left the farm."

Annie interrupted. "Tell Bryant how you buried your father, Jordan."

"Both Ma and Pa is buried there," Jordan said. "It was for the two."

"But it was after your father was covered over that you done it," Annie insisted. "It was a monument to him."

Bryant looked solemnly at Jordan for a moment. "What did you do?"

"I covered him over," Jordan said. "And then I got the axe and went back to the grave, and to the oak tree that shaded it from the west. And in the evenin' light I commenced to drive the axe into the tree, workin' till my arms was tired, but goin' on like I planned—strikin' down into the night, until there came the splinterin' sound, the givin' away, breakin', and then the crash of it."

Bryant shook his head, closed his eyes for a moment. "Why?"

"I wanted him to have a way to be remembered."

"You always liked him, didn't you?" Bryant said.

Jordan nodded slowly.

"Papa's little man," Bryant said. Then he laughed, his laughter rising until the bulb swung back and forth on the light cord.

Bryant spent almost a week in Jordan's house, snoring away the nights on the living room sofa, and spending the daytime buying presents for the boys, bringing in huge armloads of groceries, and taking Annie and the boys on trips through the countryside. Jordan would hear them tell about what Uncle Bryant had showed them, or had done for them, until he came to feel like a stranger in his own house. He became more and more anxious for Bryant to go.

He left one morning, just after breakfast. Jordan carried his luggage to the car.

"Are you coming back to Leafwood, Bryant?" Annie asked him. She and the boys and Bryant were standing on the porch.

"I don't know. I don't know. Doin' well up in New York. Hate to leave, but I hate to be away from all of you, too." He looked down on the boys. "Goodbye, sons," he said—and stopped short, for he realized what he had called them. He was flustered for a moment, then quickly he turned and went down the steps to his car.

Jordan swung into the car, too. They drove up the street toward the coalyard, Bryant honking the horn at the neighbors as he went by and waving his hand out the window. At the coalyard he pulled over to the side of the road.

"I enjoyed it, Jordan. Nice visit, boy."

"Goodbye, Bryant," Jordan said, suddenly deeply moved.

"You got a good family. I hope you make out better for them."

"I'll make out, Bryant." He closed the door easily.

Bryant smiled, then his car slid up the street and around the curve as it headed back into the North.

He didn't say anything about taking Annie and me and the boys with him, Jordan thought. I sent him up there, Pa and me, but he said nothing about it.

That day Jordan worked frantically. Some of the older men noticed it, and Jenkins came over to him late in the morning.

"What you doin'?" Jenkins said. "That ain't no club, it's a shovel."

Jordan didn't say anything. When Jenkins moved on, he went back to work as before.

The trouble was that Jordan knew he had to hurry, but he wasn't sure toward what, and he couldn't put his finger on the reason why.

7

He found out part of the reason soon enough, found it out when he went home. He walked down the road happy enough. Wasn't Bryant gone? Wasn't he going home to his own family? Things would be as fine as they had been before.

So he reached the house and nobody met him. The boys were in their room. He knew that was the way it had been in times past, but he didn't like it at all now. Annie came to the kitchen door and glanced at him, as if assuring herself that it was indeed Jordan, then she went back to the stove without speaking.

Still, he figured, he couldn't ask for the sky. It was enough that Bryant wasn't there.

Supper was hominy grits and sausage. It was the first time the family had had that since before Bryant came to visit them. Well, he hadn't expected a banquet in celebration of their freedom. The fried meat looked all right, and the light bread would put flesh on a man's bones, same as hot rolls. But he noticed with dismay that Fletcher and Harris made faces at each other as they stared down at the food.

There was a deep quiet about the place, too, since Bryant was gone. There had been no car trip that afternoon for the boys, and nothing to talk about. Nor was there the booming voice of Bryant, as he laughed at his own stories or at a mistake Jordan had made.

There was not his huge bulk sitting at the table, dominating it, either. Now the family was back together and back alone.

Jordan ate more than usual to show everyone he was glad to get back to a regular diet.

"I shoveled coal straight for four hours this afternoon," he said. Nobody else at the yard could do that, but it did not impress the family.

"I'm goin' to take you boys to Durham," Jordan said, "first chance I get."

"We been to Durham," Fletcher said, bitterly staring down at his food.

Harris pushed back his plate and glared at the table top.

"Worked durn near so hard today that Mr. Crawford told me to go easy, or I'd wear myself out." Jordan chuckled.

"You want some more coffee?" Annie said.

"Huh? Oh, no. Plenty here."

"Your cup is empty. You've not poured any in it yet."

He ran his tongue nervously over his lips, then chuckled at his mistake. But nobody else did. He pushed the cup part way across the table and Annie filled it.

"I think things is going to be better now," Jordan said. "I can see good days ahead this winter."

"Eat your food, boys," Annie said.

Harris pulled his plate back to him, grudgingly picked up his fork, and poked about in the grits.

"Good food," Jordan said. "Put muscles on you."

"Uncle Bryant had muscles. He didn't eat this."

"Ahhh," Jordan said, trying to hold his temper. "Uncle Bryant had muscles of a sort, but not like you need."

They ate only for a moment before Fletcher looked over at his mother. "Uncle Bryant is goin' to buy a new car, another Buick or a Cadillac."

"Asked me to pick out a color," Harris chimed in.

"Asked us," Fletcher said. "I told him black."

"I told him dark-green," Harris said, forgetting for a moment his anger at the food and eating freely.

"Dark-green ain't right for a big car like a Cadillac," Fletcher said.

Harris shook his head, his mouth full now. "I told him dark-green and Uncle Bryant said he might get dark-green."

"Shut up!" Jordan said suddenly, his eyes flashing. Both boys sat back in their chairs, stunned and motionless.

Annie said quickly, "Yes, be quiet, boys."

They looked at her, surprised to find a reprimand coming from that direction, too, and then began glaring down at their food again.

"Eat," Jordan said sharply.

Their forks began to dig into the hominy grits.

"Don't take it out on the boys, Jordan," Annie said.

"Huh? What? Not takin' anything out on the boys."

They ate in almost silence for a while, the boys throwing side glances at their parents. Finally Harris leaned back in his chair and said, "Uncle Bryant promised to take us fishing when he comes back."

Jordan lay his fork aside, glared at Harris. "He's not comin' back." Both boys looked at him as if he had spoken a sacrilege. "Well, is he, Annie?"

"I—don't know."

"God, he said nothin' to me. Why the hell—"

"He is comin' back," Harris said.

Fletcher added, "And he told us he would take us on a trip into the North."

"Huh?" Jordan looked around nervously. "Godamighty, who does he think he is? Does he think I'll—just—"

The boys stared at him incredulously.

"Jordan, let's not talk about it now," Annie said.

"Huh? Not talk? Hell—"

"He is comin' back, and he is goin' to take us to the North," Fletcher said, leaning across the table and speaking directly to his father.

"No, by God!" Jordan said.

"He is!" Fletcher screamed, then darted from the room as Harris began to sob, his head bowed down almost to the top of the table, his fists over his eyes, his little body heaving with fear and disappointment.

"Harris—" Jordan said. The boy did not look up. "Harris, I don't care about—about your goin' to the North, but you're a little boy and—"

Harris sobbed on. Annie looked about helplessly and breathed deeply, as if the pressure of the place were crowding in on her. "I'll—I'll get the boys to bed now, Jordan. Wait until tomorrow to—"

"I don't care if you go to the North," Jordan said. He put his hand on Harris' chin and tilted it up so that they were looking at each other. "Harris—Harris, whatever you say, boy. You just tell me what you want."

Harris burst into tears and started to run out of the room. Jordan caught him by the shoulders and held him back. "Harris, just tell me. Whatever you want. What do you want, Harris?"

Through his tears the little boy spoke. "I want Uncle Bryant back," he said. Then he fled freely from the room. His father had released him.

The next day Jordan asked Patrick for twenty dollars. It hurt his pride to do it, but he did it anyway, and Patrick seemed to take pleasure in loaning it to him. Then he asked Mr. Crawford if he could get off an hour early. Crawford gave it serious thought, and agreed he could go at four-thirty if he would get his work done. He outlined the work in detail, and it was more than for a usual day, but Jordan did it.

Then he went downtown, his fist clenched around the money. He hurried along, looking in the display windows for a present that would serve his need; but it was hard to find anything just right. He went from store to store. Finally he saw a badminton set at a little shop.

He went in, realizing that he was the only Negro in the store and that he had on his work clothes covered with coal dust. But he stood to one side until he saw that one of the girls wasn't busy, and then went up to her. She was blonde, and usually talking to a blonde girl bothered him, but he wasn't thinking of that now.

"That—uh—that paddle set in the window—" Jordan said.

She looked up at him. "Yes?"

"How much?"

"You want to buy it?" She didn't believe that he would want to, evidently.

"I do, yes."

"I'll have to get it out of the window."

She went to the window and pulled it out of the display. It was only a minute before she was back.

"Let's see….Shall I wrap it up?"

"But—how much is it?"

The girl looked down at the price. "Only sixteen dollars."

Jordan nodded, because he was surprised it cost that much, and she took that as a sign that he wanted it.

She wrapped the paper around the box. Jordan wanted to tell her that he didn't want it, but she was wrapping it up, and he was the only Negro in the store.

"I don't want it," he blurted out.

She looked up sharply, startled by the tone of his voice.

"I mean—what I mean is, I just got twenty dollars."

She shook her head. "I don't understand. This is only sixteen."

"But I got to buy food."

"What?"

"I got to buy some food—and a dress."

She looked quickly around the store until her eyes came to rest on the manager, who was standing not far away. She sighed, somewhat relieved. "Do you want the badminton set?" she said.

Jordan swallowed hard. "I want a present for my boys."

She moved the badminton set aside, keeping a watchful eye on Jordan, and pulled out a box from the shelf behind her. "This is a Chinese checkers set," she said. "We find that it is very popular with children."

It was a red board and had marbles in six colors. It was just the thing and he hoped it was not too much.

"It's—only three dollars and ninety-five cents," she said.

He nodded. "Yes," he said. "Yes."

With shaking hands he gave her the twenty-dollar bill, now dirty from being carried in his work clothes. She returned the change.

"Thank you. Thank you," he said, and started out.

"Your package," she called after him.

He came back, shamefaced, started to reach for the box.

"You want it wrapped?"

He nodded dumbly.

The girl took out some nice paper and wrapped it up. Then she put a bow around it. He watched her flying fingers, fascinated; then he looked at her face as she worked, and was startled by the beauty of it—the simple beauty of it. She was like a little girl, he thought, a very little girl; and he was afraid of her—he, Jordan, afraid of her, when he was not afraid of a Negro in Leafwood.

The ladies' dress shop was crowded with women who had gotten off work and had come by to see what was on sale. The women milled around in the small room, and Jordan had a hard time even getting into the place.

Then one of the women saw him and stopped dead in her tracks. The other women, one by one, turned to look at him, and silence fell on the place. A saleswoman stepped from behind the women and came closer to Jordan.

"What is it?" she said.

"Uh—I want a dress," he said.

She smiled uneasily. One of the women tittered, but recovered. There was a nervousness about the room.

"A dress—for whom?"

"My—my wife."

The saleswoman nodded, glanced at the other women, then braced herself. "What kind of dress?"

He grinned foolishly. "Just…to wear around—that's all."

"A party dress?"

"Huh?"

"Do you want a party dress, or a house dress, or—"

"I want—I want a dress to go to church, I guess."

A couple of the women tittered now, and he thought he should get out of the place; but suddenly the saleswoman smiled, as if she understood more than he had told her. It was a good smile, and made him feel like he would stay, and that the cold stares of the other women didn't matter.

"Come right this way, sir," she said, and she led him to a rack of clothes. "How large is your wife?"

He looked at the dresses dumbly. "I dunno, exactly."

"Is she—about my size?"

Jordan didn't want to look the woman over to see. He had seen a colored man look a white woman over once, and there had been a big row about it. Then too, he didn't like to look at women like that.

"Sir?"

The woman just stood there, and Jordan held his ground. Finally he said, "She's your size"—not knowing one way or the other.

The woman took a dress from the rack. "This dress is—" She stopped as a thought came to her. "How much money do you want to put into it?" she asked softly.

He ran a tongue over his lips. Every woman in the place was staring at him. "I…I want to put in—maybe—" Then he said, "How much are dresses?" Actually he wanted to get a good dress, but he hoped it wouldn't run more than ten dollars.

"Dresses are—all prices. How much do you have?"

He clenched a fist around the money. He knew the perspiration had come out on his face. "Ten dollars," he said in a low voice, hoping the other women would not hear him.

"How much?"

"Ten dollar," he said, still whispering.

She smiled, a warm smile. "That's just exactly what this is. Shall I wrap it for you?"

He nodded, a wave of relief coming down on him.

Then he looked at the dress for the first time. It was pretty. It was made with flowers in the design and was white. Annie had never had a dress like it, he knew. It looked like silk.

He went over to the counter where the woman was working away. One of the other customers had been standing there, and now she gave the salesgirl an angry look and stomped out the door; but the salesgirl only smiled, as if she had done something that held immeasurable pleasure for her.

She gave him the dress, neatly gift-wrapped. "Come back," she said.

"Thank you, ma'am." He felt he owed her more than he could figure out. "Thank you—very much, ma'am."

"I hope your wife likes it."

Jordan backed to the door, almost walking into a rack of dresses. He looked at the other women, and everyone was watching him. Quickly he left the place.

At the grocery store he had to wait until three or four other people had been waited on before he could tell the butcher what he wanted.

"Four T-bone steaks?" the butcher said.

Jordan nodded.

"I'll have to cut 'em. About an inch thick?"

Jordan nodded.

A while later the butcher said, "That will be—uh—four dollars and twenty cents."

Jordan was dumbfounded. He had bought a Chinese checkers set for less than that. But he took the package. Then he looked around on the shelves for some other food. He got down a can of applesauce, that being one of his favorite foods, but he decided that perhaps the boys were tired of it, so he put it back in place. He bought a can of pears, instead, and a can of fruit cocktail.

He figured he had a dollar left, so he bought a bottle of red wine for sixty-five cents. They would all drink wine that night. They would have a party—he and the boys and Annie. Everybody would drink a little wine.

He paid for it all, and was surprised to find he had eighty cents left of the twenty dollars. With that he bought a box of chocolate bars because Annie liked them.

In spite of all his hurrying, Jordan was late getting home. He knew Annie would have supper ready, but he also knew she would be happy to fix supper again when she saw what he had bought.

He burst into the house and called to her. She came to the hall door and looked at him critically, then in surprise.

"What you got?"

Jordan was loaded down with packages. "Wait'll you see." He dumped the packaged on the sofa and pulled out the one with the steaks. "You fixed supper?"

"Yes."

"Well, Annie, I got—got something." He shoved the package into her hands, feeling proud.

"Jordan, what in the world?"

"It's food, honey. Open it."

Annie went back into the kitchen and put the package on the table. She began unwrapping it as Jordan moved to the boys' room and threw open the door. "Hey, boys, come see what I brought home."

They came out moodily and stood in the kitchen doorway just as Annie folded back the wrappings on the four T-bone steaks. She looked up amazed.

"And that ain't all," Jordan said. He hurried back to the sofa and got the bag with the fruit cocktail in it and came back in, the boys parting to make way for him.

"Here," Jordan said, giving Annie the bag.

Dumbly she peered inside it, then brought out a can of pears, another of fruit cocktail, then the box of chocolate bars. She laid the articles in a row on the table.

"It's good, ain't it? Jordan said. He was proud already, and they didn't know yet about the other presents. He would give them to them when the time came.

Annie took out the bottle of wine, setting it to one side as if she didn't know what to do with it.

"Well it's good, ain't it?"

"But—where did you—" She looked up at him. "Jordan, you didn't spend your money for this!"

He stared at her. "What—" He looked to the boys, seeking support.

"Oh, God," Annie said, and slumped down on a chair.

Jordan didn't eat any supper. Instead, he roamed the house, going from the living room to the bedroom to the kitchen, demanding to know what the reason was.

Finally he went out on the porch and sat down in a wicker rocker, sat there for half an hour, thinking of the high hopes he had had. Then he went into the kitchen again and got the bottle of red wine.

Annie looked at him moodily. "Jordan—"

He took the cap off and drank deeply. It felt good in his stomach.

"Jordan, I'm sorry, but you don't have the money for this, not the money Bryant has."

He went back to the porch and sat the bottle on the floor within arm's reach. Bryant hell....A few neighbors went by on the street and called to him, waving at him, but he didn't answer.

I wonder what Mona's doing, he thought.

Then he remembered the Chinese checkers set and the dress. What can I do with the dress? he wondered.

But the checkers set was for the boys, and they were all right. He drank another swig of the wine, and went back into the house, and got the boys' package out.

"Hey, boys," he said. "Hey, Fletcher, Harris, come out here."

There was not a sound from them. Frightened, Annie hurried in from the kitchen. "Leave them alone, Jordan."

Jordan threw open the door to the boys' room. "Hey, boys, come on out, huh?"

Fletcher looked up nervously from the bottom bunk where he had been studying.

"I got you a present," Jordan said. He held out the box with the ribbon around it. "Come on, huh?"

Harris propped himself up on his elbow, looking appraisingly at the box.

"Come on, boys—"

He helped Harris down from the top bunk. "Come on into the living room."

The boys followed him, hanging back, with Annie watching protectingly.

"Here." He held out the box to the boys. Neither moved. "Come on, boys—"

"Take the box, boys," Annie said.

He looked up at her sharply, but both boys suddenly reached forward and grabbed the box. Jordan stood back, waited expectantly.

"Go on," he said, "open it."

They set the box on the floor and untied the ribbon. The two of them tore off the wrappings.

"It's a good present for boys," he said proudly to Annie.

The box was well colored and the boys took to it at once. They removed the top, and there was a large bag of marbles and the colored board, all laid out before them.

They could not help fingering the bag of marbles.

"Open 'em up, Fletcher—Harris. They're a present."

The boys looked up at him, as if to make certain, then they fell to work opening the bag. They dumped the marbled down on the board, glancing up at Jordan proudly. Deeply affected, he slumped down on the floor beside them and fingered the shining marbles.

"It's a good present for boys," he said.

"What—what is it?" Fletcher asked.

"Huh? A game. A game."

He took up the instruction leaflet and gave it to Fletcher. "Here, you can learn about it. It's a good game."

Fletcher opened the leaflet hungrily and started to read. Annie stood nearby, leaning on the post of the doorway, biting her lip.

"Here, let me see that thing," Jordan said, taking the leaflet from Fletcher. "It says here—"

The two boys came up beside him, one to each side. They stood there as he read the leaflet to them. Then the three of them set to playing, Harris grabbing for the green marbles.

"I'll take the black," Fletcher said.

"I'll be blue," Jordan said. "Let's put the other marbles over here." He dumped them into the bag, casting another glance at Annie, but he didn't ask her to play with them.

After the game, when the boys where in bed, Jordan stumbled back onto the porch and finished off the bottle of wine. I could tell Mona about the checker set, he thought. The game had been a big success, and he wanted to talk about it.

But soon Annie came out on the porch and sat down in the other rocker. She sat there for a long while without speaking.

"That checker set is a good present for boys," he said. "Them damn marbles."

He put his feet up on the porch rail. Mr. Hogan went by on the street and Jordan called to him, "Hey, Hogan, how's everything—all right?"

Hogan looked up at him, surprised. "Sure." He trudged on up the street.

"Hogan's a good man," Jordan said. "Damn shame about him bustin' himself few years back."

Annie rocked on, until the sound of the rocker got on Jordan's nerves; but the wine steadied him. Let her rock. Let her sit on the porch and rock her life away.

"Jordan, it won't work," she said softly.

"Huh?"

Her rocker stopped. "You have to give the boys time, Jordan."

"Time? Huh?"

"The boys will forget soon and—"

"I'm doin' all right. Let me be." He glared out at the street. "I was hopin' we could give them that checker set together, but you got mad, and so I give it to 'em."

"Jordan, don't lie to me."

He took his feet down from the rail angrily. Then he stopped before speaking, because it was a lie, and he hadn't known it until then.

"And talkin' about that," Annie said.

"No. I know. Just because the boys liked the checkers game, you get mad at me. I didn't do nothin' to you."

"All right, Jordan."

The rocker started again. He glanced over at her. She was frozen in the chair, her eyes looking ahead. She was his wife and that was strange, he thought. Annie was his wife and was jealous of him because of the boys.

"I stayed in Carolina for you, Annie. And I done worked my best. I did wrong, didn't I, Annie, because I stayed for you."

Her rocker stopped. He thought he heard her gasp.

He shook his head angrily. "So you make one choice, just one. That's all a man has, by God."

She stood stiffly erect, staring at him. "What choice you mean? You speakin' of that day—" She stopped, momentarily panicked, then abruptly swung around and hurried inside the house.

Stunned, Jordan stood up, bracing himself on the porch rail. "Annie," he shouted. "Annie, what day do you mean?" He saw through the glass part of the living room that she had gone into the kitchen. "Annie!"

He saw her moving around the kitchen and shouted her name as loud as he could, but she didn't flinch or even look toward him.

"Cold, by God!" he said. He stumbled off the porch and made his way up the street through Tin Top.

Mona's house was dark when Jordan came to it, but he pounded on the door until he heard her coming down the stairs. When the porch light went on, he stepped close to the screen so that she could see who it was.

She hesitated only for a moment, then unlocked the door and pulled it open. He stepped inside and they looked at each other for a while, as if each were remembering the last time they had stood there.

"Mona—I—"

She clicked off the porch light. He felt her before him and her hands came to clasp themselves at the back of his neck.

In her room upstairs Jordan lay on the bed while Mona undressed, then he got up and went into the bathroom and turned on the shower. He was grimy with coal dust and wanted to wash up first.

This was the life—hot water splashing down on him. He would have a shower bath put in his house when he got everything going right. He had given it some thought since Bryant left. While shoveling coal, he had thought about starting a business, maybe the taxicab company he had mentioned to Coltrane. The colored people in Leafwood used the cabs more than the whites, because the whites had cars. He knew that. And there was no taxicab in the town run by a Negro.

He wasn't going to mention it to Coltrane again, though, or to anybody else. He was going to do it himself.

Mona came to the bathroom door, and looked on as the water splashed over him. He didn't mind her looking.

"Would you wash off that make-up?" he said.

She moved to the sink, fastening the loose robe around her, and washed her face, then wiped it dry on a towel. He saw that she did have a fine figure, and that there was beauty to her face, just as he had remembered. And he knew she wanted him. He had stood on the porch and called to Annie, but she had not come. But Mona was there and wanted him.

Mona went back into the bedroom, glancing at him as she passed. He stepped out onto the tile floor and dried himself, rubbing his skin until it tingled.

He went into the room, and from the bathroom light he saw that she was lying on the bed with a sheet thrown over her. He left on the light.

"Turn it off, Jordan."

He went back to the bathroom door and turned off the light. Then he lay down beside her, pulling the sheet over him. Mr. Crawford had told him she was experienced. Well, that was all right.

His hands reached for her and groped over her. She reached for him.

"Just hold me close for a minute Jordan."

"Yes." But his hands moved over her. He couldn't stop his hands. "I came to you, by God," he said.

"Yes, dear, I know."

"I came to you, Mona."

"Yes, Jordan."

And he thought of Annie, and the time they had fallen into the moss-covered ground more than ten years before. He wondered if it would be like that. He wondered how much love is needed. His mind got turned on that, and he didn't know what to make of it. He didn't know he could love Mona, and as he lay there, he loved Mona as he had loved Annie—but he had known Annie.

"Jordan—" Mona whispered.

"Did you know I would come back?" he said.

"Yes, dear."

"I had to come back."

"I wanted you to come back. When I heard the knock, I said, 'That is Jordan,' but I was afraid to believe it and told myself it wasn't. Until I saw you there, I told myself it wasn't."

She held to him.

"Jordan," she whispered.

He held her tightly, but his mind was not set. He remembered the taxicab company and having a shower bath in his house. She's rich, he thought.

"Jordan, for God's sake," she whispered.

He held her tightly to him, his hands moving over her.

"Ben," she said. "God, Ben," she said.

It was almost dawn when Jordan got back to the house. He went inside, sober now and his thinking clear, and as he turned on the living room light, he saw the dress he had bought for Annie spread out on a chair. For an instant the day passed before him: what he had wanted it to be, and what it had been.

"Ah, Lord," he said.

He stumbled into the bathroom and washed carefully. Then he pushed open the bedroom door and was about to turn on the light when Annie spoke to him.

"Jordan—" Her voice was low, and he thought for a moment that a sob broke through it. But she couldn't have been crying—not Annie. She was stronger than a tree turned into the wind.

He took his hand off the light cord and started undressing in the dark.

"I saw the dress, Jordan."

He flipped his work pants over the nail.

"It's—very pretty."

"It's a good dress."

Perhaps she was sobbing, after all. He threw his shirt over the bedpost. "It's too large now, but—that's all right."

He sat down on the edge of the bed, not knowing what he ought to do. Then he got up and went into the bathroom and splashed cold water on his face and neck. He brushed his teeth, then came back into the bedroom. Finally he lay down and pulled the covers up under his chin, feeling the cold sheets on his skin.

Annie moved slightly on the bed. "It's a pretty dress," she said, "one like I always wanted."

He felt her hand as she touched him. "I'm tired, Annie."

"Yes," she said, taking her hand away.

They lay there for a while, Jordan thinking of the plans that had been going over and over in his mind since before Bryant had come to Leafwood. "I'm goin' to leave the coalyard soon," he said to her. "I can't get anywhere down there."

"But—"

"It's all right. I know what I'm about."

She was quiet for a minute. "But it's not easy to count on what's not sure."

"Goin' to be sure."

"And I can't go on carryin' the weight of it by myself."

He thought about that, wondered about it. "Weight of what?"

Annie spoke softly, her voice shaking. "The family. And I'm goin' to have another baby, Jordan."

Suddenly he felt very tired. He was going to try to make a place for himself in Leafwood, and he thought he could do it; but now there was to be another baby, and doctor bills, perhaps, and food to buy for it. It was the wrong time.

"Jordan—" Annie said anxiously. "Jordan, I was so afraid you wouldn't want it, but tonight when I saw you with the boys, I knew I should tell you. Do you want the baby?" She was weeping now.

He looked at the ceiling, dimly outlined by the reflected dawn light. He thought of Mona and wondered if he could love Annie the same again.

"You don't want it," she said, sobbing.

He thought of the taxicab company. He could tell Annie about that, but she wouldn't understand, not when she was thinking about a new baby.

Finally she stopped crying. Jordan heard the Hogan boys next door as they ran into the back yard of their house to feed the chickens. It was dawn, and soon Annie would have to get up.

"I'd best get some sleep, Annie," he said. "I been awake all night."

He closed his eyes, but he couldn't go to sleep. His mind went from one thought to another, so that he got weary thinking. Perhaps if he found a night job, as well as the coalyard job—

Then he remembered Bryant, and he wondered if he would come back. He pulled the covers closer around him. What if Bryant were to come back?

"Jordan," Annie said, her voice so low he could hardly hear her. "I can't carry on alone, I tell you."

"What you say, Annie?"

She went on in the same voice. "I try to believe that something will come and help out. But it's the weight inside me, Jordan. I don't know. Every day I wonder what will come of us."

I wanted her to like the presents, he thought. It would have been better if she had liked the presents.

8

Through the winter he worked on and worried, did odd jobs as he could. He painted some, cut at the wood lot, helped move new furniture into the hospital. He lost weight from working. Crawford had raised him back to fifty a week. But when spring came he had only seventy dollars.

That wasn't enough for anything, and it made him angry. One day he fretted about it so heavily that, when five-thirty came, he pounded his way downtown. He would go to Mona's. Several times he had been by there, and Mona had comforted him, made him forget the hard times that went on outside her big house. But each time, when he left her, it had been harder to return to the problems and harder to do anything about them. Mona was like a soothing medicine. But one that cut his courage down.

He could go home to Annie, but that wasn't any good now, not as tired as he was, not to grits and sausage. Lord 'a' mercy, not with no more hope inside him for helping his family than he had.

Before he got to Mona's house, he slackened his speed, however, and finally turned toward Jake's. He would get a beer and think about it. Or maybe he could drink enough beers to forget about it. That would be better than going to Mona's, for the beers would make him sleep finally, and when he woke, even if he had a pain in his head, his mind would be clear. A man could always work a pain away in the coalyard.

At Jake's he drank four beers. He was supposed to break up logs that night at the wood lot, and Jake reminded him of this, but Jordan said nothing to him. None of Jake's business. Damn Jake and everybody else who didn't have a wife bearing and who was free to go as he pleased. "Lord 'a' mercy," Jordan whispered. Then he pulled around a man standing beside him at the bar. "Look here," he said, "what do you do for a living?"

"What?" He was a tough boy, part of a large family calling itself by different names, which had spawned three hundred yards down the railroad tracks.

"You got worries?" Jordan said to him. "Why you ain't got worries?"

"You go to God-damn. Take your hands off me."

Jake reached over and yanked Jordan's hand off the freight-yard man, shoved a beer before him. "Drink that, big boy, and cut out arguin'. What's the matter with you tonight?"

"None of your damn business."

"Give me that beer back then," Jake said, picking up the mug and dumping the contents in the sink. He shoved the empty glass into the dishwater and went about waiting on other customers, leaving Jordan staring at him fiercely.

The freight-yard man began to laugh. Jordan swung on him, but just as he turned, he heard a click and glanced down in time to see that he would be stepping into a five-inch knife blade. The freight-yard man smiled, held his place at the bar, the knife gripped tightly. Jordan heard another knife blade open somewhere. He turned back to the bar, a cold sweat on his face. God-damn, they had it in for him, all the young ones who know of his old days.

But Jake did, too. Jake was his best friend, but he had it in for him. Jordan had always liked old Jake, and for him to pull the beer-glass stunt on him, when they had always been friends—

"Jake, God-damn it, give me a beer," he said.

Jake poured one slowly, pushed it to him. "Twenty-five cents," he said.

Jordan drank a swallow, then slowly found a coin in his pocket, shoved it across the bar. "I didn't mean nothin', Jake. Why you do that to me?"

"I didn't like the way you was talkin'."

"Had no damn right."

"Now, Jordan, come off it now. Haven't seen you like this in months."

"You go to hell you hear me?"

The freight-yard man Negro spoke up, moving the words slowly over his tongue. "Poor old Jordan," he said.

"What you say?" Jordan kept his eyes on the half-glass of beer before him.

"Lordin' it around like a damn king in Africa. But you ain't got no tribe, Jordan. Just king o' you."

Jordan finished the glass of beer, twisted his head moodily, trying to decide what he should do to him. "You shut your mouth," he said.

"Just like a damn king in Africa."

Jordan nodded slowly, thoughtfully, aware of the open knife blade. He pushed his glass toward Jake. "Fill that up for me, Jake."

Jake wet his lips, looked at Jordan, then at the freight-yard Negro. Everybody in the bar was quiet now. "You had enough beers, ain't you, big boy?"

"No, I ain't," Jordan said.

"Uh huh." Jake filled the mug. Jordan flipped a quarter out on the bar, then blew down on the beer in the glass and made it twirl so that the light reflected on the foam. "What your name?" he said to the man at the bar next to him.

"Robert E. Lee. Ever heard o' me?"

"Uh huh," Jordan said softly. Somebody in the group began to laugh uncomfortably.

"But some calls me Zepher."

"Why they call you Zepher?" Jordan said.

"Like to move, mister. Like to move straight on through."

Jordan peered in the small mirror behind Jake, trying to get a closer look at Zepher without glancing at him. "Which direction you like to move in?" he said easily.

"Forward—that's my nature."

"No. I mean right now," Jordan said. "You want to go up against the side wall or do you want to walk out through the front door?"

Jake stared uncomfortably at the two men. Several others stepped away, leaving Zepher and Jordan plenty of room. Three of the freight-yard Negroes huddled to one side, each with a hand in his jacket pocket.

"King Jordan," Zepher said softly. "Yeah, I know. You was the one always held up to me—Jordan could drink more than anybody, fight quicker than anybody, hit harder than anybody, gamble harder than anybody. I used to believe all that, but this year you been losin' out, and right now—"

Jordan brought his elbow up under Zepher's chin. Zepher reeled twice and fell across a table, his arms spread out, his body limp. He didn't move a muscle.

A gasp went up from the freight-yard men. Jordan pushed through them, pulled Zepher up and was about to slap him awake when two freight-yard men tackled him from behind and the four of them crashed into the wall. Jordan swung around, clubbed one man as another came in. He caught the second man with a blow to his stomach that sent him sprawling back across the room. Two men jumped to Jordan's side and suddenly everybody in the place was slugging and falling about. Jordan waded through the group, fighting his way, until he had his back to the bar. His fists hammered at any moving target. Jake was bellowing at the top of his voice, "Don't break the front windows," evidently believing they were more important than all the rest. At the same time he was working his way into the crowd, ordering back fighters as he came, until he had half the men standing off.

But Jordan wouldn't quit. He stood at the bar, slamming the freight-yard boys as they came in, feeling stronger by the minute. Then Zepher, who had had two or three glasses of water dashed in his face, loomed into sight, came plunging toward him. Jordan, catlike, stepped aside, let him slam into the bar, then tightened his arms around Zepher's chest, lifted his feet from the floor, and squeezed until Zepher cried out in pain.

"Hey, there!" Jake shouted, pulling at Jordan's arms. "Hey, let him go."

"Good Lorrrd!" Zepher cried, struggling in Jordan's grasp. The others stood back now, terrified.

Jake and two freight-yard men pulled Zepher free and the men carried him to a back booth.

"Now look here," Jake shouted at Jordan, "You stop, you hear, afore real danger comes!"

Jordan pushed past him, took somebody's glass of beer and finished it.

"The rest of you men get to your booths," Jake ordered, "or get out o' here."

The men moved to the edges of the room, putting chairs back in place, moving quietly, as if afraid of sound. Some of them nursed their arms and fists. Two or three had their shirts torn half off their backs. One man, a cut bleeding at his shoulder, stumbled to the door, hung there a moment, then straightened and staggered out.

"Now, Jordan," Jake said, "next time you need a fight, you fight on the street, not in my place."

"Jake, don't you turn against me more than you have. Weren't my fault that this—this kid—"

"A man ain't called to fight kids. So next time take to the streets."

"God-damn," Jordan said, his voice deep and angry. "God-damn you, Jake." He struck out with his fist and caught Jake square in the mouth. Jake fell back with the blow, then righted himself, stared at Jordan incomprehensively.

"Ahhhhh," he said, seeking language. "What—what did you—" He turned to the others, big tears standing in his eyes. "Why—" Jake stumbled past Jordan, got the bar cloth in his two hands and scrubbed it over the bar.

Jordan looked around, baffled by his own action. Zepher and the others were half-grinning at him from the side. "You get out o' here," he said to them.

Zepher glanced around at the others. Jordan braced himself. "Get out o' here."

The men slowly pulled back, Zepher being the last to break; but he left, too, and the beer hall, except for Jake and Jordan, was empty. Jordan staggered over to a booth, heavy of body now, sank down on a bench. "Jesus," he said, rolling his shoulders slightly to get some of the strain out of them.

Jake went on rubbing the bar, going over what didn't need to be gone over at all, pressing down hard on the cloth.

"What the hell's the matter with me, Jake?...Jake?"

Jake mumbled moodily, then, after a while, came over to the booth. "You—you ever hit me again," he said, "and I'm goin' to kill you in return."

"Ah, God, Jake, I didn't mean to hit you."

"Whether you mean to or not don't excuse it next time."

"But why did I hit you, Jake? You're the only friend I got, by God."

"Never mind explainin'."

"I want to know why I hit you."

Jake sat down across the table from him. "Because your mother must o' bore you in a storm. Leastwise, there's always a storm brewin' 'round you."

"Yeah, and in me. Work, work—never get anyplace. Get ideas that never can come to nothin'. Not an end in sight."

"What your ideas, big boy?"

"Taxicab's best idea I got. Got so I can't dream 'cept it has taxicabs in it, riding down the road, one after another."

"You want to start a taxicab company?"

"In my mind I do. But I'll never get there."

"Uh huh." Jake looked at the pictures on the wall. "Fellow in here the other night said he had come back from Durham in a cab with his girl, and he had had her three times on the way over here."

The remark went past Jordan.

Jake reached over and punched him lightly on the chest. "Come on, big boy, come out of it. Lord, you done enough damage in here for you to be happy now!"

Jordan tried to smile.

"If you need money, tell you what—ask your brother for it."

"Naw. Besides, he ain't even in town."

"Well, he was in here last night, talking about business," Jake said.

"Huh? What you say?"

"Your brother. Right here, him and the three white men that own this beer hall. I had gone to bed upstairs, but I peeked out an saw 'em."

Jordan felt his body grow weak. His brother had been in town and hadn't even come by the house.

"He was here about twenty minutes. That was after the place was closed. Those white men won't come in here when it's open, you know."

Jordan's mind whirled around. "I thought you owned this place," he said, not knowing how to phrase the other thoughts he wanted to talk about.

"Naw. What the hell would I be doin' owning a damn nigger beer hall?" Jake wiped the table top for a moment. "Three white men own it, but they put my name up because they don't want people to know. The white men can rent to a nigger, repair his car, handle his diaper service- but not run a nigger beer hall. So I run it."

"And my brother—you talkin' about Bryant?"

Jake stared at him for a moment, as if trying to make him out. He whistled softly. "Yeah, Jordan. Didn't you—didn't Bryant—"

"Bryant and these three men—what they doin' here?"

"I figure Bryant might be buyin' the place. I thought you'd know."

Jordan suddenly downed the remainder of the beer. "You know where he is now?"

"No."

Jordan shook his head angrily. Then he leaned across the booth and grasped Jake's arm in his big hand. "Jake, loan me some money."

"Huh?"

"Look, I got to get this cab started—right now. It's the one idea I got, and my brother is goin' to come in here, and after that, I don't know."

Jake nodded briefly. "How much you need?"

Jordan took out the stub of a pencil. "I got my eye on a Ford that's about five years old. Is that too old for a taxicab?"

"No."

"I can get it for six hundred dollars, Jake. The man said it would cost me one-third down. That means I got to borrow a hundred and thirty dollars."

Jake nodded.

"Then I got to have enough to put in a telephone."

"Well, what percentage you give me, Jordan?"

"Huh?"

"I want to buy in. You could use a partner, couldn't you?"

Jordan looked at Jake hard, then grinned. "You goin' to leave the beer hall?"

"No. I just want to invest. I think you're goin' to make more money in one year than this beer hall make. You're goin to strike gold this time, Jordan."

Jordan wet his lips with his tongue. "I know." He tapped the table top for a moment. "We can do it, I think. Better for two of us than one, since you know everybody. I tell you, Jake, I'll let you have a third of the company, and I'll get it started without much pay for the first few weeks— except what I got to live on."

"Yeah? What you makin' now?"

"Fifty a week."

"That's fair," Jake said.

"So I'll take a chance on the fifty. And I'll sell you one-third of the company for two hundred dollars—the down payment on the Ford."

Jake thought about it for a minute. "What you goin' to do with your seventy?"

"Buy a light for the taxicab and put in a phone at the house."

Jake nodded. "Use my phone. This'll be the office."

"Good," Jordan said. "I'll keep my cab parked here from early mornin' to late night."

Jake tapped him on the hand. "We're partners," he said. "When do we start?"

Jordan looked away, fear coming to him. That was something else again—actually getting under way. It could be the wrong move, then what would he do? Not easy for a Negro to go plowing ahead into business.

Yeah, but the boys. He wanted to do something to make them look at him like they looked at Bryant, as if he were beyond them, yet close by. That was well enough and might come about, if he won. If he lost, it would be all over. Even his job at the coalyard would be gone, and there was little hope of another one. Everything to lose.

"Say, Jordan, when do we start?" Jake repeated.

He closed his eyes, blinking out the thoughts. "Got to start soon." They talked for a long while, even after the customers began drifting back in, surprised to see the two opponents bending their heads together over the table, talking amiably. Then, right in the middle of the conversation, Jordan's eyes suddenly darted over Jake's face. "Three times?" he said.

"Huh?"

"Three times from Durham to here?"

"Oh—you mean that boy. That's what he said."

Jordan looked thoughtfully at Jake. "Lord 'a' mercy," he said, "it ain't but eleven miles."

"I know. Not quite four miles a time."

"Maybe he meant Raleigh."

"Well, it ain't but twenty-five miles from here to Raleigh."

Jordan considered that. "Still not enough distance," he said. He turned on the bench and stared unconcernedly at Zepher, who was leaning on the bar and watching him. Lord, why had he gotten into a fight with that fellow? Didn't seem to be too much to him, except his tongue and speed. Looked just like his brothers and half-brothers, too—all of a clan.

"Jake," he said, "what would you do if you was drivin' a cab and had this boy and girl in the back seat. What would you do?"

"I'd keep count," Jake said.

"Would you keep on drivin'?"

"Sure. Adjust the rearview mirror and drive right along."

"How could you, with that goin' on three feet away?"

"Hell-fire, they ain't on the highway. No obstruction to it."

"I dunno how you could," Jordan said. "I wouldn't know what to do. I would be so hacked I wouldn't be able to move, I reckon."

"God, it's done every day, Jordan. No trick to it. Every Tom, Dick and Harry and every Mary and Sally does it. Couldn't be anything very much of a secret."

"Yes, it is," he said slowly. "It is, Jake, for some reason."

Jake laughed, leaning back in the booth and glanced around at his waiting customers. "God," he said. "Let's not get off talkin' about that or we never will get a taxicab company started."

Jordan looked away suddenly. "Yeah," he said, "the taxicab company."

He made a check at the rooming house, but Bryant was not staying there, and so far as he could find out, nobody except Jake had seen Bryant in town. He said nothing to Annie or the boys about it.

He didn't say anything to them about the taxicab company, either, but from the next night on, he spent his time figuring with a pencil on expected expenses and reading in a borrowed book about how to care for and repair a car.

He read painstakingly, going over a page several times before turning to the next one. Whenever he thought of finishing the book and having no reason for delay in opening his cab company, his mind filled with shadowed fears. He almost memorized some of the pages and interrupted his reading whenever he had an excuse, telling Annie even the slightest bit of news he had heard, or pestering the boys about their schoolwork.

One night Fletcher, who had come to the end of his patience with an arithmetic problem, took advantage of his father's interruption to turn the problem over to him. Jordan approached it cautiously. "If a chicken and a half lays an egg and a half in a day in a half," he read, "how many eggs will three chickens lay in three days?"

He sat down at the kitchen table and put his mind to work on it. Fletcher chatted away about the half of a chicken, but Jordan saw that it was a fair problem and determined to overcome it.

Annie at one point glanced at his figuring. "It's simple, Jordan. Each chicken laid one egg a day, so three chickens laid three eggs in three days."

"No, not so," he said. "Don't do to fly into space before you've judged the landin' spot, Annie."

"How do you know it's not right?"

"Not the answer that's in the back o' the book."

"Well, what answer is there?"

"Never mind. You just go on. One mind is enough to figure out a problem." So on he worked, fretfully marking down the numbers until he filled one side of a piece of paper.

In time he determined that one chicken laid one egg in one and a half days. The half chicken laid half an egg in one and a half days. The two together laid one and a half eggs in one and a half days.

The next step showed that the three chickens laid six eggs in three days, and he was so excited to come out on top of the problem, that he could hardly explain it to Fletcher.

Then Fletcher, deeply impressed, took the book away, and Jordan was left to return to his plans for the big challenge that threatened him. He got to thinking about it, fretting over it, and thought how easy it would be to go on working at the coalyard, where he was the best worker on the lot; he was good for many more years at the yard. He got to thinking about the North and how easy it would be to open up a business there. In the North, a man could harness himself and get a firm grip on responsibility and carry it well. But not in Leafwood. North Carolina was like a sieve that drained his strength away.

Of course, if he went up North, he could start a company easily. He could go right on up there and start in, and when it was running smooth, in a week or two, he could write for Annie and the boys. Annie would fret about his leaving, but she would have to accept. And the boys would look forward to the North. Lord, they wouldn't miss him, anyway.

The thought brought him up short. He could see them sitting down at the kitchen table, not even noticing that his place was empty. He could see Annie smiling at them, as she always did when she wasn't worn out, and he could hear them chattering away, not a word being said about him.

Well, leaving them and going North was out, he decided. Have to wait until he made enough money to take them along.

But no way to do that, except with the taxicab company.

All right, he would start the taxicab company that very week. He would make a big pile of money in a month and leave that town. He wouldn't think about the taxicab company being a failure, of people pointing at him as he drove by and saying, "There he goes; thought he could beat the world, and he got nowhere." Wouldn't think about that. No, he would ask Patrick the very next day for the loan of his car and would try out for his driver's license.

Maybe Patrick wouldn't loan it to him anyway. That would decide the whole thing, because Coltrane was the only other man he knew who had a car, and he wasn't going to ask Coltrane for a favor. And even if Patrick agreed, there was a good chance the driver's test would trip him up. He was out of practice, and he never had driven much except trucks. Or maybe he would fail the eye test, or the ear test. One of his ears was almost senseless, and that would keep him out, for sure.

Thing to do was ask Patrick the next afternoon. Patrick would refuse. And even if he didn't, chances were it would come to nothing anyway.

But Patrick did not refuse, and the patrolman giving the driver's tests, a lanky, quiet-spoken man who was bored with his duties, passed Jordan within half an hour and licensed him as a chauffer. Jordan came out of the town hall distressed and, at the same time, elated—almost overcome by the combat of emotions inside him. He turned the car back to Patrick without a word of thanks—nothing to be grateful for—and made his way home, thinking about how easily he had passed the tests, and that he hadn't even been asked about his hearing. He had answered all the questions right on the written part and had driven as well as he ever had. All the time he had been so sure he would make a mistake and flunk out, that he had rested back with assurance, and he had come through with as high a grade as a man could make.

Well, that was something to be proud of. He had done as well as could be done, and he would have to tell the boys about it. He would tell them about the taxicab company, too, and hear them carry on. Annie would realize that he was on the high road at last. She had said he was no-'count and this proved her wrong.

So that night after supper, while the boys hung on every word, he told Annie what he had done and what his plans were. He kept on talking, even when Annie got up from the table, nervously wiping her hands on her apron, and went to the sink. Finally he wound down and waited for replies.

Annie's was not long in coming. "It's not right, Jordan," she said. "It's too big a chance."

"Huh? What, Annie? Lord, don't talk against me. My mind is already done, and it's all I can do to hold it to the point."

"You have a job now."

"God, what are you afraid of? Why you hold me back?"

"You don't seem to be so sure yourself, Jordan. And with two boys—"

"I plan to work to come to somethin', and why, God-damn it, Annie, do you want to hold me back?"

After work the next afternoon, a Thursday, Jordan bought the Ford car. His fingers were trembling so much he could hardly get the ignition key in the lock. He drove past Jake's place, where he had planned to stop, and kept on driving, and he didn't care. He kept on, trying to shake off his fears, until he was ten miles out. Then he stopped on the highway and called to a white man who was plowing a field. "Hey, tell me, what direction am I in from Leafwood?"

The white man stopped his tractor and looked over at Jordan. "Toward the north," he called.

The words went through Jordan like a pain. As the other cars on the highway sped around him, some of them blowing their horns and some of the passengers staring back, he sat still and thought about the direction he had taken. His hands gripped the steering wheel as he stared straight ahead at the long, narrow road that stretched through the valley. His breathing got deeper, then finally he moved the car forward, driving slowly.

After a while he stopped, took out his money and counted it. He had four dollars. Maybe that would buy him enough gas for him to get to Washington or New York. He didn't have a map, but that didn't matter. The road was going North, and once he got up there he would know it and could find his way. It would be easier to find his way in the North than to find his way in Leafwood, where he had lived for years. Leafwood was a jungle to him now, with traps set to snare his hopes. Leafwood had let him get his license and buy a car, but the traps were all around him and somehow would put an end to his taxicab company. He would lose the car, his savings; Jake would turn against him. Annie already had told him he was wrong. The boys would look down on him.

But ahead was the North, shining, beckoning him on. There he could succeed. It was clear enough what he had to do, even if it meant leaving Annie and the boys for a while, leaving Jake and going off with his and Jake's car.

He would send for Annie long before the baby was born. It could be born in the North, in the good country, and would never grow up knowing what an empty pocket was. Going North was the best thing he could do for that baby.

There was not a reason on earth for going back to Leafwood. Lord knows four dollars' worth of gasoline should be enough to reach Washington or New York. Bryant had said Washington was closer; well, that would be the place. He could be up there, maybe in an hour or two—maybe in a day. No reason to go back.

But he stopped the car at a filling station and turned it around. He drove back toward Leafwood, tears in his eyes—hateful to him, because tears were for children. He drove back toward Leafwood, saw the outskirts approach. He was going back even though he knew he ought to go North. It wasn't that he wanted to go back. He wanted to go North more than his mind could know, but he wanted to beat the town, too. Right then he wanted to drive the car to Jake's and park it and then walk home to his house and go inside there and close the door and ask Annie to come to him. He wanted to pull her tightly to him, hold to her. Then the next morning, he would put his fears aside as if they were a dirty rag that had bound him, and would go out and beat Leafwood and make his way.

Later he would leave that town, drive out of there free.

When the sun was almost gone from sight, he told Crawford he was quitting the coalyard. Crawford looked at him for a long moment, then nodded curtly, accepting it. "It's too bad the niggers can't seem to keep to their own knittin'," he said. "Got to get over in the whole pie, but that's the way with Carolina these days and no reason to expect Leafwood to be different."

Smith came into the coal shack and sat down on the edge of the table, almost blocking from sight the stunned and silent Patrick. When Smith found out Jordan was leaving, he became angry at once. "What we goin' to do to replace him?" he demanded.

"Just have to hire that small nigger back," Crawford said.

"You fired him yourself."

"That don't matter, so long as he comes back askin' for a job. Does good to fire 'em from time to time. Keeps 'em in line."

"He won't come beggin', not that one."

"That's what you told me before Jordan come back askin' for work— that we would have to go to him. Well, we didn't. He come in here as fine as you please, right in the nick o' time. This other nigger will do the same."

"Not this one, Mr. Crawford. I tell you—"

"Well," Crawford shouted, "let's not sink the ship until we see it go down." He stomped out, slamming the door after him.

Smith remained quiet until the sound of Crawford's footsteps had disappeared, then he glanced up at Jordan. A sigh came out of him, as if he could not put up with the worry that fell to him. "You moved coal, mister," he said. "You were the best man ever to work this lot. But listen to me, if you ever want to come back, even if I had a world o' orders I won't put you on. I'll shovel coal myself, mister, before I'll put you on. And I don't think another place will have you."

Then he left, and a chill came to Jordan, but it was almost like a fever. He was one Negro that was his own, but, Lord, the weight of it.

The car was a four-door Ford custom, and Jake hand-printed the letters *J and J* in red paint on the front doors and the trunk lid, with the word

TAXI beneath. Then he and Jordan went over the engine and the workings. They waxed the body until it sparkled. This took most of Friday and Saturday. When it was done, Jordan said he would walk home and get his supper.

"Walk?" Jake said. "Take the cab."

Jordan shook his head angrily. "Don't like to drive it just yet," he said.

"Take the damn taxicab. Ain't we in business?"

"Well," Jordan said, "when I get back—"

"Now," Jake roared. "What the hell, Jordan! We can do a big business tonight and more tomorrow mornin' at Sunday school and church time. So take it home and let's get under way. I'll spread the word in the saloon tonight, in the Baptist church tomorrow. You cover the Methodist church. That ought to take care of the nigger population of Leafwood—two churches and a saloon."

"Goin' to take care of most of 'em twice," Jordan said, grinning in spite of himself. He got behind the wheel of the new cab and drove onto the street, cut down to the corner and turned left. He made all the proper hand signals. Couldn't take a chance on getting into trouble.

He drove slowly and with pride. It was an old car, but it had a shine to it and was clean. However, his fear that everybody would single out the cab and point to it, and call their friends to see it, soon changed to the fear that nobody would notice at all. So he began to blow his horn whenever he saw somebody he knew.

Before long, by traveling slowly and blowing his horn, and by waving and calling out to his friends, he won a following for the maiden voyage of the cab. A warm, almost carnival-like feeling came inside him. He felt like laughing, like singing-out.

When he reached home, several of the neighbors came over to see the car and ask about the taxicab business. Jordan showed them the engine and the upholstery, and told them that his rates were the same as those of the white company: thirty-five cents in town and fifteen cents for each mile outside the town limits. "Jake is in the beer hall twenty-four hours a day," he added, "and I'll be there as much of that time as I can."

They slapped Jordan on the back and sang out their praise of the cab company. "Don't let anybody run you off," a woman whispered to him.

"No, ma'am," he said confidently.

Then Annie and the boys came out of the house. Jordan stepped apart from the others and waited as Annie, showing her pregnancy now, came down the steps, the boys behind her. The neighbors stopped talking and stood back. Everybody listened for what Annie would say.

She walked part way around the car, then came back to Jordan. "It's—it's a very pretty cab, Jordan," she said. "I do declare, Jordan—" And a mist came up into her eyes.

Fletcher touched the car, then looked at his father. "It's good, Pa," he said.

But little Harris stood back a ways.

"What do you say, Harris?" Jordan called out. Everybody turned to Harris.

Harris looked at the car for a long while. "It's dark-green," he said at last.

And a slow smile came over Jordan's face.

That was the way it started. It was Jordan's own. He had felt no ownership when he had helped other men build a house or lay a walk, but now he had done something for himself.

That first night he and his family ate supper proudly. They ate with gusto, pushing down the grits and sausage. The boys laughed easily, and Annie smiled in spite of her fears.

"But what if it don't work, Jordan?" she would say.

He would chuckle. "It drove this far."

And the boys would laugh.

After supper he went out once more to the green cab, swung in behind the wheel and turned her around, careful not to get the wheels muddy. He went on up the dirt road and, as he did, a woman came down the road, Miss Myrtle, a talkative busybody. She waved him to a stop.

"What you want, Miss Myrtle?" he said.

She stared at him openmouthed. "I want a taxi, you durn fool. I been waitin' for you to finish eatin' supper so I could go baby-sit at Doctor Grover's house."

Jordan helped her get in, then drove up the street, his throat almost stopped by the hard knot that was there. He drove slowly, stopping at every stop sign and keeping his eyes open making all the signals. Finally he got there.

"How much is the fee, Jordan?"

"It's a mile outside the city limits, Miss Myrtle."

"The others charge me fifty cents. Is that what you want?"

Jordan started to say he would take a quarter, but she handed him a dollar bill.

"I ain't got no change, Miss Myrtle."

She took the dollar bill out of his hand. "Come back at eleven o' clock, Jordan. You can drive me home. I'll give you the full dollar then." She was gone, walking primly. Jordan looked after her. He had made a dollar. He had made a dollar!

He turned the cab around carefully and went back uptown to tell Jake he had made a dollar. He and Jake laughed about it, carried on happily, like children. "God-damn," Jake said, "goin' to be rich as hell." He roared with laughter, and several people standing around started laughing. Jake jumped up on a chair and yelled for order in the beer hall.

"I want to announce the existence in this damn town—this is a damn town," he said. "I seen better towns than this in Virginia, for God's sake—"

Two men at the far corner roared with laughter, and Jake glared at them until they quieted down. He was serious.

"But there is now a nigger cab in this town. It's run by Jordan, but by God it's run right. It's run damn near twenty-four hours a day by Jordan, and he's always ready for a trip. Now this is something for the nigger and the white—and it's run by Jordan."

There was wild jubilation then. Many of the men already knew about the cab, but they hadn't had a chance to celebrate it yet. Suddenly beer and wine were being offered as toasts to the nigger cab company, and Jake was pushing a mug of beer into Jordan's hands.

"I got to drive," Jordan said, pushing it back. Jake drank it in two huge gulps.

Jordan got up on the chair. "I want to say—" But nobody would let him speak. They were toasting the nigger cab company.

"I want to say—"

Nobody could hear him over the shouts.

"I want to say that my partner in this cab company is Jake—"

A few heard him, but not many. Jake heard him, though, and laughed out his triumph. He started giving away beer, running the faucet continuously, and carrying on, people talking to him and egging him on. Then somebody said, "I want to ride—"

"I want to ride," somebody else said.

Then they all stared. "I want to ride in a nigger cab." It was a chant now.

They pulled Jordan out into the street and four of them got in.

"Around the damn block," they said.

Jordan, grinning from ear to ear, drove them around the block.

He drove around the block a hundred times that night, carrying drunk Negroes. Some of the rode five times. They paid him thirty-five cents each time he made the round, and it was only because he had to drive to Doctor Grover's and get Miss Myrtle that he left them.

It was a good night. It was the best night ever. He went to bed thinking of what he would buy Annie and the boys, and how fine a place Leafwood was.

It was the week before Bryant came home to stay.

9

B ryant came back in early spring. He had the same car, and now it
was stacked tight with clothes and personal possessions. Jordan's
living room would hardly hold the wealth of material it inherited on his
arrival—coats, suits, shirts, linen underwear, and all the rest.

Annie went through his clothes, hanging them up in the hall where
they would be out of the way; yet in going from one room to the other it
was necessary either to go under or around Bryant's things.

But Bryant was as gay and generous as ever, bringing in bottles of whiskey
and wine, and shouting the great good tidings that he had come back.

Jordan was not glad to see him. Annie wasn't as warm in welcoming him
as Jordan had expected her to be. But the boys jumped up and down jubilantly.

"Uncle Bryant! Uncle Bryant!" they shouted.

"Yes, sir, I got up there and got to wonderin' about how you were
doin', Annie, and about the boys here, and Jordan—" Bryant was sitting
on the living room sofa as if he owned both it and the room around it.
Fletcher peered at him from the other end of the sofa and Harris sat on
the floor, looking up.

"And I said— 'Why not go on back down to Leafwood and see the
family a while longer? What's holdin' you in the big city? Break away and
go back home.'"

Little Harris giggled in delight. Annie looked helplessly at Jordan, who
gazed strongly at his brother, wondering why he had come back and
when he would leave.

"As I drove down through Jersey and Virginia, I said to myself—

'Bryant, soon you'll be home. Soon you'll be back with Annie and the boys…and with Jordan.'"

He went on like that, talking away. For the next few days, whenever Jordan came home, Bryant was talking, and the boys were listening.

"Ain't you got homework?" Jordan would say to them.

They would shake their heads and look up critically, then Bryant would go merrily on with whatever story he was telling.

"Godamighty," Jordan said to Annie on the third night, "don't he ever get up off that sofa except to eat?"

"He took the boys shopping this afternoon."

"Shopping, for the Lord's sake? What'd they buy?"

"I don't know. Bought groceries, but they hinted that that wasn't all. Bryant's got some surprises."

Jordan didn't know what she meant, but he knew he didn't like it.

Annie said, "Shouldn't you eat quick and get back up to Jake's with the taxi?"

"Huh? No, I'll stay, Annie. I got to stay for a few minutes."

"But the people who phone in—"

"Never mind," Jordan said. He had to see what Bryant was up to. All through supper he wondered about it. The boys would exchange anxious glances, poke one another; and Bryant would wink at them until Jordan got put out almost beyond his endurance.

Finally he blurted out, "Bryant, heard you come back into town a couple of weeks ago and didn't come by here, not even to see the boys."

Bryant, his hand stopping in mid-motion, slowly looked up at Jordan. "No, couldn't 'a' been me."

"Yes, it was," Jordan said bluntly. "Over at the beer hall."

"No."

"You was seen clear enough. What you doin' back?"

"Mistake made. Who saw me?"

Jordan didn't want to get Jake into any trouble. "Never mind. You was with three white men."

A slow smile came over Bryant's face. "Not me, boy," he said evenly, then he fell to eating again.

Annie shook her head nervously as if to say that the conversation was bothering her. The boys looked around somewhat critically at their father.

But Bryant soon looked up, as unconcerned as ever. "Tomorrow we'll go to Durham, boys," he said.

"They seen Durham," Jordan said. "They don't want to go over there."

The boys' eyes widened in disappointment.

"Do you want to go back, boys?" Bryant asked.

Both boys nodded enthusiastically. "Yes, sir," Harris said.

"Well, right after you get out of school then. We'll count on it."

Jordan ate the rest of the meal in silence, thinking all the while that it was Bryant's food he ate, and not liking it any better for it.

After dinner he waited for the surprises, but Bryant found his place on the sofa again and began talking. Jordan saw that he planned to go on indefinitely, making up stories about the North. He made up story after story.

"...So I saw this little kid for the third time, just standin' there on the street corner lookin' lost, with people passin' every which way. I went up to him this time, and I said, 'Boy, where's your home?' He didn't say nothin'. 'Look here, you got parents?' He just looked at me with them moon eyes. 'When did you eat last?' He didn't say anything again. 'Not very talkative, boy. You want some food?'

"He didn't say anything to that, either, but he took hold of two of the fingers on my right hand and just looked up at me. 'I'll tell you, boy, I'll give you a steak if you'll say somethin'.'

"He drew in his paw. Just looked at me.

" 'Just say one word.'

"He shook his head as fine as you ever saw. Just stood there.

" 'All right, boy,' I said. 'Come on, I'll buy you a steak.'

"We went down the street to a steak house there in Harlem, and I set him up. He ate big, like he was starved. I tried to question him, but it did no good. Finally, when he was done, he got up, said 'Thank you' and went on back to the corner. He hadn't said another word to me, and so help me God, I couldn't figure it out."

Jordan couldn't figure it out, either, and didn't want to stay till it was explained. He kept thinking about poor Jake telling the customers that the cab would be back any minute.

"What the hell happened?" Jordan asked, after a while.

"Happened?"

"What did you do, for God's sake?"

"What could I do?"

"Hell-fire," Jordan said, deeply irritated, "bound to be a reason." He glared at Bryant.

"I'll tell you, Jordan. I put two men on it, told them to follow that kid, to find out why he wouldn't talk to me. They come back that same night and explained it."

Bryant ran his tongue around the inside of his cheeks and looked at the boys, then at Annie, then back at the boys. Jordan kept thinking of that taxicab business going to ruin.

"They told me the reason all right."

Jordan uncrossed his legs and ran his hand nervously over his face. He was sure that Bryant was the most aggravating storyteller for people in a hurry that he had ever run across.

"Yes, sir, these two men explained it simple and right off."

The boys were in a nervous state, but nobody said anything to Bryant, who sat on the edge of the sofa, his hands on his knees, peering around, soaking up every ounce of suspense.

"Would you like to know what they told me?" he said.

"Godamighty," Jordan said, getting up angrily and stalking out the front door.

All that night, as he took the passengers to where they were going, he wondered about that story and kept getting more and more angry because of it. It was a lie and he knew it, but he felt that Bryant had some sort of ending in mind, and he wanted to know what it was.

"Might be that the boy could speak just those two words," Patrick suggested, his chin resting on a beer mug and his eyes focused on the television set in the corner. Since Jordan owed him money, he was always taking part in his conversations at Jake's, even though his debt was now only three dollars and a quarter.

"Speak two words?" Jake said incredulously. "Naw. He was just bein' aggravatin'. God, I was an aggravatin' kid!"

Jordan knew they didn't have it right. As for himself, he didn't suggest a solution, and wouldn't unless he could bring up one he knew would be better than Bryant's.

"To hell with it," Jake said at last. "Did you ask what he was doin' back in town a while back?"

"I asked him, and he said he wasn't here."

Jake plopped his open palms down on the counter top. "Has he got a twin?"

"No, he ain't," Jordan said. "He's the only one of his kind."

Patrick interrupted. "You take one of these foreign kids and maybe all he learned was how to say 'thank you.' So he's out there when Bryant comes up—"

Jordan and Jake turned wearily to stare at Patrick, as if to say that he had brought up a subject that should have been left undisturbed.

That night when Jordan got home, Bryant was still holding out in the living room, and Annie and the boys were up, even though it was past the boys' bedtime by more than two hours. The boys glanced at Jordan and went on listening. Jordan motioned for Annie to come with him and led her past Bryant's things to the kitchen and closed the door.

"Ain't it damn near time for the boys to be in bed?" he said.

"Now, Jordan, what can I do? It's your brother—"

"Ain't it time, I said!"

Annie sighed deeply. "Yes, it is."

He stalked back into the living room. "All right, boys, let's go to bed."

They looked up fearfully, but Bryant nodded. "Right this minute, Jordan. Just let me finish this—about this man, Jordan, who traveled all over the world, and when he was in Harlem, he would walk right down the middle of the street—not using the sidewalks at all—"

"Bedtime, by God!" Jordan said.

The boys got up grudgingly, hesitated for a moment, then trooped toward their room.

"Oh, yes, the surprises," Bryant said, as if he had forgotten them.

Everybody stopped, watched as Bryant slowly reached behind him on the sofa and pulled out a small package. "Says something here on the wrapping," he said. "Let's see now—appears to be the word 'Harris.'"

Jordan saw that he couldn't make the boys go to bed, not before they had the surprises, so he sat down.

Then Bryant called out jubilantly, "Annie, come here! We got presents."

Annie came in from the kitchen as Harris took his package from Bryant and untied it. Inside was a fine watch. It was a boy's watch, true enough, but Jordan had never had a better one himself.

"This one says—'Fletcher,'" Bryant said. Fletcher came forward and took it, undid the wrapping and took out a watch of his own, smiling up happily, as was Harris.

Jordan was disappointed in him. Nothing would have pleased him more than to see Fletcher turn down the gift. He didn't know quite how it could be done, but it would have made him glad.

"This one says 'Annie.'"

Annie hesitated only for an instant, then went to Bryant and took the gift. It, too, was a watch, the smallest Jordan had ever seen. He was sure Annie would turn it down, but she put it on her arm, throwing Jordan a quick glance, as if to see what his expression was. Jordan knew he was going to turn down the present given to him. He would refuse it on the spot—even if it was a watch, and he needed a watch to keep his cab schedule straight.

He sat there braced to refuse. But Bryant sat back on the sofa, a contented look on his face, as if he were done.

"Now don't thank me," he said. "Just let's all keep time. No excuse now for one of you not knowing when dinner is ready, when school begins, or whatever. So be prompt, boys. Now, you'll notice by your watches that it's way past bedtime. Your father won't like that if we keep it up. So from now on, when it comes to ten o'clock, you can excuse yourself and go to your room. Good night, boys."

Jordan was stunned. He had never heard anybody tell his boys what they could do before. He got up from the chair, glaring down at Bryant. Annie suddenly came up to him.

"Jordan—I—Jordan, look—"

He thought she wanted him to look at her watch, but when he looked at her, she had the watch behind her. But her face showed worry.

So he took a deep breath and said nothing. She led the boys out of the room.

"No surprise for you, Pa?" Fletcher whispered to him at the door.

"No. No. I ain't no child."

"Mama ain't a child."

"Never mind. Let it be. Go to bed."

That night Jordan tried to tell Bryant he would have to leave, but he couldn't get the words out. Bryant kept interrupting, talking about how fine the boys were, and what it meant to him to be able to live in that house. Jordan finally explained that it was very crowded and let it go at that.

The next night, he realized he shouldn't have done it quite that way. When he came home for supper, Annie took him to one side.

"Jordan, the boys didn't go to Durham with Bryant. They've been lookin' at houses here in town—"

He didn't get the point at first. "Is he leavin' us?"

"The boys told me he's buyin a house, and we're to come and live with him. Bryant thinks it's crowded here."

Jordan sat down weakly on a chair. He had never heard of such a move. It made him angry right off, and the more he thought about it, the more heated he became. It was clear as new glass what Bryant had in mind.

He stood stiffly. "By God!"

"Jordan, please—not now—not now—"

"What do you mean, not now?"

"Jordan—you've got to—to hold yourself. I can't stand all this!" She ran out of the kitchen and closed the bedroom door after her.

He felt worse than he could bear. He had his cab company going, was making a little more than fifty a week, even after car payments. He was more than holding his own, and now this came up.

But he knew how hard everything was on Annie. So he ate what he found heating on the stove and made his way back uptown.

The next afternoon, the five of them went to see the big house. When they got there, two Negroes were painting the hall walls.

"I figured white for the hall, 'cause it's not well lighted," Bryant explained, "but I want you to tell them what to paint the other walls, Annie. I just got them started with the hall."

Annie said nothing.

He led them through the house, which had eight rooms and two baths. Jordan saw that it had a large kitchen with a gas stove and a good sink, and the cellar had a sound coal furnace with a stoker. It would be easier on Annie in the new house.

The boys were everywhere, laughing and carrying on, their voices echoing in the empty rooms. When Jordan got upstairs they were in the attic, shouting back to their uncle Bryant.

"Listen at that," Bryant said proudly to Jordan.

When they came to a big corner bedroom, Bryant said, "I thought this one would do for you and Annie. Good closets in here."

Once more they heard the boys. "Good place to play up there," Bryant said. "It's a fine house for them."

They saw the whole place, even the wide expanse of lawn. It was three doors down from Mona's house, Jordan noticed, and in the best neighborhood for Negroes in the town. But if they moved there, he knew what it would mean.

Yet he had seen Annie run her hand over the sink and stove. He had heard the boys laughing. It was a bad business, all beyond him. He wanted them to be happy, but he didn't want it all to be lost.

He ate very little supper that night. Finally he pushed back his plate. "We ain't goin'," he said.

The boys had been talking about the new house, and now their laughter stopped short.

Bryant looked up slowly. "Now, Jordan—"

He shook his head, his face hard and set.

"Jordan, I do think you're put out because I didn't buy you a present last night. If it's that, why—"

"We ain't goin'!" There was no doubt in his voice at all.

"Now, look—" Bryant started.

But Annie broke in, her voice controlled and low. "Bryant," she said, "we ain't goin'."

Jordan was so surprised he didn't know what he ought to do. He stood up, his eyes fastened on her, vaguely aware of the startled expression on Bryant's face and the stunned faces of the boys. He saw Harris lean forward, his tiny chest on the table, as tears welled up in his eyes.

Then he sat down weakly. It was all right. Annie had helped him. He didn't understand it, but Annie had helped him.

That night, Jordan got one of the Hogan boys to drive his cab. It was the first time he did that, but he wouldn't leave the house and give Bryant a chance for a new try. Bryant sat on one half of the sofa, his brooding eyes turned first to the floor, then to one wall, then to the ceiling; and Jordan sat in the soft chair; keeping a steady gaze on him. If he made a move, no matter what it was, Jordan knew he had to squash it.

Annie was in the bedroom and the boys were in their room.

Finally Bryant sighed deeply. "No matter," he said. "We'll make out here."

Jordan said nothing, even when Bryant glanced over at him.

"We was happy here. I'll rent out the house."

Jordan said nothing.

"I'll put it up for rent tomorrow. Let it go by the board. Old places are best."

"Where you goin' to live?" Jordan said.

"Why, right here," Bryant said easily.

"No. No you're not, Bryant."

Bryant seemed to have expected this. "All right, Jordan, if you want it that way. If you want the two of us parted—"

"The two of us is parted now. I don't want no more part. But I want my own family."

"You're deciding it, remember that, Jordan. You're throwing me out."

"I want my own home, Bryant."

"I have no choice but to go."

"You have no choice, Bryant, that's a fact. And I don't, either."

Bryant looked away, then suddenly he turned to Jordan, now enthusiastic. "I got it, Jordan. By damn, I got it. I tell you what, boy, we can work together still. Let's just forget about today—the house, what we said. I tell you, you have a fine idea in that cab company. But you can't pull it off with one cab, because—hell, Jordan, people want service. I phoned in twice yesterday to Jake's—didn't say who I was—just wanted to see how things were running. Told Jake I needed a cab right then, and neither time was you there to come over. You can't run a cab company that way. Has to be right on the button. So us two can pull it off, because I got money, Jordan. We'll put four or five cabs on the street. You can run it."

Jordan knew what Bryant was doing; but it was a fine idea, and he didn't know how to come to grips with it.

"Who's goin' to own the company, Bryant?"

Bryant frowned at him. "Split as to value. You own what's yours and I own what I put in it. Then from that point on—"

"You own most of it then?"

"Well—I tell you, boy—what's wrong with that? Your part would be worth more than what you got now, 'cause the profits would be heavier."

"Jake and me is goin' to build our company up next year."

"Well—" Bryant was confused for a moment only. "Well, I'll give you a third. Now, that's fair enough; and you can run it."

Jordan wet his lips. "Where you goin' to live, Bryant?"

Bryant flashed a smile. "We're goin' on from this morning, Jordan—just as before. You and me—and Annie and the boys. I'll see that those boys are given the best of—" He caught himself, knowing right off that he shouldn't have said that.

Jordan's eyes narrowed. "You just go, Bryant," he said.

Bryant started to speak again, but reconsidered. He seemed to be fighting back a well of emotions inside him, then suddenly he turned his huge body on the sofa, turned so that Jordan couldn't see his face. He lowered his head into one big hand and began to sob.

It was beyond Jordan. It was the boy again out on the farm, following his mother. The boy was crying. It was pain, and it troubled him. "Ah, Bryant," he said, getting up stiffly and staring toward him. "Bryant, what is it? Godamighty, Bryant, what is it?"

He put his hand on Bryant's shoulder, and was about to speak again when Annie interrupted from the doorway.

"Jordan," she said, now with a sternness in her voice, "let him be."

He looked back at her. "Did you hear what—"

"I heard. Let him be." She led him into the bedroom and closed the door.

"But Annie—Bryant is—he's all mixed up—he—"

"Jordan, you were right in what you said, and a long time sayin' it. There's no other way. It'll hurt him, and maybe he'll try to hurt you in return, but there's no other way, do you hear?"

He went over to the window and raised the blind, looked out at the road, wondering why he was sorry for Bryant after all Bryant had done and tried to do.

After a while he was startled to see Bryant go down the walk, carrying a load of clothes in his arms. Bryant threw them in the car, then came back.

"He's leavin' tonight, Annie! He's bad hurt."

"Don't you go out of this room, Jordan."

"Annie, Godamighty, not even my pa would—"

"Jordan!" She stopped him at the door. They stood there together as Bryant softly closed the front door and tiptoed to the hall. They heard the coat hangers move ever so lightly outside their door, then his footsteps went away. Jordan returned to the window and looked out.

Bryant made four trips. As Jordan stood at the window, watching, he felt a pain grow inside him. He wanted to go talk to him, yet he knew Annie was right. And Annie was still standing with her back to the door, tears in her eye—he didn't know why she was crying, unless it was for Bryant. He wanted to cry for Bryant too.

He was going away angry, deep hurt.

After the fourth trip, he stopped at the car, looked back at the house. There was a deep stillness. He spoke and Jordan didn't hear the word. Quietly Jordan raised the window. Bryant spoke again.

"All right, by God, we'll see," spoken soft and angrily. Then he got in his car, turned it around, and drove off up the street in a cloud of dust.

Jordan sank weakly on his knees by the window. The cold air seemed to wet his face and neck. "Ah, Mama," he whispered. Annie knelt beside him.

"He liked the boys," Jordan said. "He don't know what it is to have boys. He's all mixed up."

Annie put her arm around him, lowered her cheek to his shoulder. "Don't—don't hurt yourself."

"He could tell a fine story," Jordan said.

"Yes."

"Did he ever say why that little kid wouldn't speak to him? He liked kids."

"He told it."

"What was the reason?"

"Nothin' much that you can believe. It was that the little kid had a brother that couldn't talk, and he felt sorry for him and acted like he couldn't talk, too. It was because of the love for the brother."

Jordan shook his head slowly. "That poor little kid," he whispered.

10

It was spring now. To Jordan, the best season. Out on the old farm the new tenant family opened up long cuts in the body of the earth and dropped in seed, letting each find its place, then turned in new dirt—leaving the fields looking as if they had been swept by a big cleaning woman. The mid-South rains came down in the afternoons and once or twice through the night. The moist seed split. Sprouts shouldered their way up through the crust of ground and got their leaves to the sunlight.

On every trip through the countryside, or even through town, Jordan smelled spring. He kept his eyes open for the bursting forth. "What flower is that?" he asked a woman one day, as they drove along from the bus station.

"Azalea."

"What do you know about that?" he said, craning his neck around to look. "Purty flower."

"I like those tulips, myself."

"Yeah," he said. "I'm goin' to plant me some tulips sometime." His fingers were itching to get down into the soil. When he was home he would look hungrily about for places to plant seeds, and he measured again and again an area in the back yard that came out twenty by twenty feet every time.

One night after supper he set to planning, marking out rows on a piece of paper for tomatoes, peppers, okra, snap beans, potatoes, lima beans, and corn.

"Goin' to plant pumpkins?" Fletcher asked.

"No. That takes—Well, maybe pumpkins. Maybe we can run us a pumpkin through the corn patch. But Lord, we hardly got room for the corn."

He went over the plan several times, deciding where everything was to go and what kind of seed to use. Finally he was satisfied that the problems had received proper thought.

The next afternoon the boys were given a spade and a pick and told to break up the back-yard area. They sweated and complained, but there was considerable excitement, too, for neither of them had ever been in on a planting before. Annie was happy about it. She puttered about, kicking rocks out of the garden plot and showing the boys how to break up the clods of soil, instructing them all the while with stories about her work as a girl. She seemed to take more interest in the new garden, Jordan noticed, than she had in the continued success of the taxicab company. Although the company had now become so popular it took almost every minute of his time, and even though his profits were reaching towards seventy dollars a week, Annie never had much enthusiasm for that topic.

But the garden was different, and together they watched the boys try to break up the ground.

"Pa, can't you get a horse and plow to do this?"

"Pshaw," Jordan said, "for twenty by twenty? Get that ground broke up, or I'll horse you." He laughed as he went back to the cab and started out.

The next afternoon Jordan had planned to get the boys to mark the ground off into rows, but that was the day the court summons came. It said he was to appear in Recorder's Court the following Monday to answer to a charge of driving a taxicab without a franchise. He'd come back to the beer hall to see about the calls, when the deputy served him.

Jake was staring at the pictures of the Negro athletes on the opposite wall as Jordan reread the summons.

"Your brother don't lose much time, does he?"

Jordan looked up at him.

"It's bad, Jordan. We're in trouble."

"No," Jordan said. "We'll just go to court and—"

"Deep trouble," Jake said. "And when we was doin' so well."

"But look, Jake—"

They stopped short because Bryant came into the beer hall, speaking cheerfully to a couple of men in the front booth, calling to them as if they were old friends. He came back to where Jake and Jordan were and greeted them warmly, but Jordan noticed a quiver to his lips. Nobody said anything to him.

"Let's all have a beer," he said.

Jake grudgingly poured out a beer.

"No, I mean the three of us. Here's a dollar, Jake. Fill 'em up."

Jake considered that for a second, then poured two more beers.

"Say, Jordan," Bryant said, "I'm goin' to have a housewarming next month, and I want you and Annie to come."

It was the first time Jordan had seen Bryant up close since the night he had left the house, and his sudden friendliness embarrassed him. "No, don't think I can make it," he said, pulling away.

Jake cleared his throat and looked at Bryant, as if asking for an invitation. Bryant knew what was going on all right, but he ignored it, finished up what was left in his glass and shoved it across the counter. "Fill it up," he said.

Jake let the beer start foaming down the glass. "What time is this housewarming?" he said.

"Oh—middle of the evenin'."

"Uh huh. What day?"

"Ain't decided that yet, Jake."

"I'd like to come."

Bryant sniffed the beer as the bubbles burst and sizzled. "Fine beer," he said finally, turning and going over to a booth. "Come on over here, Jordan."

Jordan stuck around where Jake was.

"He ain't goin' to invite me," Jake said, "and him probably ownin' my place, I'm sure."

"Forget it, Jake."

"Jordan, come here a minute," Bryant called to him.

He walked to the booth and sat down.

"Look, I do want you and Annie there, boy. I'm goin' to have people over from Durham and Raleigh. Goin' to be a big party."

Jordan started to object.

"Now, for old time's sake, boy," Bryant said, extending his hand. Jordan hesitated; then, remembering the scene of a few nights before, shook hands with him.

"Annie and me will come," he said.

Bryant met his gaze for a moment, then got up from the booth with an expulsion of air, and wended his way toward the door.

Jordan remembered about the court summons. "Oh, Bryant," he called, "what kind of license you need to operate a taxicab?"

Bryant looked back, scratched one ear in a detached manner. "I don't know. Do you need a license at all?"

"Yes, you do."

"Well, I'm surprised about that."

He turned and went out. Jordan looked over at Jake, who nodded a couple of times, as if to say he still suspected Bryant for turning them in.

Jordan was far from at ease in the heavily shuttered hall of the town court. He caught himself staring at the empty jury box near the front, wondering if there was ever a jury trial in Leafwood. Rumor had it that the town officials had known so little about what they were doing, that they had had the wrong kind of courtroom installed—and at considerable expense, because the jury chairs were leather-upholstered.

Jordan didn't know about that one way or the other, but he did know that the only justice he had ever heard spoken there was from a single judge, a wizened old man of sixty years, bitter of eye, with a small mouth through which came a thin, grating voice, who sometimes handed out sentences and fines before a witness had taken the stand.

"We should 'a' gotten a lawyer," Jordan whispered to Jake.

"Lawyer would irritate the judge."

"I dunno. I dunno."

"That's right. Make him think we was gangin' up on him. Just try to get along, Jordan. They can't do nothin' more than fine us ten dollars, can they?"

The judge banged down his gavel at this point, and found another man guilty, fined him heavily—fifteen dollars and court costs.

"How many men does that make for today?"

"So far he's had four up before him, and all was guilty."

The next man up was a white man who was trying to start a wood lot just beyond the western town limits. He was known to drink more than he should, and the wood he sold was never dried out properly. The judge found against him before he had hardly gotten a word out, and he moved right up to the judge's desk and banged on the top of it. "By God, how do you win an election? I'm askin' you how you win an election, when you ain't got any idea of what's right and fair? How do you win?"

Two cops grabbed him and pulled him back, leaving the judge leaning as far back in his chair as he could. Suddenly he sat erect, as if coming back to life. "Don't let me catch another one of you out of line!" he said. "I'm here for justice, by God, and justice has a hard bite! There are no weak teeth to justice; she clamps down and hangs on!"

He sat back in the chair, staring at the wood-lot owner, who was dropping money on the clerk's desk, paying his fine, his eyes averted. Jordan felt sorry for him. He had done a strong thing, but now he seemed to be ashamed of it.

"They say he had his wife fixed when she was twenty so she wouldn't get no children," Jake whispered. "And now that he knows it weren't needed to keep from havin' children, it gnaws at him."

"No," Jordan said. "The judge?"

"That white man—the firewood man, for God's sake. His wife left him two years ago."

The clerk unbent at one side of the courtroom, standing tall and stiff, a list in his hand. "Jordan Cummings," he read.

Jordan was too frightened to stand up.

"Jordan Cummings," he repeated.

The judge leaned forward and smote the desk with his fist. "Jordan Cummings!" he thundered. "Is he here? Does anybody know where he is?"

Jordan stood now, but the judge didn't see him.

"Is he that big colored fellow?"

"Yes, sir," the tall white man said.

"Well, why ain't he in here?"

"I'm here, Judge," Jordan said.

The judge saw him then. "Well, for God's sake, speak up, man. We ain't got but one mornin'. Come on up front where we can have a look at you."

Jordan walked to the front of the room. Everybody was staring at him. He wondered if his name would end up in the newspapers for being in court. He had never been in a court in Leafwood, except once or twice for getting in fights. But he had never broken a real law to get there.

"Well, now, Jordan," the judge began, "my report says you been operatin' a taxicab company without a franchise. That so?"

Jordan nodded.

"Speak up."

"It's so," Jordan said.

"What kind of place do you think this is, where a man can go into whatever work he wants to without a franchise or a how-do-you-do to the government? Who do you think you are?"

"I dunno," Jordan mumbled.

"Speak up, damn it. You got to speak up loud enough for me to hear you."

Jordan looked up at him and spoke in a loud voice. "I don't know."

A hush fell on the courtroom. The judge sat back slowly. "I see. I see well enough. Yes." He tapped his finger on the desk top. "Well, well," he said, his small eyes peering at Jordan. "Where you from?"

"From here."

There was a silence in the room for a while. The judge sat back in his leather chair, closed his eyes. "How many cabs you operatin' the law, Jordan?"

"Operatin' one cab, Judge."

"You knew you was breakin' the law, didn't you?"

"No, sir, I didn't."

"Ignorance of the law is no excuse here. Justice has to be firm. She ain't no lily-white maid." He opened his eyes and gazed out the window. "You ever operated a cab company before?"

"No, I ain't."

"Well, pay court costs and close down operation."

"Sir?"

"Close down."

Jordan couldn't speak. He wanted to say something for his own cause, but he couldn't do it. Then he felt Jake beside him, tugging at his sleeve.

"Come on, big boy, come on. No scene here. Don't do nothin' now."

Jordan didn't move.

The tall, lanky clerk rose. "Agnes Tetterow," he called out.

A hard-faced white woman came down the aisle, walking with a crutch. It was clear she was there on business and no fooling around.

But still Jordan was standing in front of the judge's desk, and she had to wait on one side.

"Jordan, come on," Jake begged, feeling ill at ease in front of all the people. "Come on."

"Let me be."

"Jordan, get out of here and let this woman have her say. This is the law."

"I ain't had my say," Jordan said firmly.

The judge, who had been reading his report on the Agnes Tetterow case, took off his glasses and looked up. "Just pay the court costs, I told you."

"And shut down, you said."

"And shut down. That's all."

Jordan didn't move. The judge glanced over at the two policemen who were inching forward, neither of them showing eagerness, however, to tangle with Jordan and Jake. A nervous hum went through the courtroom.

Then the clerk was beside Jordan, whispering to him. "Nothing can be done here. Not a thing till you get a franchise."

Jordan nodded slowly. "How do I do that?"

"Go to see the town board. Apply for one. Can't be done here."

"Come on," Jake said anxiously.

"Town board then," Jordan said defiantly. Jake led him out past the staring spectators and into the hall.

When Jordan found himself thrown out of work by the law, he spoke out his criticisms sharp and clear, proclaiming that no government had a right to do that to a man.

Lord, who could say what laws were written down—nobody could read them. He didn't know. Not a Negro in Leafwood knew.

But his anger made no impression on the people at the town hall. No matter to whom he talked, he received the same quiet smiles, the same contented expressions. Except for Jordan, everybody in Leafwood was satisfied with the laws concerning taxicab companies.

Finally, angrily, he applied for a franchise. "Might get in soon," the clerk told him as he filled out the form. "No demand for 'em, I'll tell you that. The white company's been losin' money for more than a year. Hell, its owner went to Florida so as not to have to know his current losses."

Weeks went by, however, and there was no word. In Jake's beer hall Jordan fretted, cursing Bryant now, whom he knew had done this to him, and cursing the town hall and the law, recalling stories from his boyhood about what police had done to Negroes he had known or heard about. "Nothin' fair about 'em," he pointed out to everyone who would listen.

Most everybody agreed, but only Bryant seemed to understand. "Had trouble up North," he said. "Up there, got to have a franchise to stand on a street corner and watch traffic. No matter where I turned, franchises were handed out with the hand stayin' open for some personal money. Had more franchises at one time than I had places o' business. But I found out there are ways to handle all that, you, and if you need some advice—"

"No, I'm not listenin' to you, Bryant," Jordan told him, starting to push himself up from the booth in Jake's.

"Tell you what, I'll do you one better. Don't have to listen. Just turn your problems over to Brother Bryant and let me handle 'em for you. In no time you'll have a franchise sewed up."

"Huh? What you say?"

"Let me see if I can't bring you through this thing."

Jordan's eyes narrowed and his breathing slowed down for a few seconds. "Bring your own self through is the way it'll be. You'll go off with it."

"Listen to that," Bryant interrupted with a laugh. "I'm your brother, boy, remember me? I'm tryin' to help you."

Jordan watched him, unable to figure it out. Finally he started on off. "Goin' to wait for the law to take its course," he called back.

But the law took time on top of time. Jordan got odd jobs at the filling station, the wood lot, and scattered places, but it wasn't enough to support him. He thought more and more seriously about Bryant's offer. "I tell you, Jake, he knows the way things are."

"Yeah, and I know the way he is," Jake answered angrily. "Don't work with him, big boy."

Jordan promised not to, but Bryant sought him out almost every day, and Annie began to complain about the lack of money. He was ready to give in and fall on Bryant's help, when word came that he was wanted at the town hall. He brushed up his clothes and put in as fine an appearance as he could, not knowing whether they still wanted some more information or to turn him down.

He found it was neither, for his franchise had been granted for four cabs, and he could buy his license for fifteen dollars.

And then he saw the beauty of the law. The piece of paper showed him the beauty of it. There was his authority, and now the law was back of him. It was a fine thing. No fault to be found with it. The law that had opposed him once and closed him down, now protected him.

He went down to Jake's with the big news, spread it around, and he and Jake celebrated the same afternoon by putting the taxicab back on the road, phoning their customers and telling them. Only Bryant seemed to be displeased, his expression moody and dissatisfied.

But even though Jordan had not been held up overlong, and though the Negroes now looked to him with added respect because he had been to town hall and come out the winner, the fear was there, around him, all around. Bryant's face was in his mind.

"Still, no matter," he told Jake as he clipped out a small item in the *Leafwood Weekly* saying that the franchise had been granted. It was the first time Jordan had ever seen his name in print, and he was more than ordinarily proud of it.

"What do you mean, no matter?"

"We'll just carry on, that's all. Maybe Bryant didn't do it, after all. He was tryin' to help there toward the end, Jake."

"The hell he was," Jake said. "You better learn how to trust, Jordan. Don't do to trust at random."

11

When they arrived at Bryant's housewarming, Jordan looked with astonishment at the guests assembled. The men were doctors, teachers, lawyers—most of them from Raleigh and Durham. The only one he knew was Patrick.

Bryant took Jordan and Annie around, introduced them. A man named Norman Cathy seemed to take special interest, looking over Annie with a practiced eye and trying to sum up Jordan. Cathy was, to hear the women tell it, a man of fine breeding and excellent taste; but Jordan disliked him on sight.

"I've heard a great deal about you, Mr. Cummings," Cathy said, after some doctor's wife had gone off with Annie in hand.

Jordan shifted uneasily, wondered where the man had learned to speak with such easy sounds.

"Mona has told me many things." He smiled, almost a hidden smile, and Jordan looked away quickly, trying to hide his expression. It was, he realized, going to be an aggravating evening, with Annie there and this man talking about Mona. The room soon was overcrowded, and twice Jordan backed into a cocktail table, almost knocking it over. In every way he was in misery. Cathy, as if in sympathy, made a point of keeping him well supplied with whisky, and soon he was feeling better. He could see, even in Cathy's eyes, some tone of friendliness, and he relaxed into the sounds of laughter and conversation, trying to remember what was said—business ventures in Charlotte, buying tobacco farms for parents, the style of new Cadillacs, talk about New York and staying in fine hotels there; and every time one of them would mention the big city, or any part of the North, he would edge closer and try to hear every word.

But they would change off subjects fast. It was like a game between them, their minds bouncing ideas back and forth.

"Say, Mr. Cummings," somebody said to him, "we haven't seen you around here much, have we?"

"I live in Tin Top."

A hush fell over that part of the room.

"Let's see. That's near here, is it?"

"Eight blocks," he said, taking a sip from his highball glass and returning their stares.

"Not far," the man said quietly, a thoughtful smile on his face. "Not far as to distance, is it?"

They turned to other topics, and he fell back to listening.

"...The Jew is more aggressive even than the northern European; but on the other end of the scale is the Negro, always rather satisfied with the world, and—"

He pushed his way through the room, wondering where Annie was, and brushed right past her without seeing her.

"...Now, Mr. Cathy, no more of that kind of story."

"...Yes, I have a maid come in three times a week to help with the housework. The woman is a glutton for work, too—name of Mabel. . . ."

"...But you see, science says a child's skin cannot be darker than the skin of its darker parent...."

"...No, I always call for white workmen when I need house repairs. They're so much more dependable..."

"...So, as an example to the class, I pointed out *The Merchant of Venice*. When Portia comes into the trial scene—"

Jordan nudged Patrick. "Who's that pretty woman with the professor?"

"Hell, that's Bryant's girl."

"Huh? Has he got a girl?"

"She's college educated, mister—and all."

"Big girl," Jordan said. "Big body on her. Breedin' stock."

"Yeah. Well, I understand she's livin' here now."

"In the house?"

Through a drunken, happy fog, Jordan saw Patrick nod.

"...And when Portia says in effect, 'Which is the merchant here and which is the Jew?' it's Shakespeare dropping a personal comment right at the climax of *The Merchant of Venice*—giving to the prejudiced English a minority view."

Jordan had sided up to the professor, trying to catch what he was saying. Now he looked around at the four or five impressed faces. Only Bryant's girl seemed to have a small, half-knowing smile as she returned the professor's stare. She probably understood it fine, but Jordan was in the dark. He touched the professor lightly on the arm. "Uh," he said, "what did the fellow say again?"

There was a slight chuckle. The professor cleared his throat importantly. "She said—Portia is a woman, of course—she said, 'Which is the merchant here and which is the Jew?'"

It didn't make any better sense the second time than the first. "Which one was?" Jordan asked.

Again a titter went around. The professor pushed himself up on the toes of his shoes, tilted forward, then rocked back to normal height. "How old are you—thirty, thirty-five?" Before Jordan could answer, he went on, "Sometimes I'm amazed at how little is known by many of our people. The awful ignorance. I tell you, it discourages me to realize—"

Bryant's girl cut in, speaking swiftly. "It seems to me a teacher shouldn't be discouraged by anyone who wants to learn."

The professor was caught off guard. He glared at her, then smiled uneasily. "Now, that's not fair, Kate."

"Perhaps not," she said simply.

The professor coughed, cleared his throat; then, giving Jordan a critical glance, turned and left, somewhat upset. The others, made uncomfortable by the incident, wandered off, leaving Bryant's girl and Jordan talking together. Rather, she was talking, rambling on about Shakespeare and the Jews, and he was listening. He was not much very interested in either of those topics. He had never heard of Shakespeare, to his knowledge, and he had never seen a Jew. As a boy, he had waited half a day in Durham, expecting to see one. His father had promised him he would, but he had missed out somehow.

Then Bryant's girl started talking about Negroes. Jordan knew a gracious plenty about them, or so he thought; but now he heard facts and opinion come out in a long, steady stream. There seemed to be no end to the torrent, and no way to interrupt it. "...The Negro upper class has deserted us, you see. They're too well satisfied with the way things are, and are really more color and class prejudiced than the whites. Sometimes I wonder if they realize that Negroes are rioting in this country, somewhere, almost every year."

"Huh?"

"So I look around at them and know I have to go on with my work."

Jordan didn't understand when the girl tried to explain about her work—some books she was studying and a book she was preparing. "It's very clear from the statistics that it's only in the Negro middle class that changes are wanted," she said. "You can trace the growth of the Negro middle class and find a corresponding increase in unrest. The lower class is too far down to revolt; the upper class is too satisfied to revolt; and only the middle class will try to work for improvement."

"Bryant's in the middle class, ain't he?" Jordan broke in.

She smiled briefly. "Maybe near the upper class."

"No, he ain't satisfied," Jordan said. "He wants changes. He wants lots of changes."

"That's good."

"No, that's bad," he said. "That's bad for Bryant."

She looked at him thoughtfully, then glanced over at Bryant. "He's— he's not what I mean," she said, her face expressionless.

Jordan left her then, anxious to escape the flow of words. He found a place to stand in the dining room and was just finishing up a drink when she came up to him agan. "Would you like to read something by Shakespeare?" she said.

"No. I don't know about the Jews."

She smiled. "I know a book for you. Wait here."

She hurried out of the room and disappeared up the hall stairs. Jordan looked after her, then glanced around at the others. Everybody was drunk now, he decided—at least, everybody certainly looked drunk to him. Bryant was wobbling about laughing in a fat voice, carrying drinks to and fro, now bringing another one to Jordan.

"Tastes like straight whisky," Jordan told him, remembering a time in Durham two years before when some men had tried to knock him out with drink. They had done it, too, along about four in the morning.

"Purple Jesus is what it is," Bryant called back. "It's strong, all right."

Jordan saw Bryant's girl come back in with a book. He tried to hide behind some people but was too big to get away with it. She tugged at his elbow. "Here it is. You'll like it."

He pushed it aside. "I ain't much for readin'. Not tonight."

"Take it home."

He took the book in his hand, but the words on the cover blurred. He dropped it into the pocket of his coat. "Hey, what's your name?"

"Kate Herring."

"You Bryant's girl?"

She smiled, nodded curtly.

"Uh huh. Bryant's not tryin' to get me drunk, is he?" When she didn't answer right off, he asked her again.

"Maybe he is. At least you've had more than anybody else here, by far."

"Why would he do that? And where's Cathy, anyway? Ain't seen him in a long time."

As if in answer, the front door was opened, and Cathy entered, helping along a woman Jordan did not recognize instantly, then did recognize. It was Mona, radiantly beautiful and obviously a bit tipsy, herself.

"Annie," Jordan said, looking around for her, suddenly realizing the danger and wanting to get her and leave. But Annie was nowhere to be seen.

Mona shook hands with Bryant coolly. "Well—" She sounded weary, as if she had come against her better judgment. Everybody was standing around watching her now.

"I knew you would come, Mona," Bryant said, nodding graciously.

"Did you?" She turned from him haughtily, and so came face to face with Jordan. She froze, then recovered, looked around at the other faces as if pretending that the look she had given Jordan was typical. But a slow smile spread over Bryant's face. He and Cathy exchanged glances.

Mona moved along, being introduced to the guests; the hum of conversation started again. Jordan made a search for Annie. He even went upstairs calling for her, but she wasn't there. Then from a back bedroom he looked onto the terrace and saw her and Patrick sitting in lawn chairs, talking and enjoying themselves.

"Ah, God," he mumbled, relieved. The thought that he could go out there with Mona and the others, set him at good-natured peace. He would go down now and get through to the terrace. He would sit down on the terrace and laugh with them and talk about the boys.

He hurried down the main stairs and into the hall. Bryant saw him, stopped him. "Hey, Jordan, here's a drink, boy."

"I got one over on the bookshelves," he lied, surprised by the drunken thickness of his own speech.

"Take this open. And, say—you know Mona, don't you. She's right over here."

Jordan took the drink, but did not even glance at Mona. He went through the small, scattered groups of guests, only to reach the terrace door just as it opened and Annie and Patrick came inside, Cathy was with them.

"Annie," Jordan said desperately, taking her arm. "Hey, honey, come on back outside."

Before Annie could answer, Cathy moved up quickly, and before Annie knew what was happening, he had Annie in tow and was leading her across the living room floor toward where Mona was.

Jordan angrily took a step to follow, when Patrick caught his arm. "Jordan," he whispered hurriedly, "there's a rule up here—no fightin'. That's a rule."

Jordan let the words take hold him. He nodded, picked up a half-filled glass from a table, somebody else's, but he didn't care, and finished it up. He was left without a friend at the party, with Annie talking to Mona, with that damn Cathy and Bryant leading Mona on. He had better get on over there himself and break it up somehow.

But he didn't move toward them. If he should join them no telling what would break forth. Already he could see Bryant was loading Mona's glass with whisky.

"We don't care about conventions, do we, Mona?" Bryant was saying to her.

"No," Mona answered, then giggled.

"Life is too short to care about what people will think."

"Yes," Mona said dreamily.

Jordan turned to one of the guests, a Negro so light of skin that he could pass for a white man, and asked what time it was. He was startled to find it was only eleven o' clock. "Good God, when do we get out?"

"I beg your pardon, Mr. Cummings?"

He had to get hold of an idea, and he knew it. If Jake were only there, the two of them could—

Jake. That was the ticket. He went into the kitchen, closed the door and looked around for the phone. He had seen a phone on the kitchen cabinet when he had gone through the empty house with Bryant, and he had little trouble finding it. Jake's number was the number of his cab company, and even deep in alcohol he remembered it, dialed, and a moment later heard the gruff and friendly voice of the old boxer.

"Hey—hey, hello there, Jake?"

"Oh, God, where do you want me to pick you up, you bastard? You sound like—"

"They got me cornered, Jake. They got me framed. Bryant and that damn Cathy and—"

"Now hold on. What's the matter?"

"This housewarming party, God-damn it, Jake. It's framed up. I ain't got a chance, and it's not near time to go home yet." He was about to ask Jake what to do when the door opened and Bryant came in. Quickly he hung up.

"Who you talkin' to, Jordan?"

"Huh? I was listenin'."

"Who to?"

"Nobody. Conversation. Somebody talkin'. Shakespeare, I think."

He pushed past Bryant and went back into the dining room, unsure what to do now, a frantic fear coming to him. Somebody had turned on a record player, and the music was coming out strong, as if made by fifty instruments at a time. The sounds stirred him up, made him wonder—

But no time for listening. Had to think, think hard. He picked up another drink and downed it. Then Kate was beside him. "Jordan," she whispered, "you better go on outside on the terrace and try to sober up. I think Cathy and Bryant are leading up to something."

"Huh? God, I know that, Kate." His voice was louder than he had wanted to be. Several people turned to stare at him.

She took his arm and led him outside. "Don't ask me why I'm doing this," she said, helping him stumble along the brick-paved terrace. "I don't even know what they have in mind. But I know they're capable of lousy stunts, and I like you. You know why? I like you because you want to learn, and you're the first person I've met in this house who didn't think he knew everything, and that goes for Bryant, too. Bryant is all right, but he's an unfeeling man, Jordan, a crude man," she said, shuddering a bit.

"Godamighty, you sure can talk, Kate."

She shoved him playfully. "That's what my folks always told me. Then when I left the house it seemed like at least six children had gone out to the fields."

He chuckled, delighted with the idea that she had come from a farm. Lord, she looked city-bred to him.

The music was still floating around in the house, some of it escaping to the terrace, and Kate kept talking. For a while he tried to listen both to the music and to Kate, and found that he could do it very well if he kept his mind free.

They walked around for ten minutes, perhaps fifteen. The night was chilly, and his head began to go around from the change inside him. Finally he was so dizzy he flopped down on a rock wall, almost pulling Kate over. "Hey," he said. "Yeah, Lord, Kate, let me ask you somethin'."

"What?" She sat down beside him.

"You're all right. Big girl. Goin' to do very well. Want to ask you seomthin'. Did you know that—that my family named me after a river?"

"I certainly did. The Jordan, a big river."

"Is it big? I never knowed much about it."

"Very important river, too. That's where the Egyptians were killed when they tried to follow the Jews into the desert, you remember?"

"Yeah. Poor damned Egyptians," he said, stumbling along beside her.

"Yes, that's right."

He pulled up short. "That's what I ought to do to Bryant." He swung toward the house, a smile curving his lips. "I ought to drown old Bryant."

Kate grabbed his arm. "Here, now. Forget that."

"Yeah," he said agreeably, "that's right. He's my brother, my little brother—little Bryant. I never did do much for Bryant. I should 'a' done more, you know?"

She finally got him walking again and she helped hold him erect and steady.

"I looked over Jordan," he sang to himself, "and what did I see— comin' for to carry me home?"

"Come on, Jordan, stand straight."

"A God-damned chariot comin' after me—" He shook his head sadly. "Ain't goin' to ride in no chariot," he said.

"Come on, walk, Jordan." She pulled him along and did as much as she could for him before Cathy came to the terrace door, two drinks in his hands. He came toward them with lazy, graceful strides, one of the drinks held out. "Here you are, Mr. Cummings."

Jordan scratched the top of his head for a moment, then shook his head. "Not me. I didn't order anything."

"Oh, I don't want to waste it—"

"I'll take it," Kate said.

Cathy frowned at her, held on to the drink. "Bryant wants you inside, Kate. Go on."

Before she cold move, Jordan interrupted. "She don't have to take orders."

"You don't know what you're saying, mister," Cathy said. He tilted his head at Kate and she, hesitating for a moment only, went inside.

Cathy held the glass out again. "Drink it, Jordan. Then come on inside."

Jordan licked his lips, studied Cathy as if weighing the problem in his mind. He had never hit a man who had a drink in each hand before. He had seen it done, of course, and it was a very effective way; but Patrick had already told him about the rule. He gave it careful thought, wanting to be sure, then and brought his left fist into the unsuspecting Cathy's face, sending him sprawling back and down onto the brick pavement.

"Good God," Cathy moaned, tossing there.

"Ah," Jordan said, "come on up, Cathy. God, I ain't got much power in my left hand."

He kicked one of the glasses out of the way and went back to the wall, slumped down, his head clearing some now.

Cathy pulled himself to his feet and limped to one side, evidently sick.

Bryant came to the door. "Hey, Jordan, didn't Cathy tell you? We want you to come on inside now."

Jordan only glared at Bryant.

"What's the matter, boy?" He came on out, then noticed that Cathy was standing nearby, his head in his hands. Bryant nodded slowly, as if to say he understood, then looked off at the treetops thoughtfully. "Uh. Hey, boy," he said, "Annie wants you."

"Huh?" Jordan stirred a bit.

"Annie. She's in the living room. She's asking for you."

Jordan pushed past him. He wanted to see Annie. By God, Annie was all right. He stumbled through the dining room and into the living room. "Annie, how are you, honey?" he said.

She looked up, startled. "What is it, Jordan?"

"Huh?"

"You're drunk. You're the only drunk one."

Mona laughed out, low and warm-feeling. "No he's not, honey," she said, reaching out and grabbing his arm, pulling him down onto the sofa beside her. "Jordan and I are both drunk. Jordan and I are good pals, and we're drunk."

Annie stared at her, dazed and slightly frightened, as if partially aware of what she meant. Kate gave Bryant an angry look, then hurried into the hall and up the stairs.

Mona said, "Jordan and I know what it is to be drunk together, don't we, honey?"

"Annie, look here, now—" He tried to get up, but Cathy, who had just entered, sat down on the other side of him brushing against him enough to force him back onto the sofa.

"Jordan and I are good friends—" She glanced around at the others. "What are you staring at? What do you care if Jordan and I are good friends?" She put her arm around his shoulder.

"What kinds of good friends, Mona?" Bryant said.

"Best of friends." She leaned over, tried to kiss him.

"What do you say to that, Jordan?" Bryant said.

It was like a nightmare to Jordan. Then Patrick started to laugh, high and uncontrollably. A nervousness crossed the room. He saw Annie's face change. Then he saw a strange thing and his mind cleared. He saw Jake standing in the archway that led into the living room from the entrance hall. Jake was standing there, and on his arm was one of

Minnie's girls—and they looked drunker than Jordan had ever seen either of them.

"Jake," he said, reaching out for them.

Jake smiled broadly, staggering a bit.

Bryant was looking at him in horror. The professor came forward to get a better view of the ex-boxer and the worn girl.

"I didn't get your invitation," Jake said to Bryant, "and you and me is such good friends. I didn't get your invitation."

Bryant made a sign to Cathy, who got up quickly and started toward Jake, but Jake pushed him aside easily. "I want to introduce all you people to my girl," he said, motioning grandly toward Minnie's oldest, who giggled sweetly. "I want you to meet my woman. Come here, honey."

She came to him and he put his arm around her and kissed her on the forehead.

"Good God," Jordan said, trying to get up and finding that he could now.

"I want you to see a real girl," Jake said, and with that he undid a bow at her neck and her clothes fell off.

It could not have been a more complete surprise. The professor backed off hurriedly. The carefully groomed man with the clipped accent suddenly drowned the rest of his drink and dropped the glass, trying to set it aside. The older women gasped in protest. In the archway stood Minnie's girl, giggling prettily, looking around her unconcernedly.

Jordan was horrified; then suddenly he was sober. He bent double laughing. He saw Bryant's face and almost went into hysterics. "Jake, you are a good man," he said, throwing his arm around him.

"Hell, I know it," Jake said. "But think o' her—what a sacrifice. Right out here in the God-damn cold—"

Everybody left soon after that, yet there was very little leavetaking. Some went out on the terrace, some through the kitchen, and a few through the archway where a stunned Bryant stood, not sure what had happened to his housewarming. Annie and Jordan left through the main door. When they went, only Mona and Cathy and Bryant were still there, and Mona was trembling, as if she were ill. She was sitting on the sofa trembling, and Jordan couldn't figure out what was wrong with her.

But he and Annie left and they started walking toward home. For the first block, Annie said nothing to him at all, and he began to wonder if she had noticed anything out of the way before Jake arrived.

"She was very drunk, wasn't she?" Annie said, after a while.

"Huh? Who, Annie?"

"The Taylor woman."

They walked on a ways. "Yeah, Lord," he said.

"Do you know her, Jordan?"

"Yeah. She's the woman that got me fired at the coalyard."

They walked on. A small, grim small came to Annie's face. "She's the one you don't like, is it?"

"That's right, Annie," he said, trying to sound casual. "I don't like her at all."

"No," Annie said quietly. The word seemed to follow the beat of her heels as they made their way home.

12

I'm afraid of that Bryant," Jake said, "because he has a friendly disposition toward me after what I done. I don't trust people that is friendly after I come to their party with a woman on a string."

Jordan looked around the beer hall, shook his head unconcernedly. A Buick slid down the street outside. For a moment he thought it might be Bryant's.

"He owns this damn beer hall o' mine. I know he does. But I can't be sure."

"Did you bring the subject up to him?" Jordan asked.

"I have. Don't do any good. He denies it."

Coltrane came in, stopped short on seeing Jordan, then gave a birdlike nod and turned to Jake. They began to whisper about whether or not Bryant owned the beer hall. Jordan knew that was the subject because Jake never was one who could keep his voice down, and words and sentences came through clear, enough of them to make out that Coltrane had had a lawyer look into it and had found nothing.

Finally Coltrane stepped back, shook his head sadly, his small shoulders stooped. "Ah me, it's a big puzzle. I be layin' awake part of ever night tryin' to figure it out. And then the other night he didn't invite Helen and me to his housewarming."

"I didn't get invited, either," Jake said, "but I dropped in toward the end."

"Why wouldn't he invite me?" Coltrane said. "I'm well established here socially, Helen and I both. He invited Patrick, even, but not me. Why is that?"

Jake ran a finger into one ear and twisted it around. "He's got bad taste, Coltrane," he said.

Coltrane smiled, feeling foolish for a moment, then turned to Jordan, stood gazing at him thoughtfully. After a while he gave him a quick nod and went out.

"You got him all nervous, Jake."

"Hell, I ain't spoke to him about Bryant. I mentioned Bryant's buyin' this place to one of the Hogan boys, and they must 'a' dropped a word to Coltrane, askin' him about it. Then he comes in here creepin' around, with those brows droopin' half over his eyeballs. He's scared o' Bryant— just because Bryant didn't invite him to that housewarming."

"I wish he hadn't invited me," Jordan said solemnly. "I ain't goin' to any more of them. Got me in deep trouble with Annie as things lie. She pesters the dust around me but acts like I'm off someplace else."

"Why's that?"

"She thinks that Taylor widow likes me. Ain't that a laugh?"

The bean sprouts made their way up first, and Jordan proudly walked the two boys down the row, showing them how a small mound of dirt would form as the bean sprout pushed on it, then how the sprout would come through. "That's a corker," Jordan said. "Look at that little fellow there— done got his head up and his eyes open. That's one goin' to produce some fruit afore he's done."

"Is beans fruit, Pa?" Fletcher said.

"Huh? Sure. Fruit or a vegetable. Look a' here at that one."

"Let's name 'em, Pa!"

"Oh, for the Lord's sake—name bean plants! That ain't no way to do. You just name things that will come when you holler to 'em. Let these bean plants alone."

Out in the small garden plot, working with a trowel as the plants got bigger, Jordan almost felt at peace with the world. His taxicab company was all right. He and Jake were making more money, and before long they would get up to a hundred dollars a week, even after expenses and the payment on the car. They were doing that well. Soon they were going to buy another car and get one of the Hogan boys employed, have two cabs on the road. Then he could take life a bit easier.

What did bother him, even out in the garden, were his family problems. Annie was a stranger to him, and Mona pressed in on his mind. Two or three times since the housewarming she had phoned the taxicab company, but he hadn't gone by. Yet he knew it would be impossible to make himself continue to ignore her, especially with Annie drawn off.

"Women is like the wind," Jake said to him one early afternoon, "sometimes hardly movin', sometimes tearin' up the place. I had a woman in Georgia that was like that. Before I would go to the mill in the mornin', she would peck me on the cheek and make a big to-do about me. When I come home after workin' myself weak, she would be throwin' furniture. Wasn't nothin' I done to her, either."

"She your wife?"

"Wife? I ain't got no wife."

"Well, why you live with her if she was like that?"

Jake gazed out the window thoughtfully. "I didn't live with her but two years."

"But why you dodge furniture when you wasn't married to her?" Jordan persisted.

"Hell, she was all right in the mornin's," Jake said unconcernedly. "I didn't care about the damn furniture."

The phone rang and Jake answered it. When he put up the receiver, he said that the Taylor widow wanted the cab to come around right away.

Jordan went up to one of the big plate-glass windows and looked out at the passing traffic.

Jake called to him, "Hey, Mona Taylor wants a cab."

"I'm not goin' for her. She got me fired at the coalyard, Jake."

"To hell with the coalyard."

Jordan watched the people walk by, his mind brooding on Mona. Then he was aware that Jake was standing next to him.

"You got a light?" Jake said.

Jordan struck a kitchen match on the window molding and held it out. Jake puffed the cigar going, glanced up at Jordan. "She sweet on you, big boy?"

Jordan blew out the match, threw it aside. He went over to one of the rear booths and sat down. "You want me to go get her, I will," he said.

"You got most o' the ownership," Jake said.

"I didn't say anything about ownership! If you make me go get her, say so!"

Jake grinned. "Make you?" He puffed at the cigar. "No, let's don't, Jordan. Let's let her worry about us."

Jordan shifted uneasily. He didn't know whether to go or not. He figured he shouldn't, because she was dangerous to be around, but he wanted to. She was the most yielding woman he had ever known. It was not like the girls at Minnie's house, who were yielding, too—but they were just having a big time. And it wasn't like Annie, who always held back some, seemed to him.

No, Mona had held to him, run her arms around him. She had been the best woman he had ever known, and now she was calling him on the phone and Jake was making jokes about it. No joking matter. It was almost more than he could stand.

If he went to her this time, though, it would be decided. He would go back whenever she wanted him to. It would be breaking with Annie.

But if Annie kept being withdrawn from him, he couldn't be responsible, and that was a fact.

He didn't know why he was trying to be responsible, anyway. Most of the men he knew would jump a dozen picket fences getting to Mona Taylor's house if she sent out a call. They would break both legs leaping obstacles.

The phone rang again. "Get that, will you, big boy? I got my hands full."

Jordan noticed Jake wasn't doing anything except leaning on the counter, but he answered the phone. It was Mona.

"Look, Jordan, I'm waiting."

"Godamighty—I got myself in trouble with Annie, and I just don't see how I can—"

"I'm waiting."

He could see her, slim and neat, standing in the hall of her house, with the phone in her hand. Waiting for him. Soft and waiting. He could hear her breathing.

Then there was a click and he realized she had hung up. Slowly he put the earpiece back on the hook.

"She's got a damn nice shape," Jake said. "Beautiful woman. Wonder what it would be like to get close to a woman like that—"

"Why don't you mind your business, Jake?"

"Feel her all cuddly, tumblin' in your arms."

"Look here, now—"

"Oh, I remember. Even now I'm not so bad at makin' love, given enough time, but I remember when I was a young fellow. I was a threat and a promise. Seemed like I sort o' fanned up desire wherever I went. Ever time a woman saw me, she just wanted to lie back on a bed. But I don't know that I ever met a woman any more warm and comfortable lookin' than that Taylor widow. She's got just about the right flick of the eyelash to me."

"God-damn it, shut up, Jake!" Jordan shouted, storming out of the place.

He drove around town, passing Mona's house three times, but he didn't stop. His mind worked over thoughts about the boys and Annie, about keeping the taxicab company moving ahead in a straight line, and Mona. Right then Mona seemed to be a challenge to all the rest.

Finally he stopped at home and hung around, hoping Annie would say something to him; but she didn't. He went outdoors, took the trowel and dug around the small plants in the garden. They didn't need work, but the ground was a friendship to him, helped him to rest. He could think of the way each plant was alive and breathing; and it made worries seem farther off, and Annie's aloofness and Mona's wanting him less painful.

When he came near the end of a row, Annie came into view, standing at the edge of the plot, acting like she wasn't watching him. He glanced up at her, feeling awkward. "Annie, this garden is goin' to be a good thing."

She turned slightly and looked up the ragged lane of back yards.

"Goin' to plant a bed of salad greens tomorrow noon. I forgot 'em before, and that's one of the best vegetables there is." He knocked some earth from his work pants. "This dirt is better than coal dust was."

"Goin' to wear out all your clothes afore long, goin' like you do and workin' in the dirt," she said.

"Don't I know!" He was glad she was talking to him. "But soon it'll be springtime clothes, anyway. I got some light stuff, ain't I?"

"You got some."

Jordan fingered the hole in his shirt seam. "Ah, Lord," he said. There was not much he could think of to say right off.

"The boys can care for the garden, anyway," Annie said.

"No, these little plants need grown care. We'll have to wait till they get their roots set."

She nodded, then turned away and went into the house. He waited a few minutes, in case she came back out, then kicked the mud off his shoes on the back steps and went inside, too. He pulled up a chair to the kitchen table and sat down.

Annie was rinsing out some of the boys' clothes at the sink, and he noticed she was getting big with the new baby now. "How does it feel to carry a baby, Annie?"

"It don't feel much."

"Lord 'a' mercy. Must be heavy, at least. I reckon a woman gets to know a kid pretty well afore it's ever born, don't she?"

"I dunno." She began wringing out one of the boys' shirts on the drainboard.

"When do they start kickin'?"

"What you care? You won't carry one." She flopped the shirt down on some newspapers and pulled the ironing board around.

Somewhat put out now, he went into the living room, casting about for an idea. He spotted the book he had been reading, the play about a Negro which Kate had given him, *In Abraham's Bosom*. He opened it to Act Two and commenced to read, mumbling the words. Before he had turned five pages he looked up. "Say, this here nigger is a fightin' man," he called to Annie. He knew she had already finished the book and thought perhaps she would be willing to talk about it. "He's goin' to get somewhere. Damn if he don't talk a good game."

No answer.

"Annie, does he win out in the end?" he called.

No answer.

"Huh. Hope he does," Jordan said, almost to himself. He mumbled some more of the words, but he kept thinking about Annie. It was a bad thing, the way she was treating him. He fell to thinking about the people he knew who were in love, most all of them young folks, seemed like. They would ride his cab here and there at night, going to Durham right frequently, particularly to the new Negro restaurant which had opened up there. They would sing songs and be happy together. That was the way love was supposed to be—like it had been between him and Annie in times past.

"Annie," he called out, suddenly demanding in voice.

She came to the kitchen door, peered at him suspiciously. "What you want?"

"Annie, damn it!" he said, annoyed with her and with himself. "God knows, Annie—" But he didn't know what to say to her, and before he could settle on anything at all, she had gone back into the kitchen.

He went to the kitchen door and watched her work, followed with his eyes the movements of her body as she wrung out the clothes and threw them on the drainboard, noticed how her breasts filled out under the blouse she was wearing. Finally he went into the room, stood beside her. Maybe he should apologize for having gone to Mona's house, maybe that would help; but he didn't think it would, and he wasn't sorry, either. A man couldn't do any better than he could do; a man was made different from a woman, had a closer limit.

"You and me, Annie—"

She started. He saw she hadn't known he was standing there.

He put his arm around her, but she threw it off. It made him angry again, but he put that aside for the moment. "You and me, we're goin' out tonight."

"What?"

"We're goin' to a nigger restaurant in Durham."

She shook her head angrily. "Just let me be. Go your own way."

Jordan clenched his fists. "You and me are goin'."

"I ain't."

He grabbed hold of her arms and swung her around to face him. "You listen to me, we're goin'!" he said.

As they drove to Durham, Jordan told her it had been a good idea to go to the restaurant together, and that he was planning to buy a steak. Annie sat on her side of the cab, pouting and looking straight ahead, fingering the buttons on her dress front. "And who's goin' to take care of the business for tonight?" she said.

"Business? Oh, Jake is goin' to explain to the customers. He said married people should have affairs together. What you think?"

Annie drew herself tighter and said nothing to that, but a half-smile came to her face.

Soon Durham was at hand, starting with scattered houses, most of them turned backward to the new, four-lane highway that curved toward the center of town. The traffic increased. Cars were going along with them and beside them now, and Annie tried to keep her eyes on everything, fearful lest somebody make a wrong move. It was her first trip to the city.

Jordan swung into an exit lane and rolled up over a bypass, headed into the business district. The houses gave way to small shops. They passed a cemetery, bordered by a high, iron fence. Inside, a young man and a girl were walking from plot to plot, reading the markers, dull gray in the early evening light.

They took another curve and were on the main street, and now the filling stations formed double lines of signs and lights. Jordan drove slowly so that Annie wouldn't be too much afraid, but she was shivering a bit, even so. She sniffed uncertainly at the first stiff odor of tobacco.

Car horns honked. The traffic congested, then opened out. They crept around a curve and the buildings lay before them. A few of the offices were lighted, their windows white, isolated dots on the brick sides. "Right down there is a Negro company," Jordan said proudly. "Biggest nigger business in the world. Insurance sellers." Annie looked in the general direction he pointed, but didn't seem to be thinking about any single thing. Her eyes were on the cars, crowding people, and the hundreds of store windows where manikins bent and stooped and sat and knelt.

Stop lights glimmered red then green; policemen waved on the traffic, pedestrians scampered out of the way as the lines of cars heaved themselves slowly forward.

Jordan turned right, crossed the row on row of railroad tracks. They approached the darkened, windowless factories, piled one beside another, rising like walls of the street.

Annie's hands were clenched. "Too many people," she said.

"Ah, listen at that. Not so many over here. Maybe sixty thousand people is all."

"All?" she said.

He turned left and made his way through a narrow street. The street widened at an intersection. He went across that and so they entered the Negro business section, lighted red and green and blue and glistening white. Loud music was playing. The sidewalks were littered with paper and filled with people, laughing, carrying on. The Negro barber, cleaning companies, real estate offices, laundromats. The shops were open, doing business, as were the tailor shops, Negro theatre had a line waiting to get in. "Goin' to attend that place again someday," Jordan said.

He cut down a side street, cruised around the block twice, looking for a parking place. Finally, he saw a car pulling out and stopped to one side, waited.

"What do all these people do?" Annie asked.

"Tobacco men. Or work in the sheet factories." He pulled into the parking place. "Come on, Annie. Restaurant's right up the street half a block." He took her arm and they hurried through the crowds and noises. The odor of tobacco was close about them. Jordan pushed open a narrow front door, simply marked "The Marlin," and they stepped inside. As the door closed, the noise fell to the far background. Before them was a room somberly lighted, with private booths along one side. Nearby was a mural of fish, and in back was a tank with fish swimming in it—some of them red, some yellow, some light-green. Music was coming from somewhere, and around at the tables the fifty or more customers ate quietly.

"Yes, sir?" a waiter said, coming up to them.

"How do you do," Jordan said. "We want to eat."

"Yes, sir."

He led them back to one of the closed booths. Annie went in, but Jordan held back. "Could we eat out here in the open?" he said. "I like to get a clear picture of what's goin' on."

The waiter led the way to one of the tables. Annie sat down on one side and Jordan on the other, where he could watch the restaurant and see how everything was being done. He studied the menu carefully, mumbling the items aloud. "You want roast pork?" he asked her.

"I—I think I'll have a ham steak."

"Ham steak?" He bent closer to the menu. "What in the world is that?"

"It's ham, I guess."

"Huh," he said. "I don't want that myself. Godamighty, look at the prices. Two dollars for a ham steak."

"I know it. But it's the cheapest thing on the menu. What you want me to do?"

"Yeah," Jordan said, giving particular note to the prices now. "Four dollars for a beefsteak, did you see that?"

"I saw it."

"Lord 'a' mercy, must be good meat. He went on across the menu, finally coming to a seafood platter which interested him.

The waiter came by and took their order. A young lady came around with a tray of food which she offered. There were little bits of melon which had been colored green and purple, and there were pickles of all kinds. Jordan, curious about what they were, tried everything.

"How you get this melon cut into a ball?" he asked her. "Ain't that hard to do?"

"We have a special tool for that, sir."

"Are they hard to find?" he asked.

"I don't know, sir."

"What are those purple things?"

"Muskmelon, sir."

"Lord 'a' mercy."

People kept coming in and some people left. There was a gently festive air about everything. The waiter brought their salads and a basket of hot rolls, and they started in on that, Annie eating timidly, looking around on occasion to see what the other customers were doing.

He started to tell her that he was hoping they would get along better in the days to come, but it was hard to say it. She looked up at him every once in a while, and once he thought a tiny smile fleeted across her face, then she ate some more of the salad.

"Good salad," he said. "Good idea to cut up lettuce and celery and carrots and dump them in a dish together." He noticed she wasn't eating much. "You all right?"

"What?"

"I want you to be all right," he said.

Annie poked about at the salad with a fork.

The waiter came up with the main course. Annie held back, but Jordan ate eagerly, wondering aloud how the cook had prepared it.

"I tell you, I like this place," Jordan said, chuckling now. "This is all right. This food is done just right. Never had fish any better fried."

Annie nodded, went on with her eating.

Finally he said, "Did you notice the picture of the fish on the wall?" He could tell it caught her interest. "Painted on the plaster. Wonder what Jake would say about that."

"I like the blue one."

"Let's see—that one's called a—" He pushed his plate away from the place mat, on which the names of the fish were printed. "That's a blue marlin."

"I like its face, and that beak."

"Ain't that somethin'? Standin' on his tail, too. Only thing I ever saw stand on his tail like that. Only animal at all that does it, I wouldn't be surprised."

"I like that little fish, too. The one with the platter-shape."

"Yeah," he said. "Let's see here now—that's a...a ray fish."

"Which one's your favorite?"

"I tell you what the ugliest one is," he said, staring at the wall. "That's that dogfish. Don't seem to be nothin' much to him."

Annie was smiling some now.

"Let's see if I can name 'em without help o' this card," he said. "You can check me."

She pushed back her plate and studied the place mat.

"Startin' at the top left there's the ray, and the second one is—Lord knows now—"

"The sturgeon," Annie said.

"Don't tell me, Annie. Then comes—is it the short-nosed fish?"

"The short-nosed gar pike."

"Uh huh. Then the blue marlin, and uh—Knew that one without doubt."

"Sea devil."

"Don't tell me what they are, Annie; I'm tryin' to guess 'em." He was put out with her; it was hard enough trying to remember the fish without her having to break in. "Uh—next one is the...the sea horse."

"That's right."

"Next one is the flatfish—"

"Flounder—"

"Well, I heard it called a flatfish. Next one is the—" He shook his head wearily. "I don't know those last two," he said.

"No matter." She shoved her plate into place. "I wouldn't 'a' been able to do as well."

"Wouldn't you? I think you would."

"No, I wouldn't."

"Not much for names, not me. Now, that Kate, or some of them at Bryant's party—they're 'names' people—numbers, books, weighty minds. But I can't remember as well as some."

When she said no more about it, he went back to eating. Then, in the way of doing everything he could to make Annie have a fine time, he talked some about the marlin, made scattered comments about the restaurant, the food, the decorations.

She listened, nodded on occasion, but volunteered few comments. So he stopped talking, sat back in his chair moodily. He had had high hopes for the evening and few of them were being realized. Annie seemed to be ill at ease, gazing around her as if she missed the comfortable walls of her own kitchen.

"We're goin' to have to come over here more often," he said tentatively. "I like this place. It was a good idea to come over here."

Annie wiped her lips with her napkin, looked around at the other guests, saying nothing.

"This place is OK, you know it, Annie? No complainin' or carryin' on rough. No drinkin' much. I like that. That's what we needed—to get off together and—"

She shook her head suddenly, then got up, hurried toward the rear of the restaurant. Jordan, stunned, looked after her. As best he could tell, she was angry and perhaps was crying.

Driving toward Leafwood he put the accelerator on the floorboard. Annie was leaning forward, watching the road in fright. He was going faster than the speed limit, and faster than he should for the condition of his tires, too. But he didn't care now.

"If you don't want to make peace with me, Annie, all right," he said. "I'll take you home and you can go your own way, I'll go mine. To hell with all of it."

He would go to Mona's house that night.

"Jordan, stop the car."

"Huh?"

"Stop the car!"

He pulled into a dirt road, his mind turning in a frenzy. "What the hell is it?"

She sat stiffly erect, breathing deeply. Slowly she sat back in the seat. "It was the baby," she said. "I got sick, is all."

"Huh?"

"You was havin' such a good time at the restaurant, I didn't want to say anything. I'm not much on drivin' in cars, Jordan."

"You—you sick in the restaurant?"

She glanced at him, smiling faintly. "What did you think?"

They sat there in silence for a moment, Jordan not knowing what to say to her, or what to decide for himself. Going to Durham had been a fine idea after all, he realized. "Are you— are you all right now, Annie?"

"I think so." She was looking straight ahead. Then she turned to him. "Yes, I am." There was a softness about her eyes, a look of warmth and gentleness. Annie's eyes, he thought.

Awkwardly he put his arm around her and drew her to him. A hundred feet behind them, on the Leafwood-Durham highway, the lights of cars flashed by, unseen by them.

13

When Jordan drove into town, he stopped by Jake's beer hall to tell him he was back. While Annie waited in the cab, he hurried inside the place, pushed his way through the crowd of men who were clinging to the long bar, but Jake wasn't there. A strange, trim-looking Negro was working the draft-beer handle.

"Hey—hey—" Jordan said, trying to get his attention. The man nodded, filled up a mug of beer and slid it to him. Jordan pushed it back. "I didn't ask for no beer. I want Jake."

"He ain't here." The new bartender turned away and started filling beer glasses.

Jordan leaned far across the bar. "Where is he?"

"I don't know, God-damn it!" He started on down the bar, throwing a few words at Jordan as he moved. "He ain't workin' here now."

Jordan knew this couldn't be so. He looked around at the drunk faces, each seeming to laugh at another, then pushed his way to the stairs to see if Jake was in his room.

Once in the top hall, however, he couldn't find the light cord. "Hey, Jake," he said. There was no answer. "Jake."

Striking matches, he went along. Two rooms were entirely empty, two others had cases of beer stacked in them, and the remaining room had a bed and dresser in it, but not a stitch of clothing. Jake wasn't there.

The bartender, who had seen Jordan go up, met him on the stairs. "Mister, you get out o' here."

Jordan grabbed hold of him. "Where is he?"

Suddenly the man broke his hold. "Get out."

Jordan was thinking about taking on the bartender when a hard object struck the side of his head and he lost his balance, tumbled down the stairs, landing on the floor below. He pushed himself to his hands and knees and was about to get up, when somebody caught him in the face with the top part of a shoe.

When he came to, he was in the alley back of the beer hall. An ache troubled his head. He rolled his shoulders to see if they were all right, then started toward the back door. It was locked. He headed around front, then stopped on seeing Annie still waiting in the cab. Wearily, caught by the dull throb inside his head, he stumbled to the cab and sat down beside her.

"Jordan—what is it?"

"It's crazy," he said. "It ain't so." It was then he noticed that four taxicabs were parked beside the building.

A quarter of an hour later, he knocked on Coltrane's door until Helen Coltrane, his wife, answered it. He pushed past her, moved through the living room and into the hall.

"Coltrane—"

A muffled answer came from one of the bedrooms. Jordan found him there, dressing hurriedly—trying to hide the fact that he had gone to bed early.

"You get fixed quick," Jordan told him. "They got Jake." He brought Coltrane up to date, as best he could.

"All right, Jordan," Coltrane said, his nervous fingers inefficiently trying to fasten a shirt button. "It looks bad at the moment, all right."

They divided the town between them. Jordan and Annie went to the homes of three friends of Jake's; he wasn't found and no one had heard from him. They drove by Bryant's house; the lights were out. Finally Jordan parked in front of Minnie's house and, while Annie waited in the car, went inside and asked for Jake there. They had not seen him for almost a week, Minnie said.

So he drove home, dropped Annie off to look in on the boys, and was turning the cab around to drive back uptown, when she came to the porch rail and called to him to hurry inside.

Then he saw Jake, sitting in the big chair in the living room, his legs spread out in front of him, his arms dangling over the side of the chair's arms, big tears welling up in his eyes. "Ah, God-damn," he said, on seeing Jordan. "He done it, Jordan."

Annie hurried the boys out of the room.

"No, let 'em stay," Jordan called after her. "Let 'em hear who done this." But Annie was gone, pushing them into their room and going in with them, closing the door after her. Jordan wondered what she was saying to them in there.

But nothing could be done about that, because Jake, moaning aloud as he talked, began telling about what had taken place. "First two cabs come up, then two more. Bryant comes inside and asks me if I have any calls for a taxicab. I had one, and he took the note out of my hand and palmed it to one of his men. So I asked him what the hell he was doin'. I told him that phone call was for you. Then he said he owned the beer hall and it was his telephone."

"God-damn," Jordan said ominously.

"Then he said, 'All right, Jake, get out. Get your things and get out.' I explained to him that I'd worked there for thirty years. He just went upstairs, and first thing I knew my clothes was thrown down the stairs, then some o' my other things. My pasteboard suitcase come down—everything, even my toothbrush was layin' at the bottom of the steps, and I got mad and started to get him; but one of his men grabbed me off balance and by God, Jordan, I couldn't get nowhere. He ain't a legal fighter."

"I know," Jordan said, stalking about in the room. "God, how could he get a franchise and us not even know it?"

"Bought his way in. Lord, I dunno."

"Look here—" Suddenly Jordan braced Jake back in his chair. "We're goin' to fight, just like that man in the book—you hear me?"

At that moment Coltrane hurried in from outside, panting the news that Jake couldn't be found. Jake mumbled a short series of obscenities and told him to sit down.

"I ain't afraid to fight, Jordan," Jake said. "I been beat up before."

"We're not goin' to lose."

"Lost two fights by knockouts. I don't mind takin' another knockout

fightin' for my beer hall and your taxicab company. They'd know it went
beyond fifteen rounds, too, by God!"

"We got to beat 'em with taxicabs," Jordan said, turning to Coltrane.
"How much money you have?"

Coltrane quickly shook his head. "Not me," he said. "This is northern
tactics; I seen 'em used. I'm stayin' clean."

"Clean!" Jordan said. "Your business is on Bryant's list, don't you
reckon? You'll be fallin' in order, ever one of you—"

"May be. May be. But this is brother against brother—poor business."
He got up primly, pulled up his coat collar. "I'm stayin' out."

Jordan walked to his car with him and tried to talk him into helping, but
Coltrane, even in return for a part of the company, would have none of it.
He was so definite, Jordan realized there was no use pushing it further.

When he returned to the living room, Jake was waiting with two cups
of coffee, one of which he handed Jordan. "On the house," he said, smiling
as best he was able.

They drank in silence, Jordan thinking about how it all had seemed
like a dream.

Then Jake leaned his head back on the big chair. "I got over a hundred
dollars left," he said.

"How—how much more o' the cab company you want for it?"

"I'm loanin' the money, if it will be enough to buy a taxicab for me to
drive."

"It will be a right old taxicab, but it will do."

Jake nodded slowly. "Two cabs to four—that's good odds," he said.

They talked for another hour about how they were going to beat Bryant,
Jake pointing toward the day when theirs would be the only cab company
in Leafwood. Then the old man wearied of words and stretched out on
the couch, a contented smile on his face. Jordan retreated to the kitchen.
There he found a slip of paper and a piece of pencil and began marking
down the problems they had.

Buy a car.
Paint it.
Find a place for Jake to live.
Hire a telephone.

Get a neighbor to answer the telephone.

Talk around the new telephone number.

As he went back over the list, the problems mounted up so high he didn't know what to make of them.

Annie came in and tried to coax him to come to bed. She looked over the list. "Put the phone here in the house and I'll answer it."

"I ain't goin' to make my house an office. If we put the phone in Jake's room, it won't bother nobody."

"All those things on the paper—can you get 'em done?"

"Got to," he said. "That's the size of what has to give."

Jake came to the door of the kitchen, leaned on the post. "Something I got to tell you, big boy. Can't sleep till I tell you."

"Ah, God, Jake. What is it?"

Jake wiped his sleeve across his mouth. "I can't drive a car," he said.

Jordan slowly picked up the pencil and wrote a new item at the top of the list.

Teach Jake to drive.

The next day they started on that. Jake almost wrecked the cab every time he got his hands on the wheel, but he never admitted an error or a need for help. Jordan would lose patience with him altogether. "Look, Jake. It ain't hard. Now set back—"

"I am, I am." Jake leaned stiffly back in the seat, his eyes straight ahead of him at the road. "God 'a' mercy," he said, "here comes another car." He tried to take to the sidewalk.

"Look out," Jordan said, grabbing the steering wheel and getting them back onto the road as the other car went by, its horn blaring.

"Damn-fool driver," Jake said. "You just let me handle this car, Jordan. He might 'a' run us down."

Jake didn't learn to drive that day or the next, either. All the while, Jordan fretted, reminding himself that Bryant was getting further and further ahead. But all they could do, until they had a telephone and were back in business, was to talk around what Bryant had done and ask people to keep them in mind.

The third day Jake did better, but he was still tense and afraid of the automobile. "I'm doin' fine," he said. "Let's go over to Durham and buy my cab."

"Huh?"

"This money's got my money belt so tight I can't hardly breathe."

"No, now—"

"I'll drive."

"Lord help us," Jordan said, "it's over ten miles."

Jake turned over the engine. They started lurching forward, the car rocking like a crazy horse. In the first two blocks, they went through a red light and almost hit a pedestrian. Jake cursed the light and the pedestrian, and put every thought into keeping the car safe from any moving vehicles. He came to a complete stop on the main street when a bus came in view a block away, and sat there until the bus had passed.

"Playin' it safe," Jake said. "You can't trust a damn bus driver. I seen a bus driver hit three cars in a row in Alabama."

"Godamighty," Jordan said.

It took two days to paint the letters *J and J* on the car they bought in Durham, to find Jake a room and to get the telephone hooked up. The room was on the second floor of a dilapidated wooden building that sprawled across the street from the beer hall. The upstairs rooms were rented out to Negro families, and the street-floor areas were, for the most part, empty and closed up.

Jake pulled the metal cot over to the window, placing it so that he could watch the traffic passing below and keep an eye on Bryant's place. "I'll watch him in my sleep," he mumbled.

Jordan opened the window a few inches from the top. The room was damp and musky from disuse. He sat down in a wobbly chair and glanced around at the battered walls, splotched by broken plaster. So this was it. This was his office and Jake's room. Nothing hopeful in the looks of it. The room showed no signs of agreeing with the big work that had to be planned there.

"Went over and got my pictures this mornin'," Jake said, still glaring at Bryant's place. "I told him I was hired to serve beers, not draw pictures, and that what I drew was mine."

"I think you did right."

"So did Bryant," Jake said, "when he saw I was leavin' with 'em."

The bundle of pictures was now propped up in one corner of the room. "Let's put some of 'em up on the wall, Jake."

"No, no," Jake said fretfully. Then after a while he said, "Don't want to be reminded."

Before leaving the second floor, Jordan knocked at the door directly across the hall from his office. It was opened by a tired-looking Negro woman of fifty. Behind her, running around on the floor, were four or five small children, and beyond them a door opened to the other room of their apartment. The woman moved a dip of snuff across her mouth as she shifted a baby from one hip to the other. The baby made not a sound.

"Forgot to ask if you can write," he said. "When you answer the phone, you got to be able to write down where we're to drive to."

"I write well enough, and I got a boy that can, too."

From out of the debris in the other room, Jordan saw a young boy stand and come slowly toward him, his body ill, emaciated.

"Well, the phone is right across the hall," Jordan said, "but it'll probably be tomorrow night afore my partner has his license to drive."

They watched him as he stepped back and turned away.

Early the next afternoon Jordan felt that Jake might pass the driver's test, provided the patrolman didn't try to make it hard on him and Jake co-operated. He took Jake around the test block the patrolman had used on him, explaining carefully what the patrolman had said. Jake paid no attention and didn't get around the block right a single time.

"You can recite the hand signals. Why can't you use them?"

"Never mind, never mind. You take this too serious."

"It ain't no laughin' matter."

"I drive better'n most."

"Well then, stop as fast as you can," Jordan said suddenly.

Jake hit the brake and Jordan bounced up against the windshield. He sat back angrily.

"How's that?" Jake said.

"Shut up, by God!"

Jake kept wanting to go to the town hall and make his try, but Jordan held him back until the afternoon was almost gone. Even at the door of the town hall, he was telling him about the hand signals and about listening to the patrolman. "We need this license, Jake. We got to get two cabs on the road."

Jake nodded, a slow grin coming on his face. Now that he was at the town hall, he seemed to be happily anticipating the coming work, as if it were a bout. "Goin' to tell him stories about nigger women," he said, pushing open the door and moving on inside.

Anxiously Jordan waited, walking up and down the sidewalk, biting his lip. Some relief came to him when he saw Jake and the patrolman come out of the building, both laughing. Jake had passed the eye test and the test on road rules. He jumped into the cab, not even speaking to Jordan. The patrolman had not quite gotten his door closed, when the cab lurched into a start that would have proved Jake couldn't drive, without another foot being driven. The door slammed as Jake speeded on down the street, the patrolman nodding his head on his bouncing body and laughing excitedly.

Ten minutes later, Jake almost wrecked the car trying to park it in front of the town hall, but he and the patrolman were busy talking and neither of them seemed to notice. Jordan, in agony, watched the two men go into the town hall as if they were old friends. A few minutes later, Jake came out with the chauffeur's card in his hand.

"Come on, Jordan," he said, "let's get this taxi company on the road."

Jordan got into the passenger seat dumbly, his body spent.

"He gave me this license with the understanding that I just drive niggers," Jake cackled, "but that ain't no law." He shoved the old car into gear, backed up and shot out of the parking place. And lo and behold, he drove well. There was no jerking or bumping, no erratic steering.

"Jake—you…you drive all right now."

Jake peered at him critically. "I allus did, you bastard; I was just a little tense, that's all."

Notes on J and J Taxicab Co.
By Jordan Cummings

Jake got license on April 28, and it was so late in the day we didn't get much done for rest of day. Few calls.

29 April, Wed. Jake and me talked to many people today. Said we was back. Jake mad cause not much calls for his cab. Not much calls for my cab either.

30 April. Jake talked many people today who used beer hall regular. Old friends of his. I talked to people who go to Annies church. Everybody friendly. But Jake and me just made not more than 20 calls.

1 May. Jake beer hall friends come thru today. Carted them to and from the beer hall in taxicabs. Bryant saw me once today, spoke well. Bought second hand tire from Texaco station. Made half again as many calls as yesterday.

2 May. This is Saturday and always big time. Most drove us crazy tonite with calls. Turned down 7 or 8 tonite cause they was beyond us. Jake is older then I thought. Or seems to be. But hes holding up. Says its harder than beer hall work.

3 May. Church crowd about filled up morning and nite. Folks ride to church, set selves up to override sermon. Drove Harris and Fletcher with me in front seat in afternoon. They didn't make a sound.

4 May. Expected busness to fall off after weekend but it grew. We're catching on. Jake complained about feeling bad in the head. Don't know what I'll do if he falls sick. We spent $7 today on second hand arm chair for room. Got tired laying on couch.

5 May. Tues. Harris and Fletcher asked me to take them to ride in taxicab again. Did. Told them company is theres someday. Big smiles. Made 20 trips in morning, not that many in afternoon and more at nite. Jake doing most of driving.

6 May. Big nite busness of maybe 36 trips because Mr. Corbit, big white man, had party. Carried drunks till 3 in the morning then just quit. Not many calls in afternoon because stores is closed on Wednesday. Jake has got his second wind. Laughs lot now speshally when he see Bryants

cars standing idle. Stand idle lots of time now. Make Jake laugh and he go out strumming up more business. Made trip to Durham in afternoon.

7 May. Just cant keep up with busness. Talked to Chevrolet man on phone about buying bran new cab. Said he would let me have $200 off since I'm a taxicab and would put electric light on top free. Told him to hold line. But Jake didnt want to do it yet. Know the reason too. Cause he didn't think of it and bring it up. Im going to have to hire a nuther driver to spell Jake but Jake dont agree there either. Raises hell. Says hes going to grind Bryant in the dirt. Saw Bryant twice today. Big as a hog. Open up account at bank.

8 May. Friday. Jake and me almost dead. Jakes car broke down twice and I had to help him get it fixed. Finally put on new carberater. Other one look like screwdriver been ground into it. I didnt tell Jake about that and I dont know what to think. Jake didnt sleep all nite. Out using my car making calls. Dont know what total nite calls will be like but must be near 60, most of them by Jake. Tried to tell Jake hes got to take it easy. He wont listen to me. Wanted to drive all nite. Passed some of Bryants drivers today standing idle at beer hall. No smiles from them, only fists. Its Jake thats doing it. He knows everybody in town. Gets mad at his friends if he sees them riding with Bryants cabs. Cuts them down short, gives them hell. Wont listen to me. Today he agreed to order new Chevrolet. Not sure now.

9 May. Saturday. Jake wont listen to nobody. Boy across hall told me in secret to make him slow down. Driving his self hard. His car broke down this afternoon early and I have spent most of the afternoon fixing it. Jake has my cab. Am not sure how to get mad at Jake. We is beating Bryant and in shape to order new taxicab, but he is running wild. Tonite will be biggest nite yet. Shouldnt even take time to go home for supper but want to see garden.

14

"I know it's your garden, Jordan," Annie said slowly, "but I couldn't see it go without proper tendin', so I've worked the boys a little."

Even in the evening light, Jordan could see that the plants had grown well. "Corn is all right."

"It is. It is."

"Everything is up now, I reckon, and takin' hold."

They went back toward the house, Jordan shining the flashlight before them.

"Did you put that extra twenty back for the baby?"

"Yes, I did."

"That makes forty?"

"Fifty, as I recall." Neither of them had any doubt about how much it was.

"Well, maybe we can put up another twenty next month," Jordan said. "We're doin' all right, Jake and me. He works, that man—don't never sleep, seems like. Allus on the road; even tonight he ain't stopped yet. Took my cab out."

"I saw you had the old one."

"He's all right," Jordan said. "He's a good man. I don't know that there's a better one."

He put his arm around her waist and helped her up the back steps.

They were about to open the screen door when they heard the first call of the boy as he ran toward them, running hard down the street of Tin Top.

"What's that?" Annie said. "It's your name he's callin'."

They boy leaped a picket fence, dashed through the Hogan yard and into Jordan's, up the front steps. They heard him banging on the front door.

Instead of going through the house, Jordan hurried around the outside. "What you want, boy?"

"You Jordan, ain't you?" It was difficult to see through the night.

"I am."

"It's—it's Jake. He—" They boy slumped down on the steps, his face pained. Jordan saw he was the boy who lived across the hall from Jake, the one who could write. "He's had an accident," he said. "He's goin' to die."

Jordan and the boy rode in the old taxi up to Jake's place. They hurried up the steps to the room where Jake lay on the cot, his head deep in the pillows, his face turned toward the beer hall across the street where his name still shone in the window. He was moaning aloud, his face twisted in doubt. Jordan felt a trembling in his own legs as he entered.

"Jordan," Jake said, reaching out for him. "Jordan."

Pulling up a straight-backed chair near the cot, he sat down, took Jake's outstretched hand in both of his. He caught sight of the others in the room, lined around the wall—the woman from across the hall and her family. "You call a doctor?"

"I sent my girl for a white doctor," she said. "They ought to be here soon."

Jordan nodded. "Jake, are you bad hurt?"

"Naw." Tears welled up in his eyes. "But I hurt the cab, Jordan. I hurt the best cab we had, tore the front up. Ran off the road and into a creek bed, all because of that damn fool comin' from the other direction."

Across the street at the beer hall a driver came running out the front door, jumped into a front cab and headed out. "Damn him, too," Jake said. "Got our telephone number."

"Just lie quiet, Jake. We're beatin' 'em every day."

Jake's eyes rolled in his head for a moment, then he lay back, fear on his face, as if he had just seen a warning sign. His lips came back from his teeth a bit, then he closed his eyes tightly, reached again for Jordan's hand and clung to it, pressed in.

Jordan looked away, caught a glimpse of the woman, who was standing stiff near the wall, her mouth working a dip of snuff. There was worry on her face. Beside her the children stood in a row, not moving, nor crying out.

"Them kids shouldn't be here," the young boy said.

Nobody seemed to hear him.

"Look at there," Jake said, pointing out the window.

"What is it?" Jordan leaned over the cot.

"That damn doctor," Jake said, "coming with his herbs and snake medicine. I'll die for a fish, sure as hell, if he puts a hand on me."

"Did you get a good doctor?" Jordan said, turning on the woman.

"I got the one he asked for."

"Who is it?"

"Doctor Morgan."

"He's all right," Jordan said. "He's a good doctor, Jake."

"God-damn quack," Jake said. "Goin' to die, if he has his way about things."

The phone rang and the young boy answered it. "Hold the line." He looked up at Jordan. "You takin' rides?"

"Tell 'em...tell 'em to call—somebody else."

The boy spoke into the phone. Jordan looked over at the beer hall, blaring away with fast music.

"I was drivin' straight down the highway, Jordan, then suddenly this car swerves in from a side road and comes hurtlin' along headed right toward me, so I had to take a turn and run off the bank and hit the creek full force." Jake rolled his head on the pillow. "But I drove up the creek bed and got out, Jordan. I drove back here, and by God, I would 'a' found that son of a bitch that drove me in the creek if I'd 'a' been able...to—"

The boy came up to Jordan. "He was tryin' to get out of the cab downstairs when I saw him, Mr. Cummings. He was in pain, and out of his head."

"Out of my head?" Jake roared. "Get out of here!"

"Take it easy, Jake."

"I ain't never been out o' my head but three times," Jake mumbled. "I was out o' my head twice in fights, and I was out o' my head in Virginia."

Jordan grinned, felt Jake's forehead. He had a temperature, all right.

The doctor came in, the little girl leading him. He was fifty or more, with a small gray mustache and gray hair.

"What's the matter here? What's the matter?"

"I don't know," Jordan said. "Car accident, but I don't know no more."

"Let's see." The doctor sat down in Jordan's chair.

"God-damn quack," Jake mumbled, only half-coherently.

The doctor felt his pulse, then laid his hand on his forehead. He threw back the covers and examined Jake, moving practiced fingers over his feet, his legs, his arms.

"You seem to be all right for broken bones," he said.

"Sure," Jake said. And as he spoke, a small bit of blood came out the corner of his mouth. The doctor sat back in the chair, watching it. Slowly he leaned over and felt around the stomach. When he got to the chest, Jake let out a cry. The doctor drew his hand away.

"Better get him to a hospital, Jordan."

"Quack, by God," Jake said. "I ain't goin' to no damn hospital. Jordan, tell him that."

"What's the matter, Doctor?"

"I don't know. Internal bleeding. Could be anything. Might have to operate."

"Operate!" Jake roared, and now more blood came to the corner of his mouth. He sank back, coughing. The doctor bent over him suddenly and Jordan couldn't see what he was doing, but soon the coughing stopped and Jake was lying there, the look of fear on him now.

"God-damn car," he mumbled. "I weren't no taxicab driver, Jordan." He was strangely coherent. "I ran a beer hall, and that bastard took it away from me, after thirty years—threw my clothes down the stairs. My toothbrush. God-damn. After thirty years, Jordan. And he's your brother, too."

Jordan stood near the foot of his bed and looked at him, his eyes brooding. "Call an ambulance," he told the boy.

Jake tried to sit up in bed, a great pain shooting through him, and shouted out. "No, by God—no! I ain't—" He sank back onto the cot.

"Call it," Jordan said.

The doctor ran his hands lightly over Jake's chest, shook his head disbelievingly.

"Jordan," Jake said, reaching out for him. "Sit down." Jordan sat down on the chair which the doctor vacated. "Jordan, you beat 'em, you hear?"

"Now listen at that. 'Course we'll beat 'em."

"You beat 'em. Give 'em hell, Jordan. Win out. All right?"

"All right," Jordan said. "You and me."

"The accident wasn't my fault, Jordan. Not my fault at all."

"No, Jake."

"Damn driver. God-damn driver. Worse town I ever saw, except in Virginia. Worse town."

"What you got agin Virginia?" Jordan said, trying to make a joke of it.

"God-damn state," Jake said.

The ambulance came down the main street with a blaring of its siren. The boy ran downstairs to flag it down. It double-parked in front of the building and the attendants began to pull the stretcher out.

Jake kept his eyes on the beer hall across the street, from which the people came now, answering the noise and commotion. "Look at there," Jake said. "That's where I was belonged to. Got myself beat up in a creek bed. Never should 'a' gone. Should 'a' gone to Durham to find a woman, slept with her a week and then gone on back to work for Bryant. Hell, what's the difference? Hey, Jordan," he whispered, "lean over here. Look. That—that doctor. He don't know nothin'. Don't worry about what he says."

"Yeah, sure, Jake."

Jake rolled his head back over to look at the beer hall. "I worked in there for forty years."

"Thirty years, Jake."

"Forty God-damn years," Jake said. Then he laughed, a low, retching cough. "Too long," he said.

They brought in the stretcher and rolled him on it. He lay back, calling for the pillows. Finally one of the attendants raised his head and stuck a thin pillow under it. The woman stood back, her children beside her. Now she set up a low chant. "Oh, Jesus, take pity on this man. Oh, Jesus, take pity on this man...."

Her younger children mumbled the chant, and with this incantation, the stretcher-bearers carried Jake out, Jordan walking behind, his face clouded in doubt. They carried him down the steep stairs which creaked under them. Then they got the bottom door open and her words were lost in the sound of horns and traffic and the commotion caused by the crowd of spectators from the beer hall. The bearers pushed the people aside with their bodies and carried Jake through, Jake looking up at everyone, his head held firmly back on the pillow, his chin straight up, as if he would like to scream out in pain but would not do it there.

They carried him to the ambulance, the people blocking his view of the beer hall.

"Jordan," he called. But the attendants closed the doors before Jordan could get in.

"See you at the hospital," one of them said.

Jordan tried to open the door, but it was locked. The ambulance started backing up, moving into the crowd, then going forward with a whine of its siren, a rising scream as it headed across town.

Jordan turned to his old taxi, the one that had been bought for Jake to use, and started to get in when Bryant came up to him, much distressed. "Jordan, what is it?"

Jordan shook his head angrily. "Let me be," he said, anxious to get to the hospital. But part of the crowd was standing behind him, and it was hard to get through. Finally they let his car out.

When he arrived at the emergency entrance, Martha, a large Negro woman who had been working at the hospital when he'd worked there, was at the door, holding it open for him. "Come on in here, Jordan. Hurry up. Where you been?"

"I been hurryin'."

"They took Jake to the operatin' room. The doctor told you to wait outside in case he needed you or got a callin' out."

"What they operatin' for?"

"Just to find out. They're 'spectin'. I saw blood on the pillow that was left on the stretcher." She shook her head. "Bad sign. Bad sign."

Jordan paced up and down the corridor outside the operating room, the passing nurses and interns looking at him strangely. He gave them no mind, but kept thinking about the years he had known Jake. Ever since he could remember Leafwood, he could remember Jake. He could remember Jake the first day he came to that town when his father had gone by the beer hall for a single glass of beer—all he ever permitted himself—and each of the boys had been given a pretzel by the young man behind the counter, who, everybody said, could knock down a bull with a single blow of his fist.

He remembered the times since then, almost numberless, when Jake's strong left hand had struck out in his beer hall. Jake was always on the side of right, as he saw it. If right was with the underdog, he was for him; but if right was with the crowd, he let them beat hell out of the underdog, but made them go into the back room to do it, and stopped the fight before bones were broken.

Jordan suddenly turned to Martha. "When will they be done with him?"

"I dunno, Jordan."

"Can you go in there and see how they're coming?"

She shook her had, backed off. "You know you can't do that in a hospital."

He stared at her, his eyes glazed, then abruptly pushed through the doors into the emergency operating room.

Two nurses turned. The doctor looked up from the operation and nodded his head to an interne who came to Jordan, tried to lead him out. Jordan shook his head. The interne pushed a wall button several times. Jordan started toward the operating table. The doctor stopped work.

"Get out of here. You want to kill him?"

Jordan stopped. His eyes snapped clear. He looked around confused, then turned and hurried from the room.

Martha, waiting for him in the corridor, led him to a sitting room where he sat down in a leather chair.

"Ah, God, Martha," he said, sobbing. "God, what if Jake dies? I was lookin' at the garden when word come that Jake would die."

It took them more than an hour to finish with the operation, then they rolled Jake out, his eyes closed and not so much as a moan coming out of him.

They rolled him down the long hall and into an elevator. Jordan watched the hand of the hall dial stop at the fourth floor, then he and Martha started up the stairs.

"Jake's going to be all right. He didn't die in the operating room," Martha said.

They got to the fourth floor, Martha puffing and blowing from the climb, and as they did, the private elevator doors opened and the doctor came out, wiping his hands together as if there was a stain on them.

"Well, well," he said.

"How is he, Doctor?"

"Not too good. I couldn't stop it."

The doctor pushed past him and went down the hall. Jordan started to follow, but Martha caught his arm.

"Let be, let be, Jordan."

Quietly they followed the doctor, going together, and went into the room where Jake was lying back, his eyes open now and staring at the ceiling. The room had two windows, so the moonlight came in, and a small table lamp in one corner sent out a yellow light.

The doctor sat down near the lamp. Martha stood near the door. The two internes who had wheeled Jake in left without speaking. The ward nurse came in, shaking a thermometer in her hand and looking at the doctor for a sign.

"All right," the doctor said, "but don't disturb him more than necessary."

Jordan came over to the near side of the bed and stood looking down.

Finally Jake saw him. A slow smile came on his face. "Hey, big boy," he said, his teeth hitting against the thermometer. "Wait'll I get out of here and—"

"Stop talking," the nurse said.

Jake gave her a reprimanding look, but fell silent. When she took out the thermometer, he grinned again. "Is that Martha over there?"

Martha came closer.

"Martha, how are you?" Jake said. Then abruptly he became serious. "Martha—" He reached out a hand. She took it, and Jordan stepped back, not knowing what was between them.

"I always thought o' you, Martha," Jake said, "whenever I was sick, because I remembered how you was when I was in here with appendicitis, how you looked after me."

"I will again, if they'll let me."

"You took care o' me and that was fine, Martha. I meant to come by your house sometime and see you, but I got busy with the beer hall. It ties a man down."

"Yes, it would, Jake."

"Ties him day and night, except in early mornin'. I started to come to see you early mornin'.

"I wish you had."

Martha turned away. Jordan thought she was crying. He went to the bedside and saw a tiny drop of blood there, and wondered how much blood Jake had and how long it would be.

"God-damn car," Jake said. "Car come at me. God-damn driver." He rolled his head from side to side. "Oh, Jesus was the Lord with the healin' power. Jesus was the healer, Jesus was the healer—"

Jordan slumped down to the floor beside the bed, knelt there. "Jake," he mumbled. "Now, look here, Jake."

"Be true to Jesus. Ah, Godamighty, Jesus, Holy Jesus was a baby, Holy Jesus was a nailed baby. Ahhhhh!"

The nurse backed out of the room, a look of fear on her face, as if the deep feeling of the Negroes repulsed her. The doctor stood near the chair and the lamp and wet his lips with his tongue.

Martha wept near the doorway, leaning back against it, her big face heavy with sorrow.

"Jeee-suuuuuuuus!" Jake wailed. "Ah, Jesus, Lord, a king born to die with blood. Ah, help me, Father. God-damn car. God-damn driver. Thirty years. Ahhhhhh!"

Jordan touched his hand.

"Jesus, Holy Jesus! Damn the man." Jake went into a stream of obscenity.

The doctor came over and felt Jake's pulse. There was more blood on the pillow now.

"Look, Jake, be quiet," he said.

Jake cursed him, and began to pray devoutly.

"Be quiet, Jake," the doctor said sternly.

Jake fell into a chant, a mixture of spirituals and profanities about Jesus and the car and the driver who had run him off the road. He fell to cursing the beer hall, too, and Bryant, and the doctor, who was a quack. He fell to singing hymns, then the melodies of hymns, but with words he made up out of old stories and off-color jokes he had heard and told. "Have a drink," he shouted, and then he almost sat up in bed, pointing.

"Hey, you come have a drink." But there was nothing where he was pointing. Jake pointed again. "God-damn you, I don't mind losing another fight—like in Virginia when I lost and I was supposed to go North and fight, but I lost my head in a fight in that God-damn state of Virginia, hit a white bastard of a promoter. That's a sorry damn state." A moan came out of him. "Jesus, that's a damn state. Damn the state of Virginia. Ah, Jesus. Damn God, Jesus, Jesus little baby." Then into obscenity, then into a hymn, his eyes focused on the corner of the room. "I don't mind losin' one more fight, but you'll go the fifteen rounds, you sorry-faced, cold bastard. Jesus, kill the son of a bitch. Jordan, get him before he gets away—No, let him alone, let him be. Jesus, get back. I'll fight the son of a bitch—more'n fifteen rounds...."

He started to get out of bed and the doctor and Jordan held him back. The doctor called down the corridor for a nurse. Jake was bleeding badly now. The nurse came running in and the doctor spoke to her in hospital talk. She ran out, calling for someone.

"Ahhhhhhhh, fairest Lord Jesus," he sang, his voice now turning around inside himself and coming out with a strange, organlike quality. "Fairest Lord Jesus...."

"God 'a' mercy," Jordan said, the emotions flowing through him. He looked blankly at the pale doctor. "Can't you take steps?"

"I'll put him to sleep when the nurse gets here. God help us...."

"God help us," Jake echoed. He began weeping, the tears coming out of the sides of his eyes and running down his face. "Tenth round," he said.

The nurse came into the room with a hypodermic needle. She pulled up the sleeve of his gown and stuck him. Jordan watched, spellbound.

Then there was a low guttural sound. Jake looked up, a twisted smile on his face, his eyes half-closed. A wistfulness came to him. "You ain't so cold, mister," he said, speaking to the corner. "What you waitin' for? Godamighty, mister, what you waitin' for?"

It can't ever be over, Jordan thought.

"Bitch," Jake said to no one. "Son of a bitch, it's twisted." He tried to laugh, but began choking. The doctor pushed his head back and stuck a finger in his mouth.

"Get your God-damn hand out of my mouth," Jake roared, then fell back, pain racking his body, his eyes all-seeing. "What you waitin' for, you bastard?" Then he reached out and grabbed Jordan. "Jordan, hit the bastard. Jesus—"

Jordan looked around wildly, then down at Jake, fell to his knees again and made Jake lie back, ran his hand over his damp forehead. "Go to sleep, Jake. Go to sleep easy. You ain't goin' to leave."

"Jordan, is that you?"

"This is me."

"Jordan, inside my mattress at home—you hear?"

"I hear."

"I got some money. Might nigh fifty dollars. It's yours."

"Yes," Jordan said. "All right."

"And you take the cab company—all of it."

"Ain't you got no people, Jake?"

"I got you, Jordan." He smiled. "Promise me you'll get it afore that woman gets it...or them children."

"I'll go there tonight." Jordan lowered his face down on Jake's arm. "I'm goin' to beat 'em, Jake."

Jake opened his eyes. "Fifteenth round," he said. He closed his eyes and a smile came on his face. "Lost my head," he mumbled. "God-damn state. Goin' North, but lost my head and told that white bastard what I thought o' him. Jesus, damn that man." Then he opened his eyes. "No, Jesus, don' do that," he said.

He closed his eyes and breathed on. Then Jordan looked up at Martha, who was leaning against the wall, her body heaving with sobs.

"Martha, I meant to come to see you early one mornin'..." And as Jake said it, there came a great intake of air, as if his body was filling itself.

That night Jordan drove back to the room Jake had used. He threw the sheet off Jake's bed, and with his knife ripped the mattress down the middle. Inside he found the money.

The doctor was standing in the door.

"How much did he have, Jordan?"

"He got fifty here."

"I reckon—twenty-five. It'll take something to bury him."

Jordan peeled off the bills and handed them to the doctor. "Doctor, why you fool with us niggers? You can't make no money."

"Just made twenty-five." He left, and Jordan looked down at the opened mattress, then his eyes went to the beer hall, still lighted and with music blaring. As he watched, Bryant came out of the beer-hall door. Cathy was with him.

Jordan ran a hand over his face. Anger swept through him. He turned to go down to meet them, when he saw the young boy standing in the doorway.

"He's dead, is he?"

Jordan nodded.

"Did they do it?" He nodded toward the beer hall.

Jordan looked over there. "I don't know," he said, "but I reckon they could have."

"Goin' to tell the police?"

"Saw the police at the hospital. Didn't tell 'em nothin'. Things like this happen everday."

The boy nodded slowly. "What you goin' to do?"

"Goin' to win," he said.

15

The undertaker's place where the Negroes were taken was named "Home of Rest," but to Jordan, as he parked his cab on the dirt road that curved around and above it, the place was anything except restful in appearance. An unpainted wooden building made gray by time, it had spawned several rooms to the sides and rear, storage areas for the coffins and supplies of the growing business. Now in the morning light it looked like a restless spider.

The undertaker himself was a wisp of a white man, propelled by nervous energy. "No," he sputtered at Jordan. "No, I don't care for you to come in. It's bad enough to have to take care o' people who ain't got money without—without tendin' to all the niggers who want to look at 'em."

"He had a little money," Jordan said.

The undertaker eased the pressure on his side of the door. "How much?"

Jordan pulled Jake's bills out of his shirt, pushed three back into his pocket, and held out the twenty-two. "Is this enough?"

The undertaker counted it eagerly. "He's in the back room. Come on."

The undertaker led him across the huge, sparsely furnished main room and down a narrow hall which twisted its way to other rooms, and finally to the place where Jake was laid out. It didn't look very much like Jake, but it was what the undertaker said it was, he knew. He stood beside him for a few moments, trying to think through to what he ought to say. Finally words came to him. "Jake, I been drivin' this mornin'. I made ten runs so far."

The face is made of stone, he thought.

"I been drivin' your car. I ain't goin' to take the good one out till I can get the front bent back in shape. The engine's not bad hurt, though. I can get it fixed at the repair shop if I turn in your old car."

The undertaker listened attentively, nodded at the close of each sentence, as if deciding the comments were suitable.

"I'm goin' to find a way to beat 'em, Jake, and I'm goin' to find out how much of an accident it was, too. Don't you worry."

"What do you think of the way I fixed him up?" the undertaker interrupted.

Jordan started to tell him straight out, but held back some. "He ain't smilin' much, is he?"

"Did he smile much?"

"Yes, he did. Even when he was serious, those who knew him knew he was; inside he was. But now he ain't, is he?"

"I never give it a thought."

"It's all right. It's a nice job."

"They bring 'em in here. Don't have time enough. Charity cases, you know."

"Yes, sir."

"Killed in a car wreck, I understand."

"Yes, sir. Doin' his work." Jordan shifted uneasily. "Say, Jake, I'll find a way." He waited, as if for an answer. "I paid the man here twenty-two dollars, Jake. Thought that was right. Paid the doctor the rest, except for three dollars that I put back because...dead money is lucky, and I need all the luck I can get."

He looked at him for a while longer, then led the way back to the big room. "When's he to be buried?"

"His preacher was in earlier, picked out a box. Said it was to be this afternoon at the graveyard, this bein' Sunday. Ain't much better time for niggers to hold a burial, you know, 'cept Sunday."

"Ain't there goin' to be no ceremony at the church?"

"Doin' it all at the grave. You goin'?"

"No," Jordan said. "I don't believe in graves much. Leastwise, not enough to go to one."

Back in the office he left the light off and pulled the shade part way down over the window. In the near-darkness he sat down in the easy chair they had bought for seven dollars and looked about at Jake's things. There were ties and worn clothing, a comic book open in the middle, a boxing magazine, a battered radio. On the wall was a picture of a great, open meadow where sheep were grazing.

Jake will not see that again, Jordan thought.

On the dresser was a stack of pennies and nickels that had been shoved to one side, and small scraps of paper on which Jake had written reminders.

"Jake," he said aloud.

It was all a gamble and he saw that for the first time. His notions about luck didn't steady him now. The taxicab company could die in a day. Before he could get home, Annie and the boys could be gone, and he would never talk to them again, not even to say goodbye.

The ideas deadened his spirits, made him drunk with heaviness. The phone rang. Dumbly he sat in the chair, staring at it. Perhaps it was Mona. More likely it was a passenger wanting a cab. Maybe he would lose a customer if he didn't answer it. He started to reach for the phone, then sat back. Let them go to Bryant. The door opened and the boy stood there. Quickly he snatched up the receiver. "J and J Taxicab Company. Hello—" After a moment he said, "They must've hung up, Mr. Cummings."

"Maybe they wanted Jake," Jordan said.

The boy smiled briefly, saw that Jordan was serious. Slowly he backed to the door. "Want the light on?"

When he didn't get an answer, he went out, closing the door softly.

"Jake," Jordan said aloud, "they wanted you."

Jake's shoes were there, black patent leather, put back for parties and the like. His leather jacket hung sadly from a nail on the wall.

Where was Jake?

No way to phone Jake, he thought.

Across the street he saw three men come out of the beer hall and stumble on up the street. He had heard how Bryant kept women upstairs. Mighty Bryant. If Bryant had Jake killed—if he had Jake killed—

Easier to kill a man than crucify a kitten, he thought.

The phone rang, and it kept on and on. "Ring yourself off the damn table," he said. "Makes you mad not to be picked up, don't it? What you think you are, damn you!"

Finally it stopped. He sat back in the chair, sweat standing on his face. Get a drink, get a girl, get a room, let them all go. If Jake were there and it had been somebody else dead, he and Jake could do that—have a ball.

The phone began ringing again. Jordan suddenly leaned forward and slapped the receiver off the hook, let it fall to the floor.

"Jordan," he heard a voice say. "Jordan."

Slowly he reached forward, picked it up. Maybe Annie's hurt, he thought. Quickly he brought it to his ear.

"Boy, is that you?"

He said nothing. No doubt now about who was calling him.

"Come here, boy. Come here. I got to talk to you. Come here, boy."

Jordan slowly hung up the phone, stood shakily, a smile on his face, then he flopped down on Jake's cot. He looked across the street at the upstairs windows of the beer hall. "What you want, Bryant?" he said to the closed glass. "What's the matter, Bryant?"

Annie found him there hours later, still lying on the cot, his head back but his eyes open. "Jordan—" she said softly.

"Huh?" He looked over at her. "Ah hell, Annie, who are you?" She had never been in his office before, and he didn't much want her there then. "What you want?"

Annie didn't know how to answer that.

"You walk up here?"

"It ain't—ain't far."

"Huh! Is too."

"Anyway, you wasn't at the funeral. I worried about you."

"Me?"

She came over and sat down on the cot, put a dry hand on his forehead. "You feel well?"

He pulled the shade down over the window. The sun, low on the horizon, was throwing a beam into his eyes. "Did they bury Jake?"

"They did."

"Jerkin' and swayin' and shoutin', I reckon?"

"Some o' that."

"Did you shout any?" He knew she hadn't. She rarely spoke outside the walls of her own house, and she would not cry out at a meeting. "Seems like you never get the spirit, like some of 'em, Annie," he said cruelly, not wanting to hurt her, but feeling angry because of Jake, and perhaps because she had intruded on him. "Was it a nice funeral?"

"Some ways. But the open springs make it damp down in the colored graveyard. Shouldn't be at the foot of a hill like that.'

"Yeah, hell. Should 'a' carried him out into the woods myself, planted him simple. But he deserved a box." He knocked one of his pillows off onto the floor as he grabbed Annie's arm. "Annie, listen here. Do you know everybody is goin' to be put in the ground like Jake?"

She watched him warily, as if afraid of what he was about to say.

"Well, did you know it—can you think about it?"

She bit her lip, started to speak, but he went on.

"I can't. My blood goes cold. You and me and Fletcher and Harris— goin' to be put in the ground, Annie, eyes and mouths closed down, covered over with clay—"

"Jordan, be quiet!"

He lay back, glared at her, not knowing how to take an order from her. But he said no more.

"It wasn't Jake in the box. Won't be Harris or Fletcher or—"

"I saw Jake in the box."

"Was it Jake?"

"Huh?" He turned his head to face the closed shade, now golden-colored by the sunlight crowding its other side. "No," he said at last, "it wasn't Jake. But for God's sake, where is he? And why ain't God nowhere so's he can be seen?"

She took his big hand and clasped it tightly in her two hands. When she spoke, it was so quiet he could hardly hear her. "He's got heaven to live in, ain't he? God's not Tin Top born. He's not needed to come to a colored burial ground."

Jordan squinted his eyes at her. Slowly he felt what she did; it came to him what Annie felt. God was way off, unsoiled and untouched. And when she died, she would go way off to God, and there would be no problems with God.

Suddenly he wanted to be with Jake and God.

He pulled Annie down close to him and held her gently. "Yeah," he said, rocking slightly back and forth on the cot. "Yeah, Lord. Probably runnin' a damn beer hall, Jake is. My ma, she talk o' heaven like you, Annie."

"I know she did." Annie ran her hand over his chest.

"Dreamed one night she went to heaven and saw Mrs. God sewin' up Mr. God's pants." He laughed low. "Looked through the window and saw Jesus out plowin' with a golden plow."

They lay together, saying nothing more, the golden shade growing tan as the sun went down. Jordan let a peaceful spirit settle over him, and in his heart he buried Jake.

When they got home, one of Bryant's cabs was parked outside, and Kate was waiting behind the steering wheel. She seemed to want to talk to Jordan about the future of his cab company, and she had an idea—about how he could take in three partners, letting each own half of his cab. It was a fine scheme, Jordan saw right off, and his mind caught hold of it; but he knew that wasn't what she had come to talk about.

"Look, Kate—"

"With three partners who are known here in town, you could take most all the business from Bryant's outsiders. Even you and Jake had them on the run—"

He interrupted. "What you want, Kate? Why you here?"

The tension had grown inside her, and now he thought she might weep. It was more than a minute before she spoke again. "I want you not to look into the way Jake died," she said.

He ran his big hand over his face, hiding his expression. "Yeah," he said, "I know."

She hesitated for a moment, studying him, then began to speak, the words tumbling out of her. "Bryant just wanted to frighten you, Jordan, perhaps right out of a taxicab business. He sent this driver out, but neither of them knew Jake would have your cab. Jake must have lost his head, Jordan. The driver says he completely left the road. It was a terrible accident. When the driver got back, Bryant almost killed him—"

"Who was the driver?"

"Never mind that."

"Was it Zepher? That big-talker, fellow who likes to speed in cars—"

"I'm asking you not to go into this, Jordan. If you could see Bryant, roaming the house like an animal, afraid the police are going to come by."

"Yeah, I know. He has a police record up North, I wouldn't be surprised." As she started to shake her head, he abruptly said, "I don't care about Bryant."

"Then—will you let it lie for me?"

"No, I won't," he said. "Nor for myself, either. Was it Zepher that did it, Kate?"

"Jordan," she said angrily, "you say you want to beat Bryant. You won't beat him this way."

"Well, what you want me to do? Jake's dead and—"

"Get another partner. Get three good partners and go on the same way. Beat Bryant like you and Jake were beating him."

Jordan stared off down the street, the tiredness of his body evident in his face. "Maybe that's right, Kate," he said at last. "I would like to beat Bryant like Jake and me planned."

"You can. I really think you can."

"But how can you advise me like this, Kate? How can I listen to you when you live with Bryant?"

She smiled, but almost grimly. She started to answer, then stopped, reconsidering. "Good night, Jordan," she said, and drove off up the street.

He looked after her, his face shaded by serious thought, then he trudged up the bank to the yard of his house. He stopped when he saw a bird fly from one tree to another, his mind settling on a question. He wondered if God, way off with Jake, knew that the bird had moved its place.

16

Little Harris was selected for a part in the commencement program of his grammar school, one of four first-grade pupils thus honored, and he was so proud he could hardly control himself. All previous school activities of consequence had been Fletcher's. Now he had come into his own. Nothing would do but that everybody talk about Harris and the program, but Harris would release only such information as was needed to revive lagging interest.

To all of this his brother Fletcher turned a suspicious, knowing eye. His jealousy was as obvious as his disinterest was forced. Pointedly he refused to discuss the commencement program, except to point out repeatedly that few people at the school knew anything about it, and nobody knew Harris was in it. One night he became so adamant about Harris being a nobody in the program, that Harris struck him with a piece of stovewood.

Jordan was amazed by Annie's detached attitude to all this. His own feeling was a combination of those of the two boys. He was jealous for Fletcher's sake, and was jubilant for Harris'. Having one of his boys in the school program was as fine as anything could be, but it was too bad that both of them were not in it. Occasionally he would take Fletcher aside and ask him why he was not in the program.

"I didn't want to be."

"Well, was you asked? You get high marks, study all the time."

"I didn't want to be asked."

"Lord 'a' mercy, Fletcher. Got to live beyond study."

Then again, Jordan would take Harris aside and ask him how he got the part and what it was, anyway. If forced to answer, Harris would make up fantastic stories, never telling the same tale twice. One time he would be a lion, and still again he would be a soldier.

"You a soldier? You're not three foot high."

Harris would insist, describing his sword and shield.

"What you doin' with a sword? Has it got the point broke off?"

Harris stood before him, wide-eyed with fear lest he lose the point of his imaginary sword.

"I see in your face, Harris, you don't have a sword."

"I—"

"I, nothin'. You stood there and lied to me, didn't you?"

Quick as an arrow, Harris ran out of the house, moving away so quickly Jordan couldn't call his name before the front door slammed.

Then that evening it was another story.

"Goin' to be a fireman."

"Hush that noise and help your mama clear the dishes."

"Got a hose."

"You couldn't lift a fireman's hose."

"Hose a foot wide and—Ouch!"

Fletcher had kicked him from under the table.

"Stop that, Fletcher, you hear? Your brother is talkin' about the school program he's in."

"Bet he's not in it."

"Be quiet with that talk! 'Course he is. Hasn't he done told us?"

"Fireman, fireman, fireman," cried Fletcher mockingly, jumping down from the chair and scampering into the living room. "Fireman, fireman."

"Be quiet with that yellin', Fletcher!"

"Harris is in the pla—ay! Harris is in the pla—ay!"

"Shut up that kind of noise, Fletcher!" Jordan said, rising menacingly from his chair. "Annie, go lay a hand on that boy and yank him to mind."

Annie, without seeming to notice, went on washing the dishes, letting the hectic period go by with such ease as it could find for itself, knowing not to complicate it.

With a final "fireman, fireman," Fletcher broke back into the kitchen, stood sulkingly watching Jordan for a moment, then eased over to his chair, his lower lip pouting.

"Lord 'a' mercy, now hold your tongue, boy."

Fletcher glared at him. Jordan turned back to Harris. "What you fireman of, boy?"

"Fireman in the school," Harris announced, beaming.

"With a hose?"

"Hatchet, too."

"Now listen at that," Jordan said, laughing out. "Ain't he a sight, Annie—makin' up stories one after the other?" He leaned toward him quickly, grabbed his arm. "Look here, boy, you goin' to be like your uncle Bryant? He tells lie-stories, you know."

Harris laid his hands on his belly and stared wide-eyed at his father.

"You watch them tales you tell, or you be pokin' out in front like him."

"Jordan, don't lie to the boys."

"Speakin' gospel, Annie." He sat back, surveyed Harris seriously, then tilted his head away, a faint twinkle in his eyes. "Now, Harris, what you play in this school program?"

Harris wet his lips, looked furtively around.

"Come on, boy. What you play?"

Harris stared at the table top. "I play a—" Suddenly he bolted up from the table and was gone through the door.

Each night Harris had to be driven to the school auditorium, where the cast was rehearsing. It was no bother for him to walk to and from school in the daytime, but he felt that he should be driven to school at night, perhaps having rightfully concluded that no sacrifice was too great for his family to offer up for his high honor. No matter what Jordan was doing at seven o'clock, he had to arrange to get away to hurry home for Harris, who, not satisfied with a good thing, would be waiting with a list of schoolmates who wanted to ride with him.

Invariably one of them was Tinny Frazier, a slight boy of such black complexion that Jordan wondered if he had any white blood at all. Tinny, with a high, raspy voice, would sit next to the window of the back seat, and peer out at the passing sights as if he were drinking them in—these unknown wonders of his homeland.

"Tinny, are you in the play?"

"Yes, sir."

"What you play?" No answer. "Tinny, what you play?"

"Harris told me not to tell."

"Harris, what you mean tellin' that boy that! Got a mind to put both of you out of this cab this minute!"

And when Jordan had gotten them to the school, and they were running across the schoolyard to the big main doors of the brick building, he would wonder why it was he became so occupied in criticizing the boys that he couldn't find out what he wanted to know.

But actually he didn't want to know. The game they were playing was a bright spot in his life. The rest of his day was work, from six in the morning until midnight, and after midnight a call might come through, or he might work on his books, trying to figure out what had gone with his money and time.

Even Kate couldn't help him with his old books. She did show him a better way to keep the figures, so that he could tell more easily what was happening to his business; but she couldn't make out the past any better than he could.

All he did know about the past was that he was not getting ahead very fast now. The one-man cab company was not geared to service, and profits weren't high. Nowhere in sight was the start of the scheme Kate had suggested to him.

Finally, even though he didn't have the money, he called in the three men he had picked out to go into the business with him and explained his plans to them. Perhaps it was only to watch the expressions on their faces that he did it. They were young men, two of them with families, all upstanding in the community, and Jordan knew how difficult it was for them to find a job doing anything other than construction work. Now he was offering them something they could own part of, and their faces lighted up as they listened.

"I'll sell my house, you hear me?" Alexander, a black man with shiny teeth and a rapid smile, said. "Look here, sell that house and put down my half o' the down payment for my cab. Come on, Jordan, this is world-shakin', man. Get your money, hear me?"

"Now—now let me save it up."

"Come off that, man! Get that money. Lord, I can feel the good sense in this one."

But there was no way to work harder or save more out of what he made. It was a matter of time—unless he could get help from somebody. And he didn't know anyone with money, except Mona.

The auditorium-gymnasium of the school was packed when Annie, Fletcher and Jordan arrived, but Fletcher found a place with his class, and Jordan and Annie squeezed in on a bench near the back.

The program was to start at eight. Jordan, always afraid he was losing business, never sure but that the Hogan boy would let the work go by in favor of a beer or a woman, uneasily watched for the opening announcement. Finally the principal stepped through the improvised curtain at one end of the gymnasium and cleared his throat. One by one the lights in the gymnasium were cut off.

The principal began speaking, giving in measured tones credit to various faculty members for their work on the program, taking some credit for himself, and congratulating the students on their year's work. As he spoke, his eyes were glued to a spotlight which shone down on him from near the ceiling. He stood as if hypnotized by it, and before long Jordan and many others in the audience were squinting up at the light to find out exactly what attraction it held for him.

Finally he was done, and the curtain was pulled back, revealing the empty end of the gymnasium. But it was not empty for long. From either side trooped members of the fifth-grade class, who did a dance. It was not like any Jordan had seen as a boy, when some of the farm families would come together for a corn husking, followed by a square dance. This was an orderly dance. The little boys had white ribbons around their necks, and each girl wore a starched, pink dress. They twirled around a bit, held hands, formed a circle, then broke off into groups, bowing and scraping around one another. This continued for almost five minutes, and actually continued half a minute after the music stopped.

They did it all without a hitch, so far as Jordan could tell, and there was a nice round of applause as they were hustled off the stage.

The fourth grade was represented by a single young man who took his place in the spotlight that had so dazzled the principal. He spoke to the audience directly, however, using many broad gestures, and in the course of time delivered himself of the lines of the "Prisoner of Chillon," a poem Jordan had not come across before, and that he found interesting. He particularly liked the bit about the mice playing by moonlight. They had had many rats on the farm, he recalled, and although he had never seen them play by moonlight, he had seen them engaged in just about every other occupation, mostly around the corncrib. Seemed like they were always creating a nuisance, but as his father said, "where there's corn there'll be rats," and the cats, who never were interested in anything near the barn as long as there was food at the house, gave the rats a free license. All in all, Jordan liked the poem very well.

The third grade put on a song. It was a rousing rendition of "Row, Row, Row Your Boat," which was bounced back and forth among five different pairs of singers, until the audience became dizzy, and the singers—although they didn't seem to be confused—were lost voices in the babble. It was the first time Jordan had ever heard anything like that, and he was pleased with the way it was carried off; but he was quite relieved that Fletcher, who was in the third grade, had not been reduced to taking part in it.

The second-grade students appeared on stage—about twenty of them—and each had a single line to say, explaining something he had learned that year in school. Each student would step forward and recite his bit, then return to his place. Many of them forgot what it was they had learned when the time came to announce it, but this added to the general appreciation for those who did not forget.

"I learned to like all my neighbors," one boy said, and Jordan thought the boy must not know some of them very well.

Another stepped out. "I learned to count to one hundred," he said. Jordan recalled that his father had taught him to count to a hundred before he ever saw the inside of a school; but he was glad the little fellow had had his chance. It was information he would have need of, without much doubt.

"I learned to listen to my teacher," one little girl said, glancing about prettily, trying to set her eyes on the woman in question. "I learned that my father died in the army," a boy said. A titter went through the audience. Many people there knew the boy's father was not known. His mother, Sarah Whitehill, had borne five children, not a one of them legally. The little fellow stood stock-still until the laughter died out. Then, to Jordan's surprise, he spoke out again, his voice more forceful than before. "I learned that my father died in the army." This time there was a dead silence. Slowly he backed up to take his place in line. From that instant, Jordan knew, few would ever deny that the kid's father had died in the army. Who knows—maybe he had died in the army, anyway.

So through the twenty students, each one having his say, before the second-grade children filed off amid a smattering of applause.

The next performance was to be by the first-grade students.

"Harris is coming on now," Annie said. "Wonder what he is?"

As if in answer, four little angels trooped on stage, each decked out in white dresses and wings. One of the angels was Harris. The audience began to laugh appreciatively, and Jordan was about to join in, when suddenly the first boy, Tinny Frazier, stepped forward and announced, "The Twenty-Third Psalm."

The audience settled down. The second boy stepped out and spoke shakily, "The Lord is my shepherd; I shall not want."

Harris took two bold steps forward, faced directly into the audience, and spoke in a voice that must have carried outside the building. "He maketh me to lie down in the still waters."

The fourth boy stepped out, started to speak, then stopped, a perplexed look on his face. Slowly he turned and peered at Harris. "Where?" he said.

Now it became obvious to many that Harris had forgotten about the green pastures and was lying down in the still waters. The laughter was hesitant, then boisterous, then subdued, as the audience tried to find a reaction consistent with its feelings.

Tinny Frazier, knowing it was his turn to speak up after the fourth one had his say, accepted the "Where" as a cue and proceeded with the recitation. "Yea, though I walk through the valley of the shadow of death," he shouted, "I will fear no evil." The words came out as an answering declaration to the laughter of the audience, and another burst went forth.

The second boy stepped into the breach, almost moving off the low platform into the first row of chairs. "For thou art with me; thy rod and thy staff they comfort me. Thou preparest a table before me in the presence of mine enemies."

Harris stepped forward, his face still aimed straight ahead, his little shoulders stiff and true. "Thou anointest my head with oil," he declared, "my cup runneth over."

Instantly somebody down near the front laughed out, "That little kid's goin' to drown!" and the audience went into hysterics. Whatever remained of the psalm was not heard. The four youngsters completed their piece during the persisting laughter, and walked off as sure and satisfied with their performance as if they had delivered it in perfect style.

Jordan's anger subsided quickly when he heard the applause. It was an ovation. The four angels came back on stage and took a deep bow. There was knocking of wings on the upswing, but they got off without mishap, and the curtain was pulled to.

That was the climax of the evening, Jordan knew, and he was not soon given any reason to believe otherwise. A sixth-grade girl, representing the graduating class, delivered an oration on the subject of humility; and although it was nicely put together, the theme was not one in which many of the audience had an interest. Then the principal took over again, staring up into the light. "We have the awards to give out," he said, "earned through faithful service and honest effort, given to those with the highest grades...."

Jordan began wondering if he wouldn't be better off out driving people in the taxicab, but there was no way to leave. He was hardly listening to the names of award winners when the principal spoke the name "Fletcher Cummings." For a moment Jordan thought he had called on him. He was half-way out of his seat when he saw Fletcher rise and go down the aisle.

"What—what did Fletcher do, Annie?"

"Highest marks in his class," she said in a low voice.

"Huh? Highest—"

When Fletcher's applause came, Jordan sat with his mouth open, staring ahead, knocked off balance by the honor that had come to the family; and for the remainder of the evening he was lost in his own thoughts. Fletcher had won the prize for his class. How could he have the highest marks? Learning in school had been easy for Jordan, as he recalled, but he had never given any thought to it. Now his son had won the first place in his class, had done something probably beyond any other member of his family.

That night when the boys were back home, Annie and Jordan walked about aimlessly, neither knowing quite what to say. Finally Jordan sat down on the sofa and waited for words to come to him. Annie came in, looking at the floor, making no sound. It was Jordan who had to call the boys in.

They stopped near the doorway.

"I tell you," he started out, then stopped, unsure of his voice. "Look here now, that was all right." He shook his head slowly back and forth, glanced over at Annie, then at the heat stove. "I tell you that was good. I'm as proud as I can be."

He was so much taken by it, he wanted to put his arms around them and tell them they were his boys and everything was fine.

Annie spoke up. "You boys have taken the right way. I don't know of a better one. Now you'd better get to bed."

They stood there for a minute more, bathed in pride, big grins on their faces, then turned toward the bedroom. Jordan and Annie heard their door close.

"I tell you, Annie—listen here—them boys are all right. I just wish I had more time for those boys."

"I know you do."

"I tell you now, there ain't nothin' wrong with neither one of 'em." He wondered what he ought to say to her, the woman who had given him the boys; but words were not his best language. He got up from the chair and went to her, put his arms around her, pulled her close to him. "You and me, Annie, we do all right after all, don't we?"

"Better'n most, I expect," she said, suddenly proud and responsive. "It's as fine a family as anybody could have."

17

Each night when he had answered all the calls, Jordan would flop on Jake's cot and rest for a while before trying to make notes on his records. Frequently the young boy from across the hall would be there.

"You know, boy, when you get older, I'm goin' to get you a cab."

The boy grinned. "I'd like that."

"You and my boys at home. But now it's me by myself."

The boy squatted down near the telephone. "I'd like to drive a cab," he said. "Nothin' else I know anything about—'cept answerin' the phone and listenin' to the radio and goin' to school."

"You got to learn to study more, boy. Read books is what everybody advises me."

"Yes, sir. I read."

"What?"

"Funny books. Jake gave me some."

"Ahhhh, got to do better. Got to climb, do you hear me? Don't pull yourself green."

"Sir?"

"Don't pull yourself off the vine till the colorin' sets in. Otherwise, when the truth comes out, not much to you. Ain't that so?"

"Yes, sir."

"All you can hope for is that you sneak by. Got to ride your luck then, and shout out for the world to change, otherwise you might get dismissed entirely. No, don't be like that."

"No, sir."

"Grow, you hear? Then plan. Got to work, boy. Yeah, Lord. Here, hand me them pads o' books."

So he would mark down the number of calls on the pads, count the money he had taken in, put the bills in his pocket and the change in a bag, which he would take to the bank the following morning. He would check the figures over and over, estimating what he couldn't be sure of. "Work always wins," he would tell the boy. But as time went on, he found precious little profit in the business.

"Ain't that a cat's tail, though? Books can't be right. All this work."

"Mama told me to tell you that Alexander came by this mornin', wantin' to know when you was goin' to start the new company."

"Huh? No time for that, boy. No money here."

"He told Ma he had a buyer for his house."

"Ah, Lord, think o' that. He's all right, Alexander is. Him and me and Hogan and that other fellow could solve all this; but I need money. Ought to get three new cabs—take eighteen hundred dollars just for down payments, and I'd have to supply half of that. Then have to get insurance for 'em and have runnin' money."

He would sit for hours in the light of the yellow lamp and go over the figures. Yet each time the figures would take their own way. Finally, seeing that it would be years before he could save enough on his own, he phoned Mona, told her he wanted to see her. She hung up on him.

Angry, he didn't call her again that day or the next. But she didn't call him, either, so he tried again. Then he went by her house. He kept knocking until she came into the hall. She led him into the living room and closed the door, closing out the empty house from what they had to say to each other.

He had planned to tell her straight out what he wanted, but being with her confused his thoughts. So he talked about the carnival, which was just pulling into town, and about his work. He said he would have to leave soon and hurry back to the office. She listened, offered him no encouragement to continue or remain, her dark eyes brooding on him.

"You know that first night we was upstairs together?" he asked her. "That was awful real—except for when you called me Ben. But even so, it was real, Mona, and I want you to know that. And every time—"

"Not real enough to keep you."

"Mona, a man gets busy, plannin', buildin' things." He tried to explain how it had been, but she was accepting none of it.

"Better to let all that go," she said, "and deal with life more closely. Money is something you have, or somebody gives you. As for my—"

"Gives you?" he said sharply. He didn't like her saying that. The idea of being kept by a woman angered him. To buy a woman for a night was one thing, and was all right; but to be bought by a woman, even for a night, was another matter.

And she wanted him for life. He couldn't even understand that or convince himself of it. Annie wanted him like that, but she had grown up with him. Of course, Mona might want him because he was like somebody she had grown up with—at whatever time in her life she had grown up.

"I—I am here, Mona," he said, "because I want to do what's right to— to everybody, and to me. And I can't do that unless I win through this thing I'm in. I want to get three partners as good as Jake was and—"

"Aren't you through with that company yet—working eighteen hours a day, driving yourself down into a machine? Are you going on with it?"

"I am." Confidence came to him each time he reaffirmed his determination to go on with the company. It was one point he was sure of. He was going to go on and was going to win. There was not the slightest doubt in his mind.

"Then you don't need me," she said.

He looked at the smooth curves of her body, wondered what he ought to do. "Mona, I can't go on without help. I'm offerin' to sell half my interest in—"

She smiled, then laughed, but the laugh was for herself.

"It's an old story to me, Jordan, so let's not go through it. I've been here before. A man whose work is more important than life, looking to me to save his work for him, when it is his work which keeps him from me."

The ticks of the clock on the mantel seemed to grow more distinct. Jordan remembered being at the party and being drunk. He felt drunk sitting there, hearing a woman talk in a low voice about a life that must have been very long because she couldn't see beyond herself. And as the moments went by, a realization came to him, shook him with implications he could not grasp. She was, in a sense, Bryant. She was Bryant, except she was a woman, and she was driven mad for wanting to be loved and to own what loved her, and to conquer and consume what did not, until she mastered it. It was an idea too big for his mind, and didn't make sense to him about Mona, whom he still did not understand; but made sense about Bryant, whom he did understand. For Bryant only loved what he had mastered.

He rose slowly, nodded. His big hands found their way into his pockets as he sought his handkerchief, pulled it out and wiped it across his face. "Good night, Mona," he said.

He had not gotten ten feet across the room when her voice come to him, sharp and angry. "You leave me this time and you are not going to be left alone, Jordan. I have an anger!"

Now he saw the face of the woman who had cursed him when he drove the coal truck. "Shut up, Mona," he said.

"You tell me to shut up—"

"Shut up!"

"Who do you think you are, driving your way in here and—"

"Driving my way in where, for God's sake? Let me tell you something— I ain't bein' ate on by anybody. I come here to ask for your interest, because I need it, and I thought I might have it. But I don't need it if I got to stop the taxicab company. I don't need nothin' that way, Mona. I sure as hell don't need you that way, Mona! God-damn it, woman, you're nothin' but yourself, and by God, I ain't owned by you, you hear it? And I ain't goin' to stop my workin' so as to please your comfort! And if you lift one hand to stop my way, Mona, I'll fight you till I die—you and Bryant, too!"

She stared at him until he turned away, unable to look at her eyes.

18

Jordan never attended any of the oyster roasts the Methodists held on the church lawn. It was something the new preacher had started, and Jordan was against it, no matter what it was. But Annie wanted to attend the next one and became playfully insistent that he take her and the boys. She explained that a truck was to bring oysters from the coast, delivering them to the church grounds by six o'clock. By that time, members of the congregation were to be assembled and, equipped with a knife, screwdriver or some other instrument, ready to go to work opening the shells.

Jordan kept telling her he wouldn't go; but as he watched Annie and the boys making ready to attend the affair without him, he changed his mind.

The Hogan boys were there when they arrived, as were most of the other Negro Methodists of the community. There was talk about the coming feast, and much carrying on about local gossip. Coltrane and his wife came about ten minutes after six, and the forty or fifty assembled people stood around or sat on benches and waited for the pickup truck to arrive from the coast.

"It hasn't been this late before," the preacher told them, his eyes anxiously looking down the highway to the east.

"They'll be here," young Hogan said. "You can be sure these drivers will get them back to us."

From time to time during the waiting period, people would come to Jordan and try to strike up a conversation with him, and he would nod to their questions as best he could, but he would not fall into conversation with them. Coltrane also kept apart, nervously pacing near the bench on which his wife sat, rarely speaking to anyone.

Finally at six-thirty the pickup truck arrived, and high excitement took hold of almost everyone. The preacher shoveled oysters into a fifty-gallon can and soon had them steaming over a wood fire. When the first batch of oysters began breaking open at the seams, several men dumped them out onto the concrete walk and shoveled them into buckets. Each person took a bucket for himself and found a place around the long table, where he went to work opening them up. Also laid out on the table were sliced celery and carrots, which the women had prepared, and bowls of hot sauce, which the preacher had made himself. Coffee was brought out from the church kitchen, and paper cups were passed around.

Jordan had never had any experience opening oysters, and he found that the knack of it evaded him. Annie had even more trouble, and the boys were at a loss. The preacher finally came around and showed how it was done, taking Jordan's knife and inserting it between the shell, running it along until the muscle was severed, then pulling the shell open, revealing the oyster inside.

Jordan tried and still couldn't do it very well, but his fingers were powerful enough to break the oyster open if he could get any sort of start at all, so he helped Annie some.

Fletcher learned fast and soon was opening more oysters than he and Harris could eat. Fletcher would dump the oysters out into a paper dish, and when he had a dozen or so, the boys would set to work dipping them in hot sauce, laughing all the while about how fine it was to be eating oysters on the church lawn.

Before long Jordan saw that it was a good thing, and he took a bigger part in the festivities, laughing whenever anybody told a joke, and generally making himself feel at home. He joked with Annie, who ate more celery than anything else, explaining that the oysters were good, but she didn't like the idea of eating them. Jordan smiled at this and went ahead, finishing her bucket as well as his own.

By then it was quite dark, and Jordan was ready to go home. But the preacher set up a song, and the people gradually fell in.

On Jordan's stormy banks I stand,
And cast a wishful eye
To Canaan's far and happy land
Where my possessions lie....

Jordan realized these words were meaningful all right, provided a man didn't have a cab company that was running slow each week.

When shall I reach that happy place
And be forever blest?
When shall I see my Father's face,
And in his bosom rest?

"That's a nice meaning," he told Annie after they were done with the fourth verse. She nodded simply, very much pleased that he had thought so.

Then the preacher asked for testimonials from the congregation, and one after another people stepped forward to tell what the Lord had done for them. Jordan didn't say anything, and he was relieved that Annie didn't, either.

As the meeting broke up, Coltrane made his way to Jordan and Annie and the boys. "Well," he said, looking around suspiciously, as if afraid he would be overheard. "Why don't you folks drop by the house for a while?"

Jordan glanced quickly at Annie, who made no sign. The invitation might pass simply as a courtesy, but the worried face of Coltrane suggested business.

"Maybe we can," Jordan told him. "I'll take the boys home directly and drive by for a few minutes."

"Yes," Coltrane said, smiling uneasily. "Wish you would—Helen and I both." He stumbled off, nodding to first one and then another of the people in the crowd.

Jordan hurried the boys toward the car, but Annie got to talking to two schoolteachers, who wanted to comment on the boys' work, so he hung around for a few minutes more, time enough for the preacher to single him out and bear down in his direction. Jordan hurried around to the other side of the cab and began inspecting one of the tires, but it did no good. The preacher came up and laid his hand on his shoulder. "Mr. Cummings, you'll be happy to know that your name has been mentioned."

Jordan glared up and around at him. "Mentioned?"

"Yes. We have this vacancy, you know. Need a steward."

Jordan straightened up, puzzled.

"Mr. Cummings, don't you think that would be an honor?"

Jordan studied him for a moment. "Would be," he said. "But other men attend more regular."

The preacher smiled kindly. "I'm glad you brought that up. Why don't you come more often, Mr. Cummings?"

Jordan ran his hand over his face to hide his expression, then glanced off, as if wondering where the boys were.

"Mr. Cummings—"

"Well—" Jordan kicked at the tire with his shoe. "No special reason, 'cept that it's more of a silent service than I care for."

The preacher nodded, started to speak, but Jordan continued. "Seems like everybody just sits there quiet and listens, as if plain words are likely to stir up some sort of action. I tell you, I like to feel the spirit movin'."

"Yes," the preacher said quickly, "but don't you think, Mr. Cummings, that excitement is for the soul of the listeners and is each man's own? If I were to shout and carry on, I wonder if the excitement would be theirs, or mine, transferred to them. Do you follow me?"

Jordan peered at him critically, then shook his head, as if to clear it. "Maybe so. But seems like we could sing more of the old songs, at least. You wouldn't have to join in."

The preacher grinned. "I see," he said, chuckling. "Yes, let's do that." Turning, he called back, "See you Sunday, Jordan."

The Coltranes met them at the door. Helen, a light-skinned, beautiful woman, some ten years younger than her husband, graciously led them into the living room. "Sit down anywhere," she said, smiling.

The furniture was nicely made, all of it with fine upholstery, and Jordan, who had worn his work clothes to the oyster roast, hardly knew where to sit. He spotted one chair that had a hard bottom and would be easy to clean off when he left, and crossed the room to it.

"You two join us in a highball?" Coltrane asked.

Jordan looked over at Annie and she at him. "I'll take a beer," he said, "but none for Annie."

Helen went into the kitchen, which was just off the living room. Coltrane glared straight ahead of him, as if he were unmindful of the presence of anybody else. Jordan cleared his throat. "Well, how's business?"

Coltrane looked at him sharply, then began to tap the arm of his chair. "All right." Then brightening, he said, "Better than ever, in fact. How is that taxi business?"

"I got a few complaints," Jordan said easily. "I got myself backed into a corner."

"Too bad, too bad," Coltrane said unconcernedly. "Yes, indeed."

Jordan heard Helen opening the beers in the kitchen. She called out to them. "Annie, you want some coffee?"

Annie shook her head. Jordan was the one who called out, "No, thank you," because Annie didn't speak much in a strange place. He had to do the public talking for her.

He saw that Coltrane was staring off in space again, caught in thought. He was worried, all right, so Jordan decided to let him be until he spoke on his own.

Jordan glanced about the room, particularly at the knick-knacks. He had never had much to do with their like before, and there was a world of them spread out on the tables—donkeys braying, camels kneeling, cats taking off in leaps, ponies with their heads high up. He made a mental note to get Annie one or two of them sometime. Lord knows where she would put them in their house, though, with the boys tearing around and tumbling about. Let those boys loose in Helen Coltrane's house for a half-hour and there would be a big expense to pay, he could see that just from where he was sitting. Helen didn't seem to arrange much for children. Maybe she didn't know about them. She and Coltrane didn't have any. Just lived together, secluded off. Of course, maybe their business was a child to them. They had borne that. Started it in their home, too, he remembered—back in the kitchen of the house they had in Tin Top ten years before. They worked it up from there. Time was when the hiss of steam could always be heard coming from their house.

The kitchen door was thrown open and Helen came in with the beers poured in glasses. She passed the tray around and Jordan took a glass and Coltrane one, then she retreated with her own beer to the corner near Annie, and they started discussing the rugs, which Annie commented on.

Coltrane listened to them for a few minutes, then he squirmed in his chair. "Jordan, tell me, what do you know about your brother?"

Jordan rubbed the side of his head and tried to make out the pattern of the wallpaper. "He's strong."

"Can you talk to him, reason with him?"

Jordan shook his head. "Don't think so."

"Yeah," Coltrane said moodily. "I—uh—offered to sell him my cleaning business. That is, the matter came up, and I've been trying to arrive at a fair price with him."

Helen had stopped talking to Annie now and was listening intently.

"I can't seem to get a fair price out of him."

"Well, why you tell me that?" Jordan said uneasily. "Lord, you're the one that's got experience in business."

Nobody said anything for a minute, then Coltrane cleared his throat. "I can see the handwriting here," he said, "and would like to move on."

"What handwriting?"

"Well—" Coltrane sloshed the beer around in his glass. Jordan felt sorry for him. He saw that his hands were trembling and it came to him that Coltrane was not a strong man, after all, and perhaps couldn't be criticized because of it.

Coltrane set his glass aside abruptly. "I had a business up North in Washington once," he said. "Going well. But...a stand. I sold out up there. And...and Helen came with me back to this town. I don't know what I would have done without Helen."

Helen watched him quietly, with steady eyes. She was the strong one of those two, Jordan realized.

"But we want to move on," Coltrane finished.

It was all too much for Jordan to stand. "Got to run along and handle my taxicab business," he said, rising.

"Jordan, don't go—" Coltrane stood now, tired and nervous. Helen averted her eyes from him. "Don't go. Sit down a minute."

"No, Coltrane. I got to be on my way. Nothin' I can tell you."

Annie stood, looked at Jordan reprimandingly, not certain what was in his mind.

"I know what you're talking about, Coltrane, and there's nothin' I can do that you don't know how to do better."

"Look—there is. He's your brother."

"Don't matter. Fact is, I see just one hope, and that's to beat him," Jordan said. "I need to have nine hundred dollars for half the down payment on three new cabs. Let me borrow that money and with the right three men, I'll beat Bryant."

Helen pressed her dress down evenly in front of her and hid her expression.

"No," Coltrane said vaguely. "No, I'm moving on."

Jordan nodded, but then Helen spoke in a calm, fine voice. "It's something to think about, isn't it?" She held her hand out to him and Jordan shook it, not knowing quite how to hold a woman's hand.

He and Annie walked down to the car, the Coltranes walking with them. Before Jordan pulled out, Coltrane came to his door and poked his head in. "Look, Jordan, tomorrow I have to talk to Bryant. Will you talk to him before tomorrow night?"

Jordan wet his lips nervously. "I'll do what I can."

"Then can I talk to you about eight tomorrow evening? It's not just me, Jordan, it's Felix, too, with his loading company. Bryant has already asked about his operation. Don't know who else he's talked to, but it's easy to see that the pressure's coming."

Jordan listened to the hum of his car engine for a minute. "I'm goin' to the carnival tomorrow night. Done told my boys. I'll be there at eight, Coltrane." He wanted to drive on off, but Coltrane kept leaning on the car.

"You understand, don't you, Jordan? What I have to know is—is whether we can face up to him, or whether he will pull some stunts that just end up—with all hell. God knows, talk to him."

"Well—" Jordan eased his car forward slowly. "Good night," he said. "I'll do what I can."

The next day Jordan went to Bryant's house in midmorning, and talked to Kate about Coltrane's problem. Kate told him there was nothing she could do. "Bryant wouldn't listen to me on a thing like this, even if I married him."

"Well, I don't see as anybody can do much, myself."

"And this Coltrane should stand his own ground, be willing to fight on his own, before you try to help him."

"I know that, Kate," he said. "But how can you let a man drown just because he can't swim?"

To Jordan the carnival was colorful and boisterous, and, as usual, proud of itself. By the time he and boys arrived, the long row of games and rides was crowded with people looking around and seeking excitement. White and colored mingled there on almost even terms, the matter of race set aside in this place of childlike activity.

Jordan's chief interest was going behind the tents and talking to the performers. Harris and Fletcher, deep in sugar fluff, showed little interest in this until they got to the fat lady, who was fastening up a padded, plastic skin, preparatory to going on. Actually, she was not much bigger than some of the fat ladies in Leafwood, Jordan saw.

"How you be a fat lady?" Harris asked her.

"Get a suit that'll fit you. You could be as good a fat lady as anybody, young fellow," she said.

"Say," Jordan interrupted, "why don't they get a real fat lady, "stead of make-believe?"

"Nothing in a carnival is real," she said, waddling off. "That's why it's important. That's why people believe in it."

In one of the back tents, Jordan saw a crap game in progress. He lingered nearby for a while. When Fletcher and Harris begged to get back to the rides, he left with them; but his face had now taken on a disquieted look, as if the thoughts of the game could not be set by.

The boys made such a to-do over the rides, and had such a high time, that soon Jordan forgot his worries, even those of Coltrane. But before he had been on the carnival grounds an hour, Coltrane sought him out. "Did you—did you talk to him?" he asked right off.

"I did all I could, and nothin' came of it," Jordan said.

"My God. My great God, I'm done then. Get a business, they move in. Nothing's safe."

"Got to be a way to work it out, Coltrane."

"Last night I said to Helen—'If I die, they'll take it right away from you,' and she didn't deny it. They just grab."

Not so easily would they take it from Helen, Jordan thought.

"Five thousand, they offer. I make more than that in nine months—more than that clear, and have a growing business. My equipment is worth ever bit of that."

"Then don't sell."

"Ah!" Coltrane said angrily. He went off into the crowd as if to hide himself from sight.

Patrick came by, a seventeen-year-old girl on his arm, both of them laughing shrilly. Jordan let him go on by. Then he saw Bryant.

He turned away, and started over to the other side of the "Loop-the-Loop" his boys were riding, but Bryant called to him over the busy noise of crowd and machinery, "Hey, boy!"

Bryant came out of the crowd, three balloons floating on strings in his hand, a cigar jutting from his mouth, his face radiating good spirits. "Hey, Jordan, how you?"

Jordan knew right off that he was drunk as a coon.

"My little brother Jordan," Bryant said, putting a big arm around his shoulders, clawing him in close. "Say, the tent at the end has got ten of the loveliest bodies I ever seen outside the city."

Jordan nodded, tried to pull away.

"Goin' to have a little private showin' when they close down." He giggled mirthlessly. "You're invited, Jordan."

"No, I got my boys to get home."

"Boys? Where are they?" He peered around at the crowd, as if expecting to see their dark heads come bobbing through at any moment. "Boys, where are you?" he called out. "Harris—Fletcher?"

Jordan didn't look toward the "Loop-the-Loop," in hopes Bryant wouldn't see them, but Bryant spotted them soon enough and began waving. Everybody passing by stared at him, but Bryant didn't care about anything he didn't want to.

The boys finally waved back and Bryant was really set up then. "Look a' here," he called to them, handing Jordan the three balloons. Quickly he brought the lighted cigar close to one balloon so that it popped, frightening everybody within fifteen feet and sending Bryant off into peals of laughter.

"God-damn, it's good to see them again! Too long, boy. All this fightin' carryin' on. Hell! Don't get me nowhere. Each of us has a cab company and nobody needs more than one."

Jordan started to tell him he had no business owning one, but he let it slip on by.

"But look, if you get tired o' runnin' yours, Jordan, you let Bryant know, huh? That four-car franchise is something I want, you hear me? White company sold out to a Durham man who's goin' to run it crazy, and the town won't give me another cab or two. Gettin' hard to get."

A couple of Negro men went by and Bryant took time off to call to them, waving grandly. "Good boys," he confided to Jordan.

"You serious, Bryant?"

"Huh?"

"I'm not goin' to sell my franchise, you know that. And I'm not goin' to deal with you at all."

"Wait a minute. Bridle your tongue, boy. What you think I am?"

"I think you're the one that had Jake run off the road, usin' that boy Zepher, and the one that's runnin' Coltrane out of business."

"Not so," Bryant said soberly. "Neither is so. Jake couldn't drive a car, and you know it. As for Coltrane, I just asked him if he thought there was room for another cleaning company in town, and he offered to sell me his. So I told him we could combine the two businesses right off—without cost to either one of us."

"What—what two businesses?"

"His cleaning company and mine."

"You didn't have one."

"Good God, boy, I was aimin' to build one." Bryant looked around as if seeking out Coltrane. "What went with him, do you know?"

"You're a bastard, Bryant. We come from the same mother, but we was spermed different! I don't know how—"

"Now look a' here—"

"Keep your hands off o' me, by God!"

Jordan swung the balloons down and one of them touched Bryant's cigar and exploded. Bryant backed off, sputtering meaninglessly, then he began to chuckle. "Don't get excited, boy."

"Well, keep away, Bryant," Jordan said. "And let this town be, you hear me? I'm goin' to keep my franchise, and I'm goin' to start usin' all of it."

Bryant began to laugh, shaking his head. "Yeah, I know, you was the best of us—ain't that what Pa said? You was the best of us." His laughter filled Jordan's mind as he hurried away.

When the boys got off the ride, he led them home, promising to bring them back the next night or at a later time. They fretted, and it took him a while to get them into bed.

Then he took the money Annie had put by for the baby. He knew he shouldn't do it, but he had no open choice. With trembling fingers he counted it, found fifty dollars there. He might need every penny of that.

He thought of Jake's three dollars—the lucky money—and pulled it out of his coat pocket, where he had pinned it.

With the fifty-three dollars he went back to the carnival ground.

The men knelt in the sawdust, their eyes focused on the white bone cubes which were bounced out onto a piece of plywood. Only two of the players were white, and while Jordan watched, one of them threw snake eyes, losing ninety dollars, and left, his friend following.

Jordan pushed through the onlookers, selected a place in the semicircle of seven players, and knelt down in the sawdust. Some of them knew Jordan, and the game stopped for a minute.

"I thought you was dead, Jordan," a small man named Kenneth said. He was a queer, most thought, but he could play craps better than any other Negro in that section, except perhaps Jordan.

"No, I just been workin'," Jordan said. Everyone laughed.

"Last time you lost, didn't you?"

"That's right," he said, taking Annie's fifty dollars out of his pants pocket.

"You bettin' that much agin me?" Kenneth said, touching Jordan on the forearm.

He shook his head. "Playin' it safe, Kenneth."

Kenneth grinned, looked around at the others, a flashing glint in his eyes. "That's right, Jordan," he said. "We's all playin' it safe." Then he laughed, and the others joined in.

Jordan put down a five-dollar bill and rode on that. He lost it right off, and put out another. That went the way of the first. So he bet ten dollars, and that was lost, too.

But as time went on, he won a little and was ahead by the time the dice came to him. But then he lost heavily and continued losing until he had just five dollars left of the fifty. He leaned back on his heels, borrowed a cigarette from another man.

The perspiration was wet on his face. He glanced around, noticed that one of Bryant's men came into the tent for a minute, then went out. He also saw that Coltrane had joined the spectators.

Kenneth got the dice again. "Let's see here," he said. "I think I'll start off with a twenty this time."

He was covered, Jordan putting up two dollars. Kenneth won. Then Kenneth lost, and Jordan was even. He held back now until the dice came to him then put out the five.

"Godamighty, Jordan, is that all you're bettin'?"

"That's the extent of it," he said. They covered his money.

He got up on his knees. "Come on, dices, give me a seven," he said softly. He warmed the dice in his big hands. "Remember me, boys," he said, in his deep voice. "This is Jordan talkin'." He threw the dice and rolled five for his point.

"Oh, Lord," groaned Kenneth. "Now don't get unlucky and roll a seven afore you make a five."

Jordan warmed the dice in his big hands. "Come on, white boys. Get your nigger specks workin'."

Somebody cackled, and Jordan knew Patrick was watching now.

"Give me a five," Jordan said.

It was a seven, so he had lost the fifty.

He looked up and saw that Bryant was standing above him, Bryant with a small smile on his face, his big hands closed contentedly in front of him and below his belly. "Hello, boy," he said softly.

"I ain't done," Jordan said suddenly. He took Jake's three dollars from his pocket, covering them with his hand so that nobody would know how few there were of them.

The dice went around, Jordan holding back the three bills. When the dice finally came to him again, he picked them up and put the three dollars down. There was the start of a chuckle, but it died before it got going. Kenneth said, "That's right, Jordan, start little to end big. Let's see if we can cover that bet for you."

They covered it. Jordan leaned forward, the dice in his big right hand. He didn't talk to the dice this time. He didn't even press on them, just let them rattle slightly in his hand. Then when he felt ready, he rolled them out and got a seven.

That meant he had six dollars, and nobody seemed to be more pleased than Kenneth.

"Now let's see," Kenneth said. "You goin' to leave all that, or drag?"

"I ain't draggin'," he said, "not till I get where I'm goin'."

"Let's see," Kenneth said, "if I can cover my part o' that."

The men laughed again. Jordan grinned at Kenneth.

The money was out. Jordan warmed the dice again, rolled, and his point was eight. The third try he rolled an eight, two fours, and won. Now he had twelve dollars. He didn't drag, and within a minute he had twenty-four. He didn't drag, and the first try he got a seven and pulled in forty-eight. He was just five dollars loser, and now the gambling spirit was hot on him. He was the old Jordan again, riding his luck, a smile on his face. He left the forty-eight dollars in.

The men around the table met the bet and he picked up the dice.

"Oh, white mammy with little nigger babies, drop a seven now," Jordan whispered.

The men chuckled, staring at the board.

"Oh, white mammies, give me seven black babies."

He felt right and threw the dice and got a seven. He had ninety-six dollars.

"Godamighty," Kenneth said, "where you find those three dollars you had while ago?"

"Friend give 'em to me."

"He put luck on 'em."

"All he had," Jordan said, and wished nobody had reminded him of Jake. He remembered what Jake had said, for him to beat Bryant. Well, that was what he was there for, back in the sawdust, with the old smells around him. That was why he was there.

He left the money at the board—the ninety-six dollars. A hush fell on the group. They tried to match it, but twenty dollars were going uncovered. Then Bryant sank to the sawdust beside Jordan and put down a twenty-dollar bill. "Take that along with the rest, boy," he said.

Jordan started to push it back, but he didn't want to control the game like that. He sat back on his haunches and thought about it, decided he felt right enough to go on. After all, it was like on the farm when he told Bryant to be quiet—he felt as if this was his territory. He knew a crap game better than anybody else in that town.

He formed a cup with his hands and warmed the dice, shaking them around. The others were watching the board expectantly, and Jordan let them wait. Finally, when he rolled, they were ready for it, and he got nine as a point.

"Poor point," Bryant said. "But with luck—"

"I got luck," Jordan said bluntly. He picked up the dice. "I want a five and a four."

"Won't you take a six and three?" Bryant said.

Slowly Jordan laid down the dice. "I want a five and a four," he said quietly. He picked up the dice and rolled. He rolled a five and a four.

Coltrane let out a small whoop, then smothered it. The other men set to congratulating Jordan and talking about knowing real luck when they saw it. Jordan looked around at the faces and remembered how it had been when he had been in crap games all the time, and how good the feeling was. How he didn't care about anything except the cries of the men when he showed his luck.

"You draggin', Jordan?" Kenneth said, perhaps hopefully.

Jordan knew he would get a gasp if he said "No," and he said it.

The men fell to work trying to cover him. They got all except seventy dollars, then Bryant put out a fifty and a twenty. "More northern money, boys," he said.

Jordan heard a laugh, and looked up into the faces of two of Bryant's men. He brought the dice close to his lips, talked to them, looking down at the board. For a moment he thought of Annie, and he wanted to drag fifty dollars, but it was too late for that now. No time to hesitate. "You wouldn't let me down now, would you, boys? No, God, no. You friends, you two. Both speckled like hound-dogs, both know Jordan. We been same crossroad before, you and me; you friends, now, boys, you and me—rich—"

He threw the dice and shot a two, snake eyes, the worst ever, and he had lost everything.

He looked at the board not believing it. Not a word was said in the group as the players picked up their money. Slowly Jordan stood, trying to smile. He stood so that he faced Coltrane, who shook his head slowly, painfully. Then he saw the smiles on the faces of Bryant's men, and turned to go, but before he could take a step, Bryant spoke. "Hey, boy. Tell you what—if the others don't mind I'll give you a chance to win it back."

Jordan waited, stiff with tension. Everybody was watching Bryant now.

"Do you boys mind if Jordan and me has a little bet?"

Nobody said anything. Finally Kenneth shook his head, and that stood for the group.

"All right, then. Jordan, your luck is with you, but it just dribbled out for a second. I tell you what—I'll bet you four hundred dollars against that car and franchise of yours."

"That's my cab company," Jordan said, his voice almost choking. He pushed through the bystanders and started toward the door.

"Eight hundred dollars," Bryant's voice rang out.

Jordan stopped, hesitated. If he lost the cab company, he couldn't go home. Couldn't work, either. "No," he said huskily, and started out. That company was for his boys.

"Twelve hundred," Bryant said, and Jordan stopped again. There was a cold sweat on his face now, and he brushed it off with the sleeve of his coat. By God, he couldn't lose if he had to win.

"Fifteen hundred," Bryant said, hid from view by the people standing around. There was not a sound. "I want to see you win your money back, boy."

"You want to see me through."

"Ah, boy, fifteen hundred is more than your stuff is worth. You can't beat that for a bet, now can you?"

There was a pause. Jordan caught sight of Coltrane's face, and for a moment he felt his own strength. Coltrane was more afraid than he was. He had to show Coltrane.

He came back over to the crap board, the others making a path for him. "Kenneth, is your spot warm?"

Kenneth stood up, put a hand on Jordan's arm. "Warm as I can make it, big boy." He said it like Jake had always said it, as if Jordan were the big one.

Jordan knew he was, too. It was like the old days as he knelt down in the sawdust in Kenneth's place and felt the faces on him.

He took the dice. No need to talk to them. They understood well enough. They knew what was up—about the taxicab and the big plans he had for three partners. They knew about Annie and how much he loved her, and about the boys and how much he loved them. They knew about the unborn baby, and maybe they knew better than he what it all meant. They had the eyes of God, and for that moment he trusted God and threw the dice.

He threw a seven and picked up Bryant's fifteen hundred-dollar bills and walked out of the tent.

19

Jordan went out of the carnival ground thinking about the seven. It was a singing number and as pretty as a fresh girl with a red ribbon in her hair. He couldn't think of anything better than that seven, unless it was the fifteen hundred dollars.

He felt light and heavy at the same time. His mind tumbled upward with notions about taxicabs, and it weighted down with the ill-will look on Bryant's face. Well, let that be. He would take Brother Bryant's money and cram it down Brother Bryant's throat.

Lord, it was a fine night. The carnival lights were brighter than they had been. Never saw such carnival lights. The people were alive now, moving around laughing. He could see them laughing when they were just staring about. Not a thing but a song in the world.

He wanted to jump up and tell the Good Lord that he had done a fine thing in that tent—better than He did in the spring with new rains. He had put fifteen hundred dollars in the right man's pocket that time.

Crisp as lettuce under his fingers, that money. Curled up in his pocket as if it wanted to go to sleep. Well, let it rest, boy, it was going to see some fast moving in a day or two. It was going to travel.

Nothing in the way now. Carnival behind, lumberyard straight ahead, then home—the kitchen—calling Annie in, getting the boys out of bed. "I won," he would tell them. "Look at that, would you? Now, by God and salvation, look what a night this is!"

Carnival had come to town and the music was in his head. It was a good idea for the carnival to come to town. Let it come spring and fall, if

it had a mind to, and before ten years were up, he would be sailing on a
cloud with a rainbow 'round his shoulder.

"Wings on my feet," he sang out, jumping over a short pile of wood at
the lumberyard.

"Listen here," he called to the lumber, "build yourself into a house.
Plank yourself up there, get off your haunches and be about your business.
This is the night for rearin' up."

He hadn't felt so good since long before he lost that coalyard job.
Well, precious little worry about that now. Go on, coal shovels—haul by
your own selves. Never get Jordan back down there.

"Ain't gon' to fail," he laughed out.

No, just as God made little apples, Jordan was going to rise. "No-
'count," she had said. Not this boy. Not this Jordan boy. Feel that lettuce,
cold and snuggly. God-damn, wrapped up around his finger like it was
human. Hold on, everybody with a frown on! Come off that stuff and
grin enough to make your ears wiggle.

"Ah, Jesus, look at me," he laughed up at the sky.

Yeah, not since long before he lost that job had he felt so fine. "Goin'
to tell Harris," he sang to himself. "Goin' to tell Fletcher. Goin' to tell old
Annie by the sink. Goin' to stop workin'—Lord, I done pulled my load.
Got enough money to roll back in the leisure road—" He laughed out
loud, climbed up on a pile of lumber that stood in his path and jumped
down on the other side, right into a mudhole, but he didn't mind. Nothing
could dampen his ankles or his spirits that night. He looked up at the
moon, remembered the hounds his father tried to teach to hunt birds.
"Wish I could bay at you," he called to it. "Big spoon, that's what you are.
No, face of a woman. Ain't no man in the moon. You're a woman's face,
round and not a care."

He chuckled, then he laughed. He carried on in the loneliness of the
place, not feeling lonely because before him—three hundred yards away—
were Annie and the boys.

Then he heard a sound behind him.

He swung around. "Who's there? Come out o' there! Who's back
there?"

His hand tightened on the money. He looked around at the high stacks
of lumber. "Come out o' there, whoever it is!"

Then he saw their eyes—four eyes. Then he saw them, sneaking along, black men.

"God-damn," he roared, "who you sneakin' up on?"

One of them stepped from behind a woodpile close at hand. A knife flashed in the moonlight.

"Ah, now," Jordan said, "now it comes out, don't it? Where's your friend?"

He saw him then, coming up beside him at a run, aiming to knock him low with a two-by-four, but he didn't know what he was coming on. Neither of those Negroes knew what he was coming on.

Jordan let the first man swing, ducking the club, then caught him under the chin with the heels of both hands, slamming him back ten feet and to the ground. He took a leap and landed on him, rolled him over, stood him up and knocked him half-senseless into the other man.

He was on both of them and in their midst. He caught one knife hand and wrenched it open, took a kicking foot in his hand and twirled a man clean around on the ground. His fists were balls of metal and all the power of coalyard loading came out and up and into them.

"Come on back up off the ground, by God!" he shouted.

One of the men unbent and leaped, caught him around the waist. Jordan's sureness left him for an instant. He went back into a pile of lumber, felt something hard strike him behind the ear. The moon slid behind a cloud, and in the darkness he struck about helplessly, unable to get a swing. The man had him pinned against the wood and was butting his head up under his chin, kicking him with his knee at the same time.

"God-damn you," he groaned.

Then the man spoke. "Zepher, come on, help me!"

The words went to Jordan's blood right off. "Zepher!" he roared. His two big hands grabbed the man around the neck and lifted him, tossed him to one side. "Where are you, Zepher?" he shouted.

He caught sight of a knife, saw it lunge in, grabbed a wrist with his left hand and then, without even considering the knife, struck out with his right—held the man in close by the wrist and kept hitting him.

He was hitting him when the moon came back from behind a cloud and stirred his mind to thought. He stepped back, let Zepher fall to the ground in a mound of flesh.

"Look here, get up, Zepher. You ain't dead."

The other man moaned low and turned on the ground, but Zepher lay cold still. Jordan knelt beside him, pushed him over.

"You ain't dead, you hear? God-damn me. Don't you know I got no sense?"

Off in the distance he heard the carnival tinkle and rumble on. He ripped Zepher's shirt down the front, put his ear to his chest. At a mud puddle, he got some water in his cupped hands and dumped it on Zepher's face. Zepher moaned; his eyes flickered for an instant.

"You leave me alone, Zepher," Jordan said. "Just stay clear." He backed off, then turned, hurried away, afraid that he might meet someone else and not stop soon enough.

That night, after telling Annie and the boys about the money, and after patching his body so that the bleeding stopped, he dreamed of new taxicabs coming over the crest of a hill, yellow-painted with blue tops, and on the sides of each, clear for the eye to see, were the letters Jake had printed there.

"Ahhh, Jake, what do you say now, huh?"

Jake only grinned, shook his head in dreamy wonderment.

"You said to beat him. Well, what do you think? Look at that car there. See how I drive. Look at me."

"I see. I see."

"It's me in there. And look at Alexander comin' along—and that young Hogan boy. Listen to that motor, Jake."

"Hear it, hear it clear."

"Hardly a sound. Ah, God, when will they end? I bet they stretch from here to the machine."

"Turnin' 'em out."

"And see—there—drivin' that cab—that's Fletcher, ain't it?"

"Think it is."

"Turned-up nose like Fletcher's. Drivin' by. Hello, Fletcher! Huh! Doffed his hat to me. Did you see it?"

"Saw it plain."

"Well, where's Harris? Can't play favorites. Hey, Harris, hurry up! Hit the top of the hill with your car."

"Nothin' but taxicabs, Jordan."

"Far as the eye can see."

"Goin' to win."

"That's right. Hey, look at him—look at Harris driving all over the road as if he owned it."

"Don't kill yourself, Harris."

"Green taxicab all over. That's the color for him. Hey, Harris, stay in line."

"Goin' to have trouble with that boy, Jordan."

"Naw."

"Goin' to break all the rules and many a lady's heart."

"Harris? Why he ain't but a baby."

"Don't matter. Goin' to marry two or three, leave 'em prostrate with pain when he goes away. Goin' to be a seeker, that one."

"Naw."

"Fletcher, he's the steady one. Goin' to rule the roost, Fletcher is, put money by, build big and bigger. But not Harris."

"Harris is goin' to sing and carry on, you say? Well, let him be. I'll have a fortune made for him, anyway. Let him drive as he please."

"Hear the women, hear 'em pray."

"Harris comin'. But, Lord, Jake, he ain't but a boy."

"Listen to 'em cry."

"Oh, I hear it. Music cryin'."

"Women stacked up high as cordwood."

"God, he's got it, ain't he?'

"Hey, Jordan, is that your boy?"

"Oh, he's mine. Look at that nose and them eyes. World traveler, been to the moon almost!"

"May be. May be."

"Been to France and seen the Frenchmen smile."

"Wish I'd gone."

"But Fletcher keeps right on the road."

"Straight as an arrow flies."

"Taxicabs. On and on. Jake, we done it, didn't we? Was your money done it, that you gave me afore you died. Took it out of a mattress, slit it out, put it by. And now the world goes 'round and 'round."

"Carnival is comin', Jordan. Hear it in the distance. Better look to your laurels. Maybe win again."

"Ain't but one carnival, and it's done been and left me all it had."

"Hey, there's the last cab. And look who's in it, would you?"

"Annie ridin' in it. Well, think o' that. Who's drivin'?"

"Don't know."

"Hey, Annie—Annie, it's me—"

"…Ah, what you know about that—drove right on past, hardly lifted an eye. What's it mean?"

"Right on by."

"Hardly a look, 'cept of shame."

"I don't know why she shies away like that."

"Well, never mind."

"Harris was cute, though, wasn't he?"

"Yeah, forget worryin' about Harris. Harris is goin' to win their hearts, boy. They're goin' to wave to Harris."

"Yeah, Lord. Has a rovin' spirit like I had."

"Goin' to weep for Harris."

"Lord, they're goin' to weep for Harris."

20

The next day it seemed every colored person in Leafwood needed to ride in Jordan's cab, and each one asked him about his brother and how the two of them were getting along. They asked what Jordan planned to do in the way of expansion, and generally hinted around the subject of the crap game and the money.

"I almost wish I hadn't won," Jordan told Annie. He wasn't serious, and she knew it. "But Coltrane right out told Bryant he wouldn't sell. He's holdin' on now."

One of the first and loudest boosters was Alexander, who gloried in the new-won victory. "When you want my half of the down payment for a cab, Jordan? Let's get this item settled and roll the wheels, man. Goin' to sell my house today."

There was no way to hold out against his enthusiasm, and Jordan put in an order for a new cab. The other two men, young Hogan and an older man named Soloman, came in shortly, each looking peaked and eager, and somewhat afraid lest they were not going to be let in.

So Jordan threw caution to the wind, ordered two more cabs, then went to work helping the men learn the rules of driving.

Hogan and Alexander learned quickly, but Solomon was slow. A lean, serious man who two years before had tried to run a tailor shop and failed, he worried over each problem until everyone else was exasperated. Yet in his steady way he arrived at the same knowledge, and there was about him a thoroughness which prompted Jordan to believe he might do much better than well enough.

Hogan was a bother. He had but recently discovered women, and now no other thought could completely occupy his mind. "Got to make some money in this. They're chargin' three dollars a time at Minnie's."

"You mean a time or a try?" Solomon mumbled.

"You can cut down on that kind o' life," Jordan told him, remembering his own early days. "Life has more to offer than that."

Hogan nodded enthusiastically. "So I heard," he said. "But I ain't no queer, Jordan," and he laughed until Jordan thought he was going to have to put him out of the office.

The three men almost worried him to death, anxious to be under way, so he ushered them down to the police station to take their driver's tests. Of the three, Alexander and Hogan passed without trouble; but Solomon, irritated by a comment of the patrolman, spoke out too plain and was turned down.

Back in the office, Jordan sent the other two out, told Solomon to stay. He realized he might have made a mistake taking him in, and if he had, working on so slim a margin, it could all end in a bad way.

"What did the patrolman say to you, Solomon?"

Solomon shook off the question, moodily stared around at Jake's pictures, some of which Jordan had fastened to the wall.

"Come on, now, you're too far grown to be losin' out like you did. Even Jake passed the drivin' test."

"I can drive all right."

"I know you can. And you learned the rules, too. What happened?"

Solomon walked around the room, touching the wall with his fist, as if to gain steadiness. "God-damn the whites," he said at last.

It was clear enough then. One of the jumpy ones. Always in trouble, the jumpy ones. "You better go on, Solomon, and get settled somewhere else."

"I'm with you, Jordan."

"I got a business to run. Good Lord, sometimes white people call us up for a cab. What you goin' to do, get in a fight? You got your color on your shoulder?"

Solomon slumped down in a straight-back chair, his long face clouded with doubt. "You have to let me stay. I know what to do. But all the time it burns me. Ain't white, ain't white." He twisted his hands together.

"Started a tailor shop. White customers always a big problem. I acts superior, or they acts superior. Don't hit it off."

The self-pity in his voice hung around in the room, pushing Jordan down in dull spirits, making him forget for an instant his hopes. He had never worried about being black, but he had known people who worried, spent much money on dyes and pills and syrups to turn them white, even when it was known that all such was nonsense. The old people took it best, rested in their color like a comfort, a familiar quilt that protected them from bother. As for himself, all his life he had known he was going to the North, so he had given it little worry. Up there he supposed Negroes and whites were on the same basis all around. Anyway, the North had the best way, whatever it was. Everybody was happy in the North.

But now before him, head low and shoulders bent, unmasked, was a Negro, black of skin, deeply born, rebellious of what had come to him. And what was Jordan to do about it?

"I know I got to hold my tongue, but I can't seem to manage."

"Try smilin' it off, or try—"

"Like Patrick?"

"No, don't do that."

"Can't smile at times like these."

"Well, hell, you goin' to drive for me, you have to get your license and come to terms."

"Yeah," Solomon said, getting up slowly. "I can do it. I know the way. But it burns my soul."

From the day the new cabs arrived, Jordan sat in the office most of the time, keeping track of his drivers, totaling his books, answering the phone. He got into the habit of saying a few friendly words to each person who called in—nothing that would tie up his telephone line, but a greeting. Sometimes he would run his finger down the phone book when there was a quiet spell, picking out a person who never used his cab, then he would phone, let him know the company was in business, that the drivers were part-owners, and that the service was the best. Usually the people thanked him for telling them about the company.

On a busy Friday night after the cabs arrived, Mr. Crawford sent word that he wanted to talk to Jordan. The message came from one of the yard men, Jenkins, to Solomon. The next morning, when he was able, Jordan drove down to the coalyard, using one of the new cabs, and parked it beside the weighing platform. The men loading coal at the other end of the lot stopped work to wave a recognition, which he returned.

Inside the shack, Patrick, seated at the same long table, was doodling on a pad. "Ah, look a' there who's come to see us," he said, jumping up and going off into laughter. "What you doin' here, Jordan?"

Jordan recalled the last time he was in the room, and under what different circumstances he had come back. "Is Mr. Crawford around?"

"Maybe. Let's see." Patrick dialed a number on the phone, sat back in a swivel chair, smiling broadly. A coal truck pulled to a stop outside, and he glanced through the window, wrote down a figure on a ticket, waved it on.

"This is Patrick," he said into the phone. "Is Mr. Crawford over there?"

He hung up a moment later, nodded to Jordan. "Be back soon, they said."

"You didn't tell him I was here?"

"No need. He'll be here directly."

And he was. He came in, more wizened and wrinkled than at the previous meeting. He was slipping fast, Jordan saw.

He glanced at Patrick, then around the room, his eyes lighting on Jordan, flickering for an instant. "Yes," he said. "Uh huh. Been singin' any more hymns, Jordan?"

Jordan grinned. "Not lately, Mr. Crawford."

"'Amazin' Grace,'" he said cheerfully. "Loosened up the panes in the window with that one, didn't we?"

Jordan stood with his back to the heat stove, his hands entwined together, showing none of the tension he felt. It was rare when a white man sent word for a Negro to come by, and seldom blew good news. He noticed that Patrick was nervous, too.

"Seen your cab outside," Crawford said. "How many you got—two?"

"Four."

"Is that a fact? Are they busy?"

"Keep the three new ones right busy."

"Is that a fact? Makin' any money?"

Jordan started to tell him he hadn't had time to find out as yet, but before he could, Crawford jumped up, rubbing his coal-marked hands together. "Know you are, know you are—that's why I wanted to talk to you." He came up to Jordan, spoke right into his face. "I want to talk business."

Jordan knew Crawford was as slick as a fish's belly, and it didn't pay for a colored man to be dealing with a white, anyway. There was precious little out, in case something went wrong.

"You see, Jordan, I'm goin' on over soon—trustin' to the Lord for a safe passage—and I want to sell this coalyard afore I go, lest it fall into weak hands."

Jordan looked away, angry inside. It was no good even to talk of a Negro owning the coalyard. "Why you sayin' this?" he asked. "Why to me?"

"You got the money."

"I ain't got money. I got debts, is all."

"Well, don't take much to buy a coalyard. Hell, ain't nothin' to it, except a field and a fence, with a weighin' station. What you say?"

"I'm in the taxicab business, Mr. Crawford."

"Well, you can be in both. You want to prosper, don't you? I allus thought a man liked to get ahead."

"I like to get ahead, but—"

"Then this is your big chance. I picked you—"

"Why didn't you pick out a white man?" Jordan blurted out.

Crawford seemed to absorb the question, then without a word he nodded, accepting it. Patrick got up suddenly, went out, closing the door. Through the window, Jordan could see him impatiently walking back and forth over the weighing scales, something childlike in his movements.

"Tell you what, Jordan, it's a big story, so let it all go by the board, except that Patrick is...a young fellow I like very well, and I want to help him out. I could get a white man in here, sure, but I want half of this company to go to Patrick. And a white man—well, bein' partners with a nigger ain't to most o' their likings, I should imagine."

"You want Patrick to run this yard?"

"Been runnin' it, ain't he? Been doin' it for years."

This wasn't so, Jordan knew. Patrick had done all the note-keeping and had directed the operation in one sense, but the men had obeyed his bidding only because Crawford was behind him. Without Crawford, Patrick would have had a foul-up on his hands inside of two days.

"…Fact is, business is slow, anyway, and is mostly to the nigger people. Ain't hardly much business to whites. The laundry still uses coal, but I asked them if they cared if I sold out to niggers, and they said that was no concern o' theirs, so long as they didn't have to eat with 'em." He chuckled, delighted with the remark. "Don't mind to wash their clothes, they said, but they draw the limit elsewhere."

Mr. Crawford saw a good deal of humor in this, and took his time returning to seriousness. "Well, sir, that's my proposition. Last year we made almost fifty-five hundred dollars' profit in this business. I'll sell you half-interest for five thousand, of which you just need to put one thousand down."

"I ain't got one thousand, Mr. Crawford. And look here, Mr. Crawford—"

"Well, Patrick has. Patrick has near enough for both of you. Maybe you can borrow from him."

"But—but look here. I don't—I don't want—to do it."

"I told Patrick already that I won't sell to him unless he gets a strong-handed partner down here. So, what do you say?"

Jordan shook his head in distress. "I'll give it some thought."

"I've give it thought already. I've reached my mind to an end on it. I picked you out."

"Yes, sir, Mr. Crawford, but—"

"Out of all the niggers in the town, you're the only one that can hold this thing. This is a hardship business, coal in this town. People has turned to oil. But it's worth ten thousand, and I offer it with the easiest terms I can manage. It'll pay for itself, and it'll keep goin' after that. You're the man, the only man I know that—"

"No," Jordan said in a low voice. "I ain't goin' to do it, Mr. Crawford."

He walked past Crawford and on outside. As he swung into his cab, he saw Crawford standing at the open door, holding with a white hand to each doorpost, glaring at him. "You come back here and talk this over," he shouted.

Jordan had his hand on the starter button, but he got out. "Mr. Crawford, I don't want it."

"Want it! Want it!" Crawford shouted. "I put my life into this business, built it up. Patrick has his life in it. Don't tell me you don't want it; I picked you out."

"Yes, sir. But I just can't do it, Mr. Crawford."

"You listen here—"

"Yes, sir. I ain't goin' to buy it. Yes, sir."

He swung into the car and backed out, his body trembling. It was sick. It was an old white man trying to help a young Negro who didn't deserve the help, who was being kept in a place where he would fail before he knew it, go down. It was sick all around.

The next Sunday Patrick came to his house just after church and sat around the living room until Annie had to ask him to eat with them. He said nothing about the coalyard, but talked to Jordan about how lucky he was to have two fine boys and a secure business. Finally, when they had gone into the living room and the children had been pushed out to play, Patrick told Jordan that there was a bad spot in his life now. He was going to be left with the coalyard and insecurity was overcoming him.

"Well, why don't you quit the coalyard, Patrick?"

"Huh?" He looked up, startled. "What would I do, for the Lord's sake? Look here, I don't know what to say to that."

They talked a while longer, then Patrick went away, not having been satisfied, and not having said very much. Jordan felt thwarted by it, as if he had been on the verge of helping to decide something. "Didn't eat much dinner, did he?" Annie said.

"Weren't hungry, I guess."

"Funny. He didn't laugh the whole time he was here."

It was a small thing, but it bothered Annie, and now that he was aware of it, it bothered Jordan, too. He thought about it that afternoon as he spelled Hogan on the taxicab run, and was thinking about it that night when Patrick came to the door of his office, a tortured look on his face. He slumped down to a chair, staring straight ahead.

"I done quit," he said. His small chin was trembling and his fits were clenched. "Quit Crawford. Had to tell him myself. God 'a' mercy."

He went on talking, telling how he had gone to the coalyard as a boy, and had been so frightened he had started laughing from nervousness.

"Crawford liked that. He kept me on, brought me up there in the coal shack. I tell you, Jordan, I didn't know—not till you turned down the coalyard—I didn't know it was nothin'."

"What did Crawford say when you told him?"

"He almost cried. He thought I held the coal company as high as him."

"Never mind," Jordan said. "You got a duty to yourself."

"I dunno. I just left."

"That's right. You're free now. A man don't owe his life to another, just to give him pleasure, make him feel real. You got to live, Patrick—get free."

"I'm free now," Patrick said.

"Well, go on, laugh it off. You got money—start a business. How much you got?"

"Sixteen hundred dollars."

"Listen to that! You can start as fine a business as there is in this town. Start a shoe-repair shop, open a nigger movie house—we need those two things, I figure. Open a nigger grocery store—"

"Well, I have to step careful, Jordan. I went to work for Mr. Crawford so young, I ain't learned to handle myself like—"

"Ah, shut your mouth," Jordan interrupted, disgusted with him.

Patrick looked around at him as if he had been struck.

"Get hold of yourself. You sound like one of them men over at that housewarming Bryant had, like a man has got to be milk-fed. You're alive, ain't you?"

Patrick half-smiled, he was so amazed by Jordan's anger.

"Man got sixteen hundred dollars and come aroun' me whimperin'! Get on out o' here, Patrick."

Patrick backed off, bumped into the doorspot, then began to chuckle at Jordan's wrath and his own reticence.

"Cut out that gigglin'!"

Patrick began to laugh now, sure enough, and Jordan couldn't keep a serious face to save himself. "Get out o' here, damn it!"

Patrick backed off into the hall, a silhouette now. He backed down the hall, cackling to himself.

"Patrick," Jordan called out suddenly, then fell to thinking. Finally he looked up. "Come here."

He came back to the doorway.

"Come in and sit down."

He sat down, a small smile on his face.

"Got sixteen hundred dollars and you're goin' downstairs without a purpose. Don't make sense. Let's work this out."

They talked for a long time about it, going over various possibilities, but Patrick only nodded to each one and held his peace. Nothing seemed to make him enthusiastic, and Jordan knew that was the first need.

"Well, don't anything strike you, for the Lord's sake? This town needs every dollar a colored man can put in it, if we're to climb to anything."

But nothing turned up until Jordan rested his eyes on Jake's self-portrait, tacked to the wall over his desk. He glanced over at the pack of Jake's drawings. An idea formed itself. He tried to hold back suggesting it to Patrick until he could give it more thought, but it was too fine an idea not to bring out.

"I tell you, Patrick—uh—you and me—how 'bout you and me joinin' up partners on a deal?"

A big grin came on Patrick's face.

So right there, in Jake's old room, the two men set to work making plans.

The largest of the empty spaces in the building downstairs was smaller than they needed, but it was well located, so they took a lease on it. Within a week, Patrick had nailed together some booths. They bought a refrigerator and storage cabinets. When they tacked Jake's portrait to the wall, right behind the bar, Jordan carefully removed the newspaper clipping, announcing Jake's death, which he had pinned to it.

They fastened several others of Jake's drawings to the walls, and the room came alive with warmth. Jordan and Patrick opened for business, and to the men of the town it was as if Jake, himself, had come back from the dead to bring good cheer. The new beer hall was an institution reborn—not so big as it had been, but it would do.

And Jordan realized he had at last struck Bryant a steel-hard blow.

21

But all this success seemed to instill doubts in Annie, and gave her a persistence for saving which aggravated Jordan no end. It was as if she suspected that the entire business venture would fold within a month. Almost every night she brought up the importance of putting money by, and even the house money was so carefully hid that Jordan couldn't find three dollars to pay for a half-load of stovewood when Hogan delivered it.

"Well, Annie, do you think the elements are going to snatch your money away?"

"Not worried about that," she said patiently.

"Why ain't the money hid in the kitchen like it used to be? I ain't got time to look all over the damn house."

"Don't want you lookin'. I'm puttin' by as best I can, and I don't want you lookin' or I'll bury the money to hide it. Once a man gambles all he has, he will again."

He tried to make light of that, laugh it off; but her criticism hurt, nonetheless. Seemed to him that Annie was more than ordinarily hard to please. He was on his way to the top, while she was moaning and fearful. Other men's wives were able to help their husbands with encouragement and support. Never catch Helen Coltrane running down her husband. But Annie usually was on the doubtful side, holding back.

He wondered why she was like that.

It could be just the baby, he knew. Give a woman a baby and it goes to her heart too much. She pines away hoping for something it might amount to, wondering what it will be, fearing lest it be ill-formed. He couldn't imagine it—making something you couldn't see, making it without knowing how, even—not doing anything, but feeling it grow. That would stir up worries, all right.

But everybody was in similar trouble, life being what it was; seemed to him everybody got started in a dreamy way and never did shake it off. Of course, most whites were able to shake some of it off; they could hold to names and dates, places and numbers—all such lifeless things. But feelings were what caught his memory. Annie's too, maybe.

Kate was the opposite, though. She was up on ideas, but she didn't feel much of anything. She was like the whites—thought her way along. She stayed at home mostly, poring over charts showing how Negroes were doing here and there in the world, trying to find a way for them to do better; and just studying like that seemed to content her.

That was the way the world was—everybody different. No easy solution to anybody that was ever born. But Annie appeared to be more complicated than the run of the mill, nonetheless, and the only hope he saw for a solution was in his staying home, trying to be with her more.

So he reasoned. And each night when the boys finished supper and wandered outside, he would sit at the table awhile and try to talk to Annie. But no matter what topic he took up, there were only a few words said between them before he would have to take up another one. It was as if she didn't want to talk to him.

"Look here, Annie, let the dishes be. You wasn't like this when Harris was born, nor Fletcher, either, as I recall."

"Like what? What you mean?"

"Now don't go flyin' off. I just want to talk to you."

She would go on with the dishes, scarcely looking around, wiping the pots out and scrubbing down everything as if that was the only matter in the world she could give her thoughts to.

Each night it was the same problem and it ended the same way—with him going into the living room, taking over the big chair and calling for the boys to come around and tell him what they had done that day.

"Killed a snake," Harris would answer—that or some other tall tale, depending on what his mind turned up.

"Where you see a snake?"

"In the garden. He was crawlin' up the tomato posts."

"Uh huh." Jordan looked at him suspiciously. "How far up?"

"Right to the top."

"You lyin', Harris! You lyin' your mouth off. Listen to me, boy, no snake goin' to climb past soft tomatoes to get to green ones. Now, come off that. Getting' to be a habit."

"He lies all the time," Fletcher said.

"He does. Nobody goin' to believe him any more. Fletcher, what you do today?"

"He made eyes at the Alexander girl," Harris interjected.

"Did not," Fletcher blurted at him, striking him on the shoulder with his fist.

"Now, look a' here," Jordan said harshly, "don't waste my time at home with brother strikin' brother. And Harris, take care, your mouth is too big. Now keep your paw over it, if that's what it takes to hold the words in."

"Fletcher was holdin' her hand."

"Lord 'a' mercy," Jordan said. "Was you, Fletcher?"

"Pa, don't believe him."

"Well, he tells it like the truth."

"He told that snake like the truth, too."

"That's so. Goin' to yell 'wolf, wolf' once too many times, Harris."

Harris glanced around with a face of pure innocence.

"I don't even know that Alexander girl," Fletcher said.

"Do, do," Harris said.

"Well, I hope he does. But—let it—stop holdin' hands; I don't want no trouble." Jordan worried about it for a minute, then went into the kitchen, sided up to Annie. "When does the trouble start, Annie?"

"What?"

"With boys. I don't remember."

"Trouble?" She wrung out the dishcloth. "Been trouble since they was born."

"Don't mean that," he said, going back to his chair, trying to remember. "Now, you boys won't tell me what you did today, so I'll tell you about myself." He leaned his head back, looked away fondly, for he was proud of his work. "Let's see—about six I started drivin' at the rush period for the men-folk, and drove through eight as the ladies got to the house jobs...."

The boys listened attentively to this. Jordan always told them of his day.

"Then I turned to at the beer hall, cleanin' out and sweepin' up, wipin' the counters dry. That took me to ten-thirty, at which time I got the money counted from the two companies and went to the bank, put it in, picked up a statement for the month, and fussed with the bank about seven dollars till I found out it was in my favor."

The boys didn't know what that meant, and he didn't go into it, either.

"Then I argued with a white man about how much he wanted to put in a television for the beer hall, and finally decided to go through with it anyway. Then Alexander complained 'cause Hogan went to Durham last night on private business and left a hole in the cab company. So I talked down to Hogan for a while, then drove at the noon hour till two o'clock so that the other men could get fed on a sandwich. A customer come in at two o'clock, sayin' she had left a pocketbook in one of the cabs, and I had to talk to the drivers about that, and we finally found she'd been in your uncle Bryant's cab all the while. Then I set to on the books, addin' strings o' figures for two hours."

Harris began to stir restlessly, so Jordan hurried on. "Then I wrote out checks to the gasoline people, sent two cabs down for a grease job, helped Patrick load up the ice in the cooler, and stacked in the beer cans for the night. I went back to the books for the beer hall and got them all straight, except for seven dollars I couldn't find out about yet. Finally got hold of the landlord of my building and mentioned that water was leakin' from the roof and through one wall of my office. At five, the little boy from across the hall come in to take calls—boy by the name of Seth, about three years older than you, Fletcher—and I drove a cab till seven, at which time I come home for supper."

The boys were always duly impressed, particularly Fletcher. It was a rare night, indeed, when they acted unconcerned, and then Jordan would go back over the list, adding sufficient detail to make them realize he had been hitting the high spots all along.

But they usually were attentive, even eager for him to talk to them and when he was done they would ask him to sing a song. This, too, had become part of the evening ritual.

"But look here," he would say, "most of my songs are too sad or too grown-up for you boys."

"Sing about that turkey," Harris would insist.

"Lord, boy, that ain't but the one verse."

"Sing the turkey."

"All right, all right." Jordan would laugh and throw back his head—

Went runnin' down to the turkey roost
Fell down on my knees,
Liked to kill myself a-laughin',
"Cause I heard a turkey sneeze.

Fletcher and Harris would roll around on the floor and make a big to-do over that. "Sing another one about a turkey," Harris would say.

"Got no more turkeys, boy. How 'bout a chicken?"

"Chicken, chicken!" Harris would cry, going on as if that would be far better than a turkey, anyway.

"Well, here's one that will go with your 'rithmetic lesson, Fletcher—"

Old master raised a little black hen,
Black as any crow;
She laid three eggs ev'y day,
"Cept when she laid fo'.

The boys would giggle and discuss the chicken, then Jordan would help them out as they tried to sing it.

"Another one about a chicken," Harris would insist.

"Good Lord, Harris, can't stick to one animal all the time. Jump around, boy."

"What about a rabbit then?" Fletcher would suggest.

"Let's see here. May be. May be. Seems like I once heard somethin' about a rabbit." Jordan would look off at the far wall, as if trying to recall. "Yes, let's see if I can put the words together—"

O Brer Rabbit! yo' ears mighty long this mornin'.
O Brer Rabbit! yo' ears mighty long.
But hope you got 'em turned right side wrong.
This mornin', this evenin', so soon.

O Brer Rabbit! you look mighty good this mornin'.
O Brer Rabbit! you look mighty good;
But if you got sense, you'll take to the woods
This mornin', this evenin', so soon.

Jordan enjoyed these nightly sessions no end. He looked forward to them. During the day he would try to recapture words of the songs he had heard as a boy, so that he could sing them for Fletcher and Harris; and he would make mental notes of happenings of the day that might impress them.

One important matter he never brought up, however, perhaps because it made his job seem easier, was that Kate helped him some now. He had gone to her with a few problems at first, but now she came by almost every week and made his figures come out right. She would point out his mistakes as they would study the two soiled ledgers together, Jordan moaning over the poor errors that had caused him so much doubt.

Kate was to him a strong right arm, advising and correcting.

"Say, Kate, don't Bryant get on you about helpin' me, or don't he know it?" Jordan asked her the third time she came by.

"You let me worry about Bryant. It takes enough of my time doing that as it is, without having you bring it up."

"Why you live with Bryant? You like him?"

"Here, let's stay on the job before us, Jordan." She was like that—all the time working. But she would listen to his problems with concern.

"...Take them three men, Kate. All of 'em good drivers, but besides bein' drivers, they're problems."

"Every person is different, Jordan."

"Nothin' will do for that Hogan boy but that he look in every door that opens for women. Don't know if he'll ever grow up or not. Then Alexander has got so much anxiousness about him, he almost carries me out of my senses. And along comes Solomon, broodin' over every word like as if it has a deepness to it."

"How is Patrick doing?"

Jordan's face lighted up. "He's all right. He's happy."

The truth was, Patrick was a popular bartender. He would listen for hours to anybody, evidently not being able to find anything boring in any story that was spoken aloud. And whenever a drinker would get out of hand, he would step in, just as Jake had done. The men would abide by his decisions, too, as if he represented Jake and they had better obey.

"Wouldin't be surprised, Kate, if that beer hall don't make a sight more than this cab company."

"It might in time, Jordan. But you should have started a restaurant or some other type of business. You and Bryant are checking each other in both companies now. Your anger got the better of your senses."

The profits were not large, it was true. The drivers would fuss about that, unable to understand how they could work long hours and have no more than fifty dollars a week each to show for it. But Jordan told them about the payments on the three new cabs, and they could look forward to better times ahead.

Jordan started ignoring their troubles, anyway. He borrowed a guitar from Hogan and would sit in the office strumming it and singing while the work went hang. "Make me a pallet on de floor," he would sing lustily, "make it in de kitchen behind de door...."

He had over a hundred songs with which to entertain himself; and Solomon, with his sorrowful voice, could join in the words of most of them.

About this time, too, he pulled out Jake's sketching set and toyed around until he had a creditable likeness of Bryant's beer hall across the street. He showed it around and received sufficient encouragement to try his hand at a drawing of one of his taxicabs, which, except for being off-center on the paper, was as fine as he ever saw.

But Kate criticized him for drawing pictures and taking up time fooling around. "Too many people now sitting on porches about to fall in, singing songs."

"Lord 'a' mercy, Kate, that's the thing of interest. Rest of the stuff around here is numbers—white man's work."

"If you're going to get anywhere in the white man's world, you'd better stick to the numbers."

But sometimes as he would sing the old songs, particularly the slow and mournful ones, Kate would drop her pencil and listen; then she would begin to beat her fingers on the desk top in time with the music.

"Listenin', ain't you, Kate?"

She would snatch up the pencil and go back to the books; but once she broke down, laughed. "Lord help me, you'll ruin me yet, Jordan." She smiled over at him, the warmest smile she had ever given. "Look, let's get to work on those books and stay at it."

He tried, but the tedious hours deadened his spirit. Even while she would work at the bills and letters, he would be thinking of his days driving a cab and shoveling coal, his mind going fondly over the simple incidents. And of the North, land of rest and boundless opportunity. The dream of going North was still close to him, although now it had taken on another form. Now he saw himself entering the North after he had made a big success. After he had won out, he would go up there, for sure.

"Goin' to drive to New York," he would tell Kate. "Goin' to have real luggage and all. Even Harris and Fletcher goin' to have a bag apiece. Goin' to Harlem—is that the place?"

"That's one place, Jordan."

"Goin' to Harlem and settle back in comfort."

Kate would chuckle over that and shake her head, but she wouldn't talk to him about the North. Instead, she would talk about the work and about books he should read.

"Look, Kate," he would tell her, "I don't mind you bringin' one or two books in here, but does ever nigger have to fail?"

"Don't use that word."

"Read most o' one of them books and part of another, and both of 'em is on the failin' side."

"That's the way with life, Jordan."

"Not with mine." He bit off the end of a fat cigar. "By God, I ain't goin' to fail."

"Then get to work."

"I ain't goin' to fail if I have to run Bryant clean out of town and take over myself." He tilted his chair back against the wall. "Getting' tired of everybody talkin' about failin'."

So she worked on while Jordan fretted.

"It was better when Jake was alive, Kate. Then it was personal. Now it ain't. I don't hardly know whether I'm beatin' Bryant or him me. Don't have a hand in it."

"You have the big hand in it, if you only knew it."

Then one rainy Thursday, Kate didn't come in as usual. About four o'clock she phoned, asked him to come to her house at once. She sounded upset, and he hurried up there, wondering if she was done with him for not working as much as he should.

She came out of her house, a suitcase in each hand, threw them in the cab, and climbed inside. He pulled the door closed from the driver's seat. "Kate where you goin'?"

She shook her head, her face tightly emotionless. "Just—Just drive uptown. Give me time to…get hold of myself."

He was so surprised to find her like that, he didn't even start the engine. He waited there, wondering what had happened. "Is it Bryant?"

"Just…drive uptown."

"Huh? Look, Kate, did something happen?"

"Yes." Then she said, "I'm going to have a baby—Bryant's baby. But he's not to know it."

Jordan leaned against the steering wheel, the idea filling his mind. His throat tightened up when he started to speak. "He—he wants a child, Kate."

She stared straight ahead. "He'll not have mine."

He shifted around in the seat, leaned his head forward. He realized that his body was damp. Kate began to weep, softly at first, then in anguished sobs.

Now she knows deep feeling, he thought, but there was little comfort in that. He didn't dare look at her, either, even in the rearview mirror, or try to assure her. She was not that kind.

"Bryant wants a baby," he said. "Maybe he would…let the kid be. He would love it."

"Not my baby," she whispered.

He carried in her bags at the bus station and sat around in the waiting room while she bought her ticket for Rocky Mount.

"What did you do with the books you worked on, Kate—are they in the bags?"

"I left them at Bryant's."

"Huh? But that was your work."

"That's why I stayed with Bryant—the work. Only other course was to go home. You ought to see my father's house, Jordan. He has six children and three grandchildren living in two rooms."

"Yeah, I seen the like—"

"And I'm going back, carrying an unborn child."

"No, Kate—"

She shook her head fiercely. "I've thought it all over, Jordan."

"You come on up to the office. You tend my books, answer the phone. Look here—"

"No. No—"

"Well, God, Kate you can't go back to that place. You're college educated—"

"Who wants a college-educated Negro?"

"You know ten times as much as me."

"I have to do this!" She was strained almost beyond control.

Jordan left her then, went across the street to his office and got thirty dollars out of his desk, all he had put back there. He brought it back, gave it to her.

She nodded, unable to speak.

He asked for her address, and she wrote it out for him.

"Now your bus is loadin'. Look here, Kate, you take care of that baby. Don't lose it."

"I don't have money for that."

"Maybe God will strike Bryant somehow, so he'll turn in his path. Maybe even that baby would be God strikin' him. You're assumin' a lot, Kate."

"It's my baby."

"It's Bryant's baby, too."

"It's my baby." She took his hand. "You go on, Jordan, you hear me? You amount to something. You're the one who can."

"Don't say that. I don't want to hear words like that from you, not about me, Kate."

She put both hands on his, held his hand for a moment, pressed it greatly, then climbed aboard the bus. He was left to watch her as the bus pulled away.

For four days after Kate left him, Bryant was in a rage and a stupor. The sound of a party floated out of his beer hall night and day. The building vibrated with carousing. On the door Bryant had nailed the sign "Closed

For Repairs," and the blinds had been pulled. Inside, Jordan was not sure what went on, but food was delivered to the place in steaming cauldrons from one of the restaurants, and several women would go to and from. All Bryant's men were there, and some of the Durham crowd came over. Whatever satisfaction the party might have had for Bryant, it was hard on his business. Jordan's two companies were in boom time, and it was all they could do to keep up.

"Learn the names of these new customers," Jordan said over and over to Patrick and the drivers. "Get 'em and hold 'em, you hear me? You grew up together, or you know their children."

All four cabs were rolling, and the beer hall was packed up so tight the fire department inspector came down on Saturday night and made almost half the customers leave.

On Tuesday morning Bryant's party died down, and there was not a sound for hours. Finally a driver came out the front door, stretched lazily, sauntered across the street to Jordan's beer hall. Patrick met him at the door.

He was one of Bryant's men, a fellow named Godfrey, but most called him Fish Eyes. He was a hard-talking man who had come out of the North. "Jordan around?" he asked.

Patrick scratched at his throat thoughtfully, said nothing to him.

"Bryant wants him."

Jordan moved up, pulled the door open full way. Godfrey stepped back on seeing him, recovering his composure. "Bryant's over there." He pointed a thumb over his shoulder. "Will you come?"

"Tell him I will."

Godfrey accepted that, went back across the street, the light of day bothering him.

Jordan put aside a cloth he had been using to wipe off the tables. "Let's have a beer, Patrick," he said.

Patrick pulled out several cold ones and brought an opener to a booth. He took a wheel of cheddar cheese and cut off two big hunks. "You know, Jordan, Bryant could be right dangerous. You goin' over there?"

"I don't know yet." He bit off a piece of cheese and drank most of a beer.

"What you reckon he wants?"

"To know where Kate is."

"Do you know?"

"No idea."

He drank beer, one can after another, until he felt ready to talk to Bryant.

When he let himself in Bryant's beer hall, there was not a soul in sight. Bottles and cans littered the floor and a few pieces of clothing were strewn about. From upstairs he heard a lazy comment, then an answer, as if from another room.

He sat down at one of the booths near the door and watched the stairways. He waited for five minutes before he saw anybody, and then it was a woman who stared down, only to draw back sharply on seeing him. He thought it was Mona. He knew full well Mona couldn't be up there, not at Bryant's place; but it looked just like her.

Soon after, Bryant appeared, bleary-eyed and swollen of face from drink and sleeplessness. Heavily he walked down the steps, his eyes trying to focus on Jordan, as if picking him out of the debris. He came across the floor in his bare feet, his shirt open so that his belly showed, his pants creased into his flesh at the belt line. He sat down opposite Jordan at the booth. "Hey," he said slowly, dreamily, "is that you, boy?"

Jordan felt sorry for him right off.

"You come. You did right. I wanted to tell you—to tell you Kate left me yesterday."

"You lost some time, didn't you, Bryant?" Jordan said carefully.

"Huh? Oh, God, I dunno." He ran his hand inside his shirt and onto his stomach. "Just left me." He seemed to be about to weep. "But I don't care. How you tell about 'em? She's smart. Probably gone to Washington or Houston, somewhere that ain't really part of the South nor the North, where there's a chance for better. But I don't give a damn where she is."

"Yeah, that's right, Bryant."

"How can you tell? Don't blame her for leavin' this town. Say, boy, I would 'a' married her, but she—she didn't want it that way. Said wait, wait."

"Hard to tell about a woman, Bryant."

"It was the town, I think. No good. Not for her, not for Kate. She thought too much, you know it? Big mind, goin' on and on. Lord, I don't know where it took her?"

"I don't either, Bryant."

"You don't know?"

"Not a thing, Bryant."

"Looks like she would 'a' said something to somebody. Just left a note sayin' she was takin' her things. You see there how it is, desert you when you need 'em most. Hard times come, they flit away, all your friends go somewhere else, let you drop." He put his sweat-damp hand on Jordan's wrist. "But you and me, we stay together, don't we, Jordan—brothers."

Jordan pulled his wrist free. "What you want, Bryant?" he said.

"I ain't the only one that knows women are like they are. But some stay by you. One upstairs told me today she wanted to go off with me—"

Jordan started to interrupt.

"Never mind who it is—"

"I don't care who it is. What you want with me?"

"It ain't honest," Bryant said. "The world ain't honest, boy, not in this town, not in New York. Where is it? Promises, all the time promises, but it don't pay off."

He pressed his head back against the booth and shouted for whisky. A girl ran down the stairs, put a bottle on the table and hurried out of sight. Bryant drank deeply, pushed the bottle across to Jordan, who drank almost as much and screwed on the cap.

"You and me are brothers, boy. Nothing can change that." He fastened his hand on Jordan's wrist again. "You know what worries me deep down, don't you?"

"Maybe you need a family."

"What worries me all the time now is I know you and me goin' to have to part company, too, then I'll be all alone in this town." He blinked, as if trying to see the bottle clearly, reached for it and managed by luck alone to grab hold. He drank without seeming to know it. "I thought it out. So I tell you something—" He motioned for Jordan to lean closer. "You always wanted to travel, Jordan. Why don't you take off? You can make it to New York. Ain't that the city Pa wanted you to go to?"

Jordan slowly took a drink out of the bottle.

"Your cab company and that little beer hall, give you something for the two, or your part in'em, take on your debts and worries—"

Jordan kept his eyes on the whisky, reflecting light through the bottle.

"Name a price, boy."

"Price?"

"Four thousand, five thousand."

"Ain't half enough," he said suddenly, proudly.

"Uh huh." Bryant now seemed alert and sober. "That's what I thought you would say—about ten thousand. Smart business head. That's all right. Not worth near that, but you and me are the same blood. We're the same thing; be like turnin' it from one hand to the other. I'll go the ten."

Jordan tried to clear his head. He pulled at his shirt collar as if it were too tight around his throat. "I won't do it," he said.

But before he had the door fully open, he turned back. "Ten thousand?"

Bryant chuckled, finished what was left in the bottle. "You can live like a king, Jordan—just like a king in the North."

22

Patrick was waiting at the door of their beer hall when Jordan came back across the street, wobbly from the news he held. He leaned back against the bar, stared straight ahead of him at the wall, not seeing anything. It was as if fortune had bit his heels and thrown him into space. Then Patrick was before him, leaning on a broom handle, wanting to know the news.

He started to tell Patrick, but stopped in mid-sentence. It would not do to let him know that he was thinking about selling the beer hall. The three drivers came tumbling in from outside, having seen him come out of Bryant's place, and now all four gathered around.

Jordan tore loose from the group and headed for the back, but they came after him. "Look a' here," Alexander said, "What's the reason he wanted to see you? We got a stake in all this."

"We're brothers," Jordan mumbled, going through the back door into the storage room and sitting down on a stack of beer cases.

"Brothers what? What he want to say?" Alexander, Patrick and Hogan were close by, and Solomon stood by himself, looking on as from another place.

"I ain't free to tell it," Jordan said, shaking his head angrily. "I got to make up my own mind."

When they saw they couldn't shake loose his secret, they grudgingly went back into the main part of the beer hall, grumbling about the way they had been treated.

So Jordan sat on the beer cases, his thoughts tumbling about. He reflected on the long struggle he had had, and on the North, remembering for an instant the voice of his father, then the lost, lingering songs of the church, knowing that he was a man growing older, and seeing this last chance to get away. It was a life-promise tearing at him.

He went out the back way and walked slowly around the building, up the steps to the taxicab office, where he sat down in front of a stack of bills and receipts. It was a bad job he had, one he was not suited for. And Kate was gone.

His mind wandered. He remembered the books he had read, and how the Negroes had tried and had almost succeeded and had failed. He wrote across the bottom of the page, "The nigger failed."

He got up and stumbled to the dresser, looked for the sketch set, but couldn't find it, came back and drew a picture on a piece of paper of the house he had been born in. He wrote "$10,000.00" under the house, a sum that stood out bigger than all his past.

He balled up the paper when he heard the drivers come up the stairs, arguing among themselves. "Be rid of them," he muttered. He stuffed the paper in his pocket and went out, shouldering past them in the hall. Downstairs he took one of the good cabs and drove through the Negro section, the number ten thousand going through his thoughts like a half-tune. Ten thousand, he thought, as he went by a group of girls standing on a street corner.

Not to worry about anything. Nothing was a problem with that kind of money. He drove through part of the country, seeing the flowers grow, thinking about the land that must be up North—flat land, he figured, so that you could see forever out in distance. Not like North Carolina.

He drove back into town and went by Coltrane's cleaning company, but nobody was there. He drove to Coltrane's house, but his wife said he had gone down to the grocery store for some meat. Jordan started to tell her right then about what had happened. He would hardly keep from doing it, but he let her be, and drove to the grocery store. At the meat counter he saw Coltrane, standing back, waiting his turn.

Jordan stood to one side. Coltrane saw him, nodded, grinning broadly. "Decided not to sell my cleaning company," he said. "Told Bryant right out."

Jordan didn't tell Coltrane he was there to talk to him, just waited until Coltrane was going out, then went out, too, walked with him to his car and stood at the open window on the driver's side. "Goin' to leave this town," he said, and he saw fear strike Coltrane. It was a fine, terrible thing to see. "Plannin' to go North."

Coltrane wanted him to come by the house. "I want Helen to know about this. Come on by and talk to me there."

"Maybe I'll do that," he said, turning away and going back to his cab. But before he got to it, old man Hogan, sawdust clinging to his clothes, called out and hurried over, bent and worn from labor. He sided up to Jordan, licking his lips anxiously, as if in fever.

"Look, Jordan," he said, "have you got a minute sometime?"

Jordan nodded, leaned back against the taxicab door.

"I—I hear you know that Crawford is selling the coalyard. I want to ask you if you think me and my boys could run it."

Jordan scratched his head, unable to determine why the man would ask his opinion about that.

"I got the two boys and myself. I ain't wore out yet, and somebody said he might sell to a colored man for eight thousand."

"How much?"

"Eight. Leastwise, a white man told my boy that Crawford offered it to him for eight four or five months ago, but he turned it down."

A slow smile came on Jordan's face. Probably he shouldn't tell any of this to Patrick—give him the two-thousand dollar reason Crawford had wanted to sell to him. "Look, Hogan, tell you what—offer him six."

Hogan's face bobbed up, a frightened look in his eyes.

"Do like I say—tell him six thousand. Don't argue with him but be firm that you can't go beyond six." He swung into the cab.

Hogan came closer to the door. "Say, Jordan," he said haltingly, old-time Negro humility in his voice, "would you tell him for me?"

Jordan was put out with him right there. "If you're goin' to run a coalyard, you can handle the deal. Now, look here—somebody ought to buy that yard, that's the truth. If we're ever to get ahead in this town, we got to grab hold of ever chance. White man is needin' to sell to us, so move in there. Talk business. I ain't able to talk to Crawford anyhow—"

"Well, would you help us get the business started?"

Jordan almost said no, right off, but he remembered how Kate had helped him. "I will," he said, forgetting that he was leaving town.

Coltrane was in a nervous state when Jordan arrived, and Helen was feverishly trying to look at ease. They talked, Coltrane anxious to get the news straight, challenging every word Jordan said.

"If you go," Helen said, "you'll end up unhappy."

"I been to Washington," Coltrane said. "I wouldn't go back."

By the time Jordan left, he was worried. It was true Coltrane had come back without finding satisfaction, and Bryant hadn't stayed in New York.

Yeah, but he could do different and come out better. Lord, given an even start, he could beat Coltrane and Bryant put together. The North was the happy land, hadn't he always known it?

So he was smiling broadly when he reached home. At suppertime, as they ate, he told Annie and the boys about the offer and what he could do. He talked so swiftly, and was so certain of his subject, that he left his family quite far behind. Annie seemed to be strangely moved by the words he spoke, and Harris and Fletcher looked from mother to father, alert for any clue that would show through.

"Well, what do you say?" Jordan was certain they would be elated. "Ten thousand dollars."

"Jordan—are you—" She was unsure of herself, or how to answer. It was too much for Annie. "Bryant offer this?"

"Plain as day."

"Well—why do you want to leave?"

"Annie, look here?" He leaned toward her angrily. "You been set against me since the first time I told you I was goin'. Since then ever time I've mentioned it, you've turned up and away. Well, look here, now. I have a chance in this."

"Do you? Do you?" She nervously gathered up the dishes, stacking them awkwardly, and took them to the sink, slid them in the big pan. "Ah, I don't know," she said.

Jordan stomped out of the house and walked through the bearing garden. There he caught a mental picture of himself as a boy in the long fields, chopping weeds from the tobacco rows, cutting okra from the stalks—getting the itch from the plants in doing it. He saw himself pulling beans and tomatoes, hoeing potatoes from the ground. Not any more. Never back then had he thought of ten thousand dollars, even in the night dreams. Now, by God and hope, he was free from all work.

Annie was set against him. Well, he should have known that. When had she been otherwise? She had been a thorn in his oldest plans. If it hadn't been for her, why, long before, he would have been lordly rich— maybe looking down on ten thousand, as Bryant did.

Bryant was the one who understood. He was all right. He had made it possible and had done it with his heart open. He was trying to pay Jordan back for what he had done for him in childhood.

Going back inside, he told Annie what he thought about Bryant. Before, she had been hurt and confused, but now he saw the cold anger come to her eyes.

"Can't count on you!" she said. "Money sways you so much you take in your own enemies."

"That's right. Speak on. I'm goin' North."

"Well, go alone!"

She ran into the bedroom, slammed the door so hard the pots banged against each other in the kitchen sink.

"I'm goin' North, Annie!"

He drove around town, wondering how many people Coltrane had told of the offer. He traveled up and down and finally parked the cab, climbed to his office. Before he went in, he realized the three drivers were having a meeting. He waited outside the door, listening.

"Get a lawyer," Alexander said. "Hold him here."

Jordan started to bolt right in and tell them to clear out, but he held his own and was headed back toward the steps when the door across the hall opened. The woman was munching on a snuff stick, holding a baby on her hip. "Mr. Cummings," she said, "what you do to my boy?"

An image of the emaciated little fellow came to him. The idea that he could harm the boy was beyond him. "I ain't seen him."

"Come into his room, falled on the bed, cryin' and carryin' on. Thought you must 'a' knowed about it."

Jordan wiped a shirt sleeve across his face. "Is he still broke up?"

"Was now."

He had thought she would send the boy out, but instead she stepped to one side. He walked past her into the apartment, went through the littered room, saw cans opened on the table from which the family had eaten, and moved into the bedroom beyond. It was dark, except for the dim light coming in from the main room. The boy was sprawled out on a cot, his face in the blanket, his feet still in shoes, one small arm wrapped around his head protectively.

Jordan looked around for a chair, but none was handy. So he crouched down at the bed, touched the boy, then jostled him a bit, halfway turned him over. "Hey—"

The boy sat up in bed suddenly.

"Don't wide-eye me, boy. You ain't afraid of me."

The boy turned his tear-swollen face to one side, let his eyes close. He breathed deeply, like a spent animal.

"I ain't hurt you none. Your ma says you're put out because of somethin'."

The mother came up to stand in the doorway now, her body throwing a shadow over him. "He gets sick most of the time now. Ain't one for explainin' his ailments. Don't let on."

"Are you sick, boy?"

Seth folded down on the bed, broken with grief. He began to whimper. "You ain't honest, Mr. Cummings," he said.

"I never lied to you, boy."

The boy shook his head in argument.

"Never lied to nobody—not much. Look here, now. Won't do no good to bundle up there on that bed, say not a word to me when I come in here."

"You set up, Seth," his mother said. "Talk to Mr. Cummings."

Seth sat up, his lips puckered up, his eyes holding back tears.

"Always thought of you as a big boy," Jordan said. "Now what you say?"

"Told me I had to get ahead."

"You do. And you can, boy. I made it. Just today I found out how far I went. Goin' to have money put by."

"Goin' to leave. Those men said you was goin' to leave."

"Am, maybe. Why that hurt you? Times go on. You keep your job. I'll talk to my brother—he's all right now."

The boy shook his head fiercely. "Ain't."

"He's doin' me a turn. Now, look at it fair."

"Want to drive a cab."

"He let you drive when you're big."

"Don't want to drive for him."

"Why, hell-fire, boy—why—" He stood up shakily. "We'll talk tomorrow," he said, backing to the door and going on into the lighted room. The woman turned to him, the same all-accepting expression on her face.

"You—you give him some food," he said, taking a dollar bill out of his pocket. "Give him something good—give him a beefsteak, that's the ticket." He remembered how Bryant had given the little boy a steak in New York City. "He'll respond."

Jordan went out quickly and down the steps. He drove home, and when he arrived there, the lights were out except for the lamp in the living room. He sat down wearily, not knowing how to handle all he had to do.

Here he was at the top of the world, but he was the only one that seemed to know it. Everybody in town would hear the news as fast as word could travel; it was the big topic of conversation, he had no doubt—but his own house was darkened out, with just one light.

He flicked off the light.

Now the house would show up properly. Let the people see how he was welcomed home. Back from the fight, winner, offered money enough to buy his way clear. There he was, sitting in the dark, no one to join him, his family down in beds with their eyes closed, hoping that he would allow his life to slip away.

Didn't make any sense.

But he couldn't blame the boys. They didn't understand. Annie had put on a big show of fear at supper. She had made them go to bed early, no doubt, so that he couldn't explain.

He really ought to wake them up and get it straight. They had a right to know. Half the reason he wanted to go North was so they would have a future like he had wanted to have. They were the ones moving him—always had been—they and Annie.

He flicked on his light to show the way to the boys' door. For a while he stood in the hall, wondering what he would say, then he went in, closed the door behind him and pulled the light cord in their room.

They were lying in the bed, both awake, as if waiting for something to take place. He put a finger to his lips. "Don't talk loud, boys. Don't wake your ma."

"She ain't asleep," Fletcher whispered.

"Never mind. Let her be. Why the house closed up so early?"

Neither boy answered.

"Look. I want to talk to you about somethin', somethin' real. Would 'a' done it tonight at supper, but me and your ma fell out. So now I want to say about the North. Never have done that to you, but have to now. Want to, 'cause it's a good place, and I know it well. All my life I've seen it in my mind, seen the trees shadin' the ground, deep leaves, seen the big houses, seen the way the sufferin' is eased 'cause money is like water flowin', plenty for all. And the same with food and comfort, same with friends.

"This offer your uncle Bryant made me today—it's so that we can go up there—you, Harris, and you, Fletcher, and your ma and me—just take off for the happy country, leave all this bad work. I tell you, boys, I got my hands filled with books and problems."

He took hold of Harris' small hand and stroked it with his long fingers. "You hear me, Harris? You can go to school up there—learn more, be in more school programs, take part. Have oysters roasted on the ground up there often. Ain't nothin' to bother a man. I always wanted to be there, since I was a boy. Had a longin' for that country. My pa did, too, but he was old and never got there, unless maybe he went by when he left here. If such is possible, he did it. And that's where Bryant got rich. Have two brothers up there somewheres, each of 'em beatin' the world, got life by the tail, boys. And we don't live but one time through, and I want the best for you—you hear me? You and me and your ma, just the four of us, and the baby that's comin'—we're goin' to make it pay up there. Now, I want you to know and not to worry none. Just let it be. Time will come, and I'll let you know. You and me and your ma, boys—in the North."

When he was done, he thought it over and knew it was well said. He closed the door, feeling hopeful. But no sooner was the door closed than he heard a whimpering from within, or thought he heard it, wasn't sure, and finally was sure he hadn't.

Then he heard it again. It pulled him up, confused. It brought to mind his drivers, holding a session, trying to decide on a lawyer. He thought of

Coltrane and his wife, the fear they showed, and he was angry with them because of it, and he was angry with Hogan for asking his opinion about the coalyard. He was angry with Seth and his boys, too, and most of all with Annie, who had set her face against him every time.

"Where is Annie?" he mumbled, swinging to the bedroom door. But at that instant the door opened and Annie stood there in a clean white nightgown, her hair pushed back from her face, looking young—almost as young as before the labor pains and work.

"Annie, you listen to me now," he said suddenly. "I want—I want to say this once and for all, by God!"

She came up short, startled by his anger.

"Called me no-'count months ago—right in there— Do you remember it?"

"I want to say something to you, Jordan—"

"Don't change off! Right in there, in that room! You remember?"

"Jordan—"

"Do you remember?"

"I remember."

"Yeah. No-'count. And since that night I've worked myself to death, and you've not mentioned it to me, have you? I proved myself, ain't I? Ain't I done it?"

"Jordan, please—"

"I done it since then, but—God-damn, you ain't said it, ain't let on— God-damn it, Annie, you ain't never come to me."

He stalked into the living room, full of remorse, knowing that she loved him no matter what she said or didn't say. She had spoken out against the North and him, nonetheless, spoken out against them clear enough. But not a word of praise.

She came to him, touched him.

"Let me be," he said.

"I'm sorry, Jordan."

"Go on, now. Too late; this minute's past."

"I come out to tell you—I come out just then to say it."

"Naw. Don't lie to me."

"Lie? Lie to you?" She sank down on one corner of the sofa. "I come to say it, and to say I lied to you."

He went into the kitchen to get away from her, turned on the faucet and caught some of the water in his mouth, swished it around, swallowed it. Then her words came through and he could make no sense of it. "What you say?" he called back through the open door.

She was still sitting on the sofa. "The day you told me you were goin' away."

"I remember that."

"Everybody knew you were goin', Jordan. I knew you were goin'."

"Huh? Annie, you have to speak up if I'm to hear you." He moved slowly back into the room. "You knew I was goin' away before I led you to that place we talked, is that it?" he said.

She nodded slowly. "It was me that led you, Jordan."

"No, I took your hand, pulled you along."

"It was me that led you," she said. "I had it all planned. I knew how it would come out."

"You're crazy, woman. Don't talk to me about seein' that afore it took place—"

"I'm telling you, Jordan. I had to keep you! I knew you wanted to go to the North, and I knew it was better for you to go—I knew—I—" She ran her fingers softly over her face, as if feeling the features of it. "I'm admittin' what you know," she said.

"Huh? Know? Lord 'a' mercy!"

"I want it said." She bent over, one hand on her forehead. "Been shadin' all our life together. Your livin' crazy, not workin' sound, all of that was 'cause I changed your way, kept you here. I had no right—"

"Annie, now wait a minute. Let's get this straight as we go. You seem to have a world o' worry 'cause o' that day."

"'Cause I kept you when you could 'a' been a man in the North."

"Now, stop right there—"

"Let me be. Let me talk—"

"Good God, Annie!" He stomped out of the house, disgusted with her. He knew full well it couldn't have been the way Annie explained it, and she had no business lying to him. He knew Annie.

Claiming she schemed him into marrying her. Not so.

Didn't he know Annie? Since they were children, he had seen her every face, heard her talk—learn to talk, even. Don't tell him that she had tricked him into staying.

Been shading their lives, she said. Why did she lie like that? Even if it were so, it was a might little thing to be holding onto for ten years. But with a woman like Annie, it would look big at the start and would grow bigger. Annie wouldn't know how to put shame aside and go on her way.

He walked around the block, and the more he walked, the more he remembered. Maybe she was telling the truth after all. Stood to reason she would know he was going away, since his brothers had gone. If it were true, then she had no business doing what she did. Lord have mercy, what she think she is, stopping his life at half-flow?

He hurried back to the house and ran up the porch steps. But before he had his hand on the knob, he heard Annie sobbing in the living room.

Softly he pushed open the door and went it. It was a hospital ward, his house, with his family bedded down in grief. He started to tell Annie she would have to stop, because sobbing drove him crazy; but he moved on past her and into the narrow hall, then into the bedroom where he fell over the bed, unsure of what he ought to do. He heard the boys whimpering and remembered how it had been several months before when he had been isolated in that room. Then Annie had gone to comfort the boys, but now she stayed away. Perhaps he should go in this time. Always had trouble talking to the boys, though.

He heard their door open and saw Fletcher stick his head out, then tiptoe into the hall. Jordan started to call to him, but before he could get the words formed, little Harris stuck his tear-streaked face out of the bedroom door, holding back, as if the room offered protection.

"Go on back inside, Harris," Fletcher said, starting to push him gently into the room. Then Fletcher stopped and his mouth fell open. He pulled Harris out into the hall and the two boys stared at Jordan. Harris began to cry again, but Fletcher came close to Jordan.

"You—ain't gone?"

"Gone?" Jordan said, sitting up on the bed and peering at him questioningly, "Fletcher, you march in there and comfort your mama, if that's in your mind; but let me be."

Fletcher had big tears in his eyes and he shook his head to try to make them go away. "You—you started for the North just now and didn't take Harris and me."

"The North? Lord, boy, I just went around the block one time."

Harris bolted into the room, his face flushed with anger. "You went to the North!"

"Harris, not so."

"Left us—" Fletcher said.

"God knows I didn't do nothin' of that sort. Just went out the door and—"

Harris came up to the bed, within reach of Jordan. "We want to go with you."

"Well, I know you want to see that country, boys, and maybe—"

"We want to be with you," Fletcher said sharply. "If you leave us—"

"With me?" Jordan said, stunned almost speechless. "With me, is it? Is that what you said, boy?"

"Harris and me," Fletcher began.

"Godamighty," Jordan said. "Ah, look—you don't—Ah, Godamighty, why you want to be with me?"

"You goin' to leave us behind?" Fletcher asked bluntly.

"No, I swear I wouldn't do that."

"I'm goin' to be a taxicab man," Harris said. "Goin' to be like you. And if you go away and—"

"Like me?" Jordan interrupted, looking around wildly, his mind baffled by the words of the two boys before him. Then he gave way to his feeling and enveloped Harris and Fletcher in his long arms and pulled them to him. "Want to be—like me—is it?" It was beyond hope what his boys had said to him. "Ah, now, look a' here, you got to do better'n that. Why, I been a wanderer in this town, been no-'count. I tried lately to change my ways, saw I had to work my life out, wasn't goin' to fall to me. But better for you to be like—like—"

He hesitated, unable to suggest a man to serve as model for Harris and Fletcher. What Negro in Leafwood was high enough for his boys? "Ah, Lord," he said, holding them close. "You're goin' to be better'n me."

When he put the boys back to bed, he sat down near Annie on the sofa. Neither of them spoke for a while, each aware only of the other and of the need for speech. Finally Jordan said, "Fletcher and Harris, they told me—Did you hear what they said?"

"I did."

"Lord, I ain't nobody."

"You are," she said.

"Not yet I ain't."

"And maybe in the North, if I'd not—"

"Annie, don't say no more about that. You're stompin' at the wind, Annie."

"No—no."

"Listen here, blamin' yourself. Honey, it wasn't you. My pa is the one who put the notion in my head, made it stay. But he's not to blame, either. A man plays his own tune, and I played a poor one." He moved to her, touched her hand. "Annie, you think it was you that turned me wrong. Why you think it was?"

"Jordan, since that day—"

"Hush, Annie—let it lie." He put his arms around her, as he had the boys, rocked her gently back and forth.

"You—you got to forgive me, Jordan—or—"

"Sure, honey. Sure, I do that, even if it was you—"

He felt her yield her stiffness and hold to him. "Ahhh, Annie." He rocked her back and forth, tears coming to his own eyes. "Why you talk like you do? I ain't got much beside you. I ain't never knowed you blamed yourself for how I failed you. Ahhh, Annie, God, Annie, ain't no sense."

He held her tightly to him. "I forgive you, don't you know that? I forgive you, honey."

23

The next day in midafternoon Jordan put his family in the cab and, without saying a word to them, drove to the colored graveyard. There he asked Annie to lead him to Jake's grave.

He looked down at it a long time, then turned to the boys. "Get rocks, Harris, Fletcher," he said, "gather as big as you can bring 'em here."

They scattered around, picking up rocks and hurrying back with them. "Take your time, boys," Jordan said, lifting a heavy rock out of its place near a tree root. "Goin' to stack a marker for Jake. It will take a while."

It took almost an hour in all, but it was two feet high, and mounded nicely. There was no doubt but that it would stay there for a long time to come, unless kids tore it down or animals burrowed under it. For the moment, the marker was fine, at least, and was as well as could be done.

Then Jordan got his family back in the car and drove out to the family place, where he led them past the house to the hillside graves of his parents. There, without saying a word, he began to gather rocks and stack them in two equal piles. The boys, weary and perspiring, fell in to help, and Annie, big with the baby, knelt down as the piles of stone grew. She stacked them up, doing it as best she could.

Nobody said a word, although Jordan sometimes would stop and look at the grave of his father and mother as if he wanted to say something to them.

Finally the two mounds of stone were done and Jordan helped Annie to her feet. "I never knew her much, Annie." He was looking at his mother's grave. "She just went on by me, gentle-like." Jordan glanced over at the grave adjoining. "But him I knew." He put his arm gently around Annie. "It's been a long while, years over."

"No need to think on that, is there?"

"Maybe it was nonsense to mark their graves now, Annie. But this mornin', thinkin' about leavin', I decided it had better be done. Lord, we got to remember."

They were still standing there, the boys looking at Jordan questioningly, when Bryant came up over the road bank, walking heavily, waving to them even as he appeared. "Knowed it, knowed it," he called, hurrying as fast as he was able. He arrived panting, extended a friendly good morning to Annie, and put his arm on Jordan's shoulders, glancing at the graves but not noticing them.

"I knowed I would find you here. Drove out to see, and there your cab was settin'." He glanced down at the boys. "Brought Fletcher and Harris for a farewell, did you, Jordan? Well, this is the place, ain't it? Here where he lays, rest his soul."

Jordan wondered if Bryant had any love at all for their father.

"Dear ol' man, raised us right. And he was right, Jordan—get away. I owe my success to him, for he shoved me on, put me on the sound path." He pressed Jordan's shoulders. "He was right, you know it?"

"I reckon not," Jordan said, wanting to be gone and say no more.

"What's that? How did you answer?" Bryant was not accepting what he heard.

"He was wrong, Bryant, like you know." Jordan turned and started down the hill. The boys held back only for an instant, then ran after. Annie looked furtively at Bryant, then she, too, followed, as if to escape the place while there was time.

"Hey, boy, look here—" Bryant called out demandingly. Jordan went on. "Boy, wait!"

Jordan stopped. There was no running from it.

"Come here, by God!"

He swung around. "Don't order me!"

His boys, frightened, hurried from him, went off into the field, leaving the path. Annie stopped part way between the men, her hands clenched, but it was clear that nothing was to be done now that they were on their old ground. She moved away, gathered Harris and Fletcher to her and tried to get them down the hill, but they hung back, wanting to see. She forced them on.

"The world is crazy," Bryant said, stalking toward Jordan. "The world has lost its head, boy. Do you hear that?" His voice had taken on a husky quality that reminded Jordan of Jake's voice as he died.

Jordan stood in the path, holding his place, a churning dread inside. Bryant stopped within arm's reach. "Ahhhh, boy, listen to me—ain't light at midnight, ain't night at day. Somethin' has to be right. More money you want—well may be."

"No," Jordan said deeply.

"Speak up. I ain't playin' now. Had my say, you yours. You drive me around this way and that. I don't take that nowhere—not here, not in New York. I'm a big boy, Jordan. I been to the city and come back. Once you beat me up out here at will, but not now."

Jordan waited, bracing himself, his weight on both feet. "I'm stayin' in town, Bryant."

"Listen here—"

"I'm stayin' right where I am. I'm sunk in now, with two businesses, and I'm goin' to make 'em pay if I got to dig it out of them books and men. So let me be."

"More money you want—"

"Hear it—I'm stayin' here."

Bryant struck out, caught Jordan beside the head with his fist, jarring him part way down the hill and almost off his feet. Jordan came back, then stopped, let his fists fall away. "That won't do, Bryant," he said. "Won't do at all." He turned, went on anxious lest he hear Bryant's footsteps behind him.

"Hey, boy," Bryant called to him. "I didn't mean to do that. You know that, don't you?"

Jordan stopped in the path, his back to Bryant. He stood for a long while, going over the sorrow of the moment. Then he turned, feeling awkward inside. He wanted to tell him about Kate and his baby, but there was no way to say it, no hope of a time to say it, even.

"If you—if you ever—" he said, then moved away, leaving the thought half-formed.

"Hey, boy, look—hey, Jordan, wait a minute!"

Jordan kept stumbling along, almost in a run.

"Boy, you're all I got. Don't you know that?"

Jordan ran down the clay bank to Annie and the boys, paying no attention to the Negro tenant family which had come out to stand near the porch. He hurried them to the cab and drove fast down the dirt road and away from Bryant and the family place.

He would come back, he knew, but it would not be the same again. The old mill dam was down in the valley yet, and maybe it would touch his thoughts from time to time—the wearing away of what men had built. But let that go, for men were building right along. He knew full well that his own taxicab company would fall away, forgotten, in time. But there were no means at hand to write his name so that it would always stay, for his labor was with days and numbers. But to think on that only brought misery.

No, he would not come back to the old place often. Only often enough for the boys to grow up knowing where their family had started. The past was part of growth—a man is always growing up from something, he thought. Let them see where their family had been a ways back. Maybe a family is like a baby—living in the dark for the time, getting its body formed, its strength. Maybe that was true of the whole Negro race, as he knew it—trying to be safe as its body formed so that it would be strong for the birth.

He let Annie and the boys out, then drove down to the beer hall. He went in the back way, got a broom and swept out. Patrick said very little, except that he was glad to see him, hoped he would not go away.

He went upstairs to his office and worked on the books, putting his full thought on them. When young Hogan came in, he found out Crawford would sell the coalyard for seven thousand, and Hogan wanted his money out of the cab company. Jordan agreed to that and began a list of young men who might buy his place.

When Hogan left, Jordan wrote a note, worrying over the paper as he tried to make the words neat. "Dear Kate," he wrote, "I feel Bryant will leave this town soon, but you had better not come back. His men would send him word. It is a bad thing, Kate. Maybe you can come back and work for me in time. I am well. Solomon is not a sure man yet, and

Hogan will leave me for the coalyard, which his family is buying. But my company is better than it might be. I am working and will stay at it. I will go on from here."

He signed his name, took all the money he had on him—four dollars— and slipped the letter and money into an envelope.

Then he sat back, most of his work done. The evening light came into the room. He heard Seth's footsteps in the hall and called to him. They talked awhile, Jordan listening and questioning. Seth rambled on, going from one subject to another until Jordan had to smile at the wealth of things that could be known about. Perhaps if he had time, and as he was able, he would try to arrange an order for what he already knew, and go on from there. And Seth would come along and pass him, if all went well.

"Do you know the songs, Seth?" he asked.

Seth didn't know them, so Jordan leaned back, his head against the wall. "You got to learn the songs." He sang one, then another, his voice deep and vibrant, carrying the strains of the vast days past, and telling of work and worship and wonderment, reciting in a feeling the throb and pulse of the most emotional of the world's people. Seth listened, nodding to the beat of music; and then Jordan was done.

Wearily he rose. He left the boy looking after him, wide-eyed and wondering, his face searching him for answers.

On the way home he stopped at the grocery store and bought the food he wanted for supper—four T-bone steaks and a can of fruit cocktail, pears and a bottle of wine, then a can of applesauce, because he liked applesauce and was the head of the family. He took them to Annie, who fixed supper as he waited.

"Bryant came by this afternoon to apologize," she said. "He had a woman in the car—that Taylor widow, Mona, I think it was. Said they was taking a trip."

Jordan looked up thoughtfully.

"He was a sight with the boys, Jordan. Brought them candy and presents. Brought me candy, too." She talked to him now easily and quietly, as if the confession of the night before had pierced the screen between them, so that she could bring herself to look at him more clearly.

"Did he bring a present for me?"

"No," she said, smiling. "Not for you, Jordan. Just the message." He nodded. "I'll be watchin' for his return." He looked at Annie, awkward with the child. "When do you bear the baby, Annie?"

"Soon now."

"Haven't we got money for you to see a doctor?"

"No need. I know the signs." Then she said, "I feel like it's a girl. I hope it is this time."

"Yeah," he said. "Maybe it will be."

He sat there a while longer, watching her, wondering what the meaning of Annie was. Something to do with life and worrying—holding back, waiting for the fullness.

"Annie, why didn't you want me to go into business for myself?"

"Lord, what a question," she said, laughing softly.

He waited, saw she wasn't going to answer further. "Did you think it was before my time, that I couldn't carry it?"

She shook her head as if the subject bothered her. Then she smiled. "Now, you stop questionin' me like that, Jordan Cummings, or I don't know what I'll do to you—"

He grinned. "All right, honey. All right."

He sought out Fletcher and Harris in the back yard, picking limas off the dying plants. He helped them some, the setting sun coming down warm on their shoulders. Then when Annie called, they went to the house together.

Maybe one of them will be a doctor, he thought, as they tramped up the rickety back steps.

He opened the wine and poured some for Annie and himself, then a bit for Fletcher and Harris. They began to eat, the heaviness of the day around them and the coming night ahead.

"You're not eatin' much, Annie."

"Tired," she said.

"Yeah. So am I."

Might be a girl, he thought. Damn sure it would be God that would decide. Those were God's countries—birth and death. All the rest was in shadows.

"Here, Harris, don't lean over the table when you eat," Annie said. "Ain't no bed."

Harris pulled his elbows back, grinned at his mother.

Yeah, all in shadows. Wrapped up dreamwise. White man lived in the world, most likely, Negro in a dream, as if he wasn't born yet. Maybe not ready to be born. That's what Annie would say. Leastwise, she would feel that. But, Lord, got to move along. Had two boys coming up strong.

'Course, time has a way of slowness. Bothersome damn thing. Puts everything in its season, no matter—birth or falling away.

"You goin' back to work tonight, Jordan?"

"Yeah. But I'll try to get home by ten."

"Wish you would."

That's right, Jordan, stop thinking so hard and eat faster. Got work waiting. That's the ticket—work. Let the other go its way. Nobody can shape a birth nohow.

Lord, wasn't it enough that he and Annie and the boys were together? Wasn't it enough that they could see the good days coming on?

...From the *Leafwood Weekly*

BORN to Mr. and Mrs. Jordan
Cummings, in the hospital last night,
a girl, eight pounds two ounces. Mr.
Cummings is one of the town's leading
colored businessmen. The child was
named Agnes Nell after the father's
mother.

JOHN EHLE is the author of eleven novels and six nonfiction books and has won numerous literary awards, including the North Carolina Award for Literature, the Thomas Wolfe Prize, the Lillian Smith Award for Southern Fiction, the Sir Walter Raleigh Award for Fiction, which he has earned five times—more than any other writer to date—and the Mayflower Award for Nonfiction. His books have been translated into French, German, Swedish, Czech, Spanish, and Japanese.

Following service in World War II, Mr. Ehle earned his BA and MA at the University of North Carolina-Chapel Hill. He taught at the university for ten years before joining the staff of Governor Terry Sanford in 1962. He resigned from the governor's staff in 1964 to write *The Free Men,* a nonfiction account of the civil rights movement that took place in Chapel Hill, North Carolina during 1963-64. Mr. Ehle later served on the White House Group for Domestic Affairs and was appointed to the First National Council of the Humanities. He has been awarded honorary doctorates from Berea College, the North Carolina School of the Arts, the University of North Carolina-Asheville, and the University of North Carolina-Chapel Hill.

Mr. Ehle lives in Winston-Salem, North Carolina, with his wife, actress Rosemary Harris. The two divide their time between Winston-Salem and three other homes in Penland, North Carolina, New York City and London. They have one daughter, actress Jennifer Ehle.

Cover designer **MIKE DAVIS** has been an art director in the advertising and marketing industry for 30 years. He spent 17 of those years as owner of his own agency before joining Nicholson Kovac, Inc. in Kansas City, Missouri, as senior art director. Mike earned his BS in Marketing from Park University and his MLA from Baker University. He also has taught graphic design at Maple Woods Community College.

Away from the office, Mike can be found riding his Harley-Davidson, trout fishing, playing guitar, taking photographs or relaxing on his boat with friends on Lake Waukomis.